Three Bedrooms, Two Baths, One Very Dead Corpse

Three Bedrooms, Two Baths, One Very Dead Corpse

DAVID JAMES

KENSINGTON BOOKS
http://www.kensingtonbooks.com

After dedicating all my previous books to other people, I've decided to dedicate this book mainly to me. After all I've been through, I could use a little recognition. Oh, and a portion to Sandra Quinn, Realtor like me, who kicked my ass when it needed it.

KENSINGTON BOOKS are published by

Kensington Publishing Corp.
119 West 40th St.
New York, NY 10018

Copyright © 2010 by David Stukas

All Kensington titles, imprints and distributed lines are available at special quantity discounts for bulk purchases for sales promotion, premiums, fund-raising, educational or institutional use.

Special book excerpts or customized printings can also be created to fit specific needs. For details, write or phone the office of the Kensington Special Sales Manager: Kensington Publishing Corp., 119 West 40th St., New York, NY, 10018. Attn. Special Sales Department. Phone 1-800-221-2647.

Kensington and the K logo Reg. U.S. Pat. & TM Off.

Library of Congress Control Number: 2010930788

ISBN-13: 978-0-7582-0631-2
ISBN:-10: 0-7582-0631-3

First Hardcover Printing: October 2010

10 9 8 7 6 5 4 3 2 1

Printed in the United States of America

CHAPTER 1

A Woman on the Verge of a Nervous Breakdown

". . . and by morning I had a yeast infection that you wouldn't believe! (sob, sob) Then when I'm finally able to leave my house, I find that one of my neighbors keyed my Hummer. (sob, sob)"

As I sat in Judith Sackets's obscenely large living room in Palm Springs, barely listening to her unappetizing story and histrionic crying, I wondered how I got here. Not how I got to her house per se, but how my life brought me *here*. I'm sure that I am not the first person in the history of the world to ask this question, but if ever there was a time to ask such a question, this was it.

"I work so hard for the charity I started, but no one seems to understand me or what I'm trying to do!" Judith lamented. "You understand me, don't you, Amanda?"

Judith, sensing that my nanosecond of hesitation signaled that *even I* didn't want to understand her, burst into a great sob that threatened to make her lungs come out her nose, which was immediately followed by a sharp intake of breath caused by the enormous vacuum in her lungs—I feared that Judith would inhale the paper napkin underneath my glass of water. In and out, in and out, the oxygen was sucked in, then expelled by the great bellows. I smiled meekly back at Judith, hoping to show some sense of sympathy.

It's not like I hadn't been warned. My ex-husband, Alex, also a real-estate agent here in Palm Springs, told me to stay away from Judith. Jeb, the top producer in my office, said the same thing. And just about any carbon-based life-form living here in the Coachella Valley echoed the same sentiment. Perhaps even the rocks and mountains that encircled our valley warned me, but I turned a deaf ear to their cries, because I, Amanda Thorne, would single-handedly tame Judith Sackets and get the listing to her 4,500-square-foot, six-bedroom house where all other agents had failed. And the gates of success would open, and I would get listings that would startle and amaze seasoned Realtors worldwide. Crowds of agents would part as I walked in their midst, and they'd speak in hushed tones of stifled amazement. "Look, that's Amanda Thorne. She's the one who listed and sold Casa de Loco. Not even Mary Dodge would touch her!" It's amazing that I, a woman with almost no sense of self-confidence, could fantasize about taking on a client like Judith Sackets. Unfortunately, the real reason I was sitting here taking what amounted to little more than mental abuse was that I was desperate for a sizable piece of business.

It wasn't that I needed the cash. Alex had been very generous to me in the divorce. Too generous, I often thought, flooded with guilt about how much he settled on me. "Don't worry about me, Amanda . . . I'll earn it all back in a year or two," he'd said. I had little reason to doubt him—he was capable of the impossible. But I needed to show my most tireless critic—me—that I could be a big success on my own. Plus, I'd developed a reputation in this town. Alex and I had landed some of the largest sales in town. I had to prove I could land the same kind of business on my own.

But right now, my ability to discern a hopeless cause from one full of promise was rather suspect. As I looked at Judith, I marveled at how she could have the audacity to tell me she's having the worst day anyone ever had. Nothing is further from the truth. It is a little-known fact that the shittiest day ever experienced by a human being was had by C.B. Lansing, a flight attendant for Aloha Airlines. On April 28, 1988, she was serving drinks to surly assholes in her section of the cabin of a Boeing 737, when quite unexpectedly, a large section of the outer fuselage of the plane peeled back, sucking Ms. Lansing out into the void and, presumably, to meet up with the ocean a minute or so later in a manner that I won't speculate about. True story. This is, arguably, the worst day anyone ever had, so fuck you, Judith Sackets.

Not that my present predicament comes anywhere near C.B.'s, but I, too, am having a very bad day in my life. Or, more correctly, a run of bad luck lately. I moved from a profitable career in Bloomfield Hills, Michigan, to a city where I know almost no one. I'm marked by the stain of a humiliating divorce, old-time Palm Springs agents are full of jealous hatred toward me, the house I bought here is riddled with termites and dry rot, the yard is full of scorpions, my contractor has taken to living in my backyard in a tent and showering naked there using my garden hose, I have still yet to land a home-run listing by myself, and worst of all, I am a straight, single woman living in the gay mecca of Palm Springs. Can things get any worse?

Oh yes. Far worse. Very soon. But at that moment in time, the poop hadn't yet hit the fan. However, thanks to the nefarious workings of some mysterious person who was about to change the course of my life, it was definitely airborne.

In the real-estate business, one of the biggest legal landmines an agent encounters concerns disclosures. Disclosures are forms that sellers are supposed to fill out, indicating every-thing that they know about the property being sold—both good and bad. These forms are designed by state regulatory bureaus to get sellers to expose the fact that, say, the house being sold is built over an ancient Indian burial mound. Or that a family of six was slaughtered on the premises. These revelations often have a bearing on whether a buyer wants to proceed in buying a particular house, or whether to call in an exorcist or good carpet-steaming company.

The unfortunate thing about disclosures is that they apply only to real estate—not people. This is a sad thing, because it would make life so much easier. Instead of going out on a blind date with yet another psycho, you could ask to see his disclosures first.

"I see that you killed and ate your mother back in 2003," you'd point out, smiling confidently since you hold all the aces in your hand.

"True, but I'm vegan now," your date would protest.

"Ah, yes . . . well. And I see that, in 2000, you got drunk and unruly on a flight to Las Vegas and you ended up taking a dump on the beverage cart . . ." you'd finish, handing back his disclosures and sending him on his way.

My ex-husband, although I still dearly love him, didn't come with a set of disclosures, either, which is a pity. He turned out to be gay.

Finding out your husband is gay after six years of marriage is something that would make some women bitter and hostile toward all men. But not me. Without a doubt, those six years were the best of my life. I traveled more, explored more, learned more, and earned more than most people would in a lifetime.

So how could I marry a gay man and not know it? It's easy. When you look at the caliber of available straight men out there, you'd know what I'm talking about. I mean, what heterosexual woman wouldn't want a man who cooks like Wolfgang Puck, goes shopping for home furnishings with you and actually enjoys it as much as you do, never talks football with you or even watches it, and—this is the topper—actually stays in bed with you hours after he's had an orgasm, cuddling you like it was your last day on earth?

Tell me I'm right, ladies. Or, to be fair, some of you guys.

Now I don't want to go on and on about how I married a gay man, especially since my mother still brings the issue up whenever she needs some ammunition to fire across the bow of the unstable dinghy that I call my self-esteem. After all, there is a body—or two—to stumble across in the pages ahead. But the question of what does a homosexual look and act like does arise, mostly by married women who wonder about the fact that their husband has an innate sense for buying sexy and smart-fitting clothes for himself, prefers to vacation in San Francisco or New York, and keeps his crotch hair trimmed. You can see the fear in the faces of these wives. I can't tell you how to spot a gay man, since to this day, I still miss some surefire club members, but I can tell you how it happened to me.

I was working in a real-estate firm in Bloomfield Hills, Michigan, deliriously happy that I had moved out of my hometown of nearby Waterford some years ago, had a nice house in Birmingham, and a respectable amount of money in the bank. I could now live the kind of life led by a madcap heiress, but one thing was still missing: I had the means but not the skills. How do you live a life full of daring adventure and reckless abandon when you don't know how to do it?

I felt that our educational system had let me down by not offering adult education courses taught on the subject. This seemed completely illogical to me. I was never going to use the Pythagorean theorem to figure out the length of the third side of a right triangle, but when I needed to know something really useful, like how to hire a Sherpa for a Himalayan mountain climb or whether it's legal to bungee jump off the Empire State Building, I drew a conspicuous blank. So while I was busy trying to figure the solution to my problem, the answer walked into my office one day.

His name was Alexander Thorne. Besides being strikingly handsome, he climbed mountains in Nepal, had a fifth-degree black belt in Isshinryu karate, cycled 25 miles daily, scuba dived, hiked the entire Pacific Crest Trail, bought and sold million-dollar-plus houses like they were candy bars, and best of all, he was single.

I pounced on him like Kirstie Alley on a tray of sticky buns. Although I had done a little exploring and experimentation in my life, I was not on Alex's level. But I certain of one thing: I was going to be.

Anyway, to make a long story short, we married a year and a half later, and had a wild and crazy time until Alex dropped the bomb. No, not the *gay* thing, but the *moving* thing. The year was 2004, and Alex smelled money to be made in Palm Springs, California. He had looked at the limited supply of houses there, the climate, the favorable demographics, the proximity to Los Angeles and San Diego, heard about the hordes migrating from San Francisco to Palm Springs, and what it all added up to was a lot more than anything the moribund real-estate market that was Michigan could offer. So off we went.

There's an old joke: A man named Old MacGreggor is sitting in a pub in Scotland, lamenting that no one remembers him as the man who once valiantly saved the little town in which he lived from a terrible flood. Do they remember Old MacGreggor as the man who once single-handedly spared the town from a raging fire? No. And does the town connect his name with the time he warned the locals of an impending landslide? No. "But you fuck a sheep just one time . . ."

Palm Springs is like this joke. Yes, a lot of fucking goes on in this town, but that's not the point I want to make here. When most people think of Palm Springs, they think of celebrities: Bob Hope. Frank Sinatra. Cary Grant. Dinah Shore. All stars, all gone. Or they think about golfing. In doing so, they're missing the reality of what's really going on here.

The year is now 2005, and Palm Springs is on a roll. In the year we've lived here, hip restaurants, hotels, and shops were springing up like California wildfires. Dilapidated mid-century modern houses were being snapped up and renovated at an astonishing pace. Like many of its former residents, Palm Springs was being snatched back from God's waiting room and given another chance at life.

Of course, when I moved here with my then-husband, Alex, these were the things I was seeing. The drooling idiot transfixed by a shiny object.

The one thing I explained away was the heat. One hundred and six degrees normally in the summer. Occasionally, 123 degrees. Oh well, you can't have everything.

Palm Springs more than compensates for summer heat with mild winters. You could be sitting around a firepit at night warming yourself by the flames, then go bicycling in a short-sleeved shirt the very next morning. And the setting—oh, the setting. Surrounded by mountains on every side, the city is notably set right smack up against the base of 10,834-foot San Jacinto. We're not talking against foothills that eventually lead up to the mountain itself in the distance, but right up against the mountain.

So Alex and I bought a house that needed some TLC (thousands to local contractors) and began remodeling it immediately. We landed jobs at one of the best real-estate firms in town and the money started rolling in. And rolling in. And rolling in. But we didn't just work . . . that wasn't Alex's way. Oh no.

We hiked. We went cycling. We fucked like rabbits. We cooked like mad. Life, I thought, couldn't get any better. Then the other shoe dropped. Alex confessed that he was gay.

This shouldn't have been a surprise since Alex had told me that he had had several bisexual experiences in his late teens. In fact, it was one of the many exotic things about him that I found so attractive: There was nothing he hadn't tried. Little did I realize that once you try ass crack, you never go back.

So after the obligatory several-days-of-crying thing, we agreed to split up. Okay, Alex thought it would be better if we separated. Me, I pleaded for us to stay together. I mean, *pleaded*. I told him he could go out and sleep with men and I wouldn't care. It's funny, now that I think back on all those tears, I've come to realize that most of them were tears of embarrassment. No, really! It wasn't that Alex had betrayed me. He just became aware of something that was a part of him and he was powerless to change. Lack of real self-awareness, which is something we all suffer from. Plus, how could I be angry with him? In the six years we were married, I lived more than I had my entire lifetime. I saw Paris and London, New Zealand, South America, and scores of other locations around the world. I skydived, learned to scuba dive, went hang gliding—everything a little girl from Waterford, Michigan, would never even consider. Plus, we're still best friends—just like in our marriage—so what I lost is compensated by all that I gained, and continue to gain. Plus, I came up with my own definition of love: Love isn't a greedy, needy thing as in "I need you . . . or I'll die if something should happen to you." Love, for me, is helping someone become the most they can be. In

Alex's case, it's helping Alex be the most Alex he can be. Love that's unselfish, but giving. And if Alex realized that he was gay, he needed to be what he was meant to be—as long as he didn't start dating any actors.

So after leaving Judith Sackets's house, I drove back to The Curse, a name I created for the house I bought after Alex and I divorced. I was going to call it The Soul-Destroying, Money-Sucking Motherfucker house, but it just didn't have the ring that *The Curse* had. Plus, it summed up the house better than any other words I could think of. From the first day I moved enough of my belongings into the house to live there during my brief sabbatical and planned remodeling, the house had it in for me. As I found out, you didn't actually *live* there—you did hand-to-hand combat with the structure.

I pulled up in the driveway and parked my car. Stepping out of my vehicle, I proceeded to navigate the obstacle course of bricks, stacks of plywood, rolls of roofing felt, boxes of nails, and a mountain of drywall scraps in my faux-alligator Kate Spade slingbacks. The house had ironically become a metaphor of my life: full of potential, but under constant construction.

What I couldn't understand is how Alex made renovation of our previous love nest look so easy. There never was any shouting, cursing, or throwing of objects. No horrendous surprises. Like everything in his life, it all flowed smoothly and effortlessly.

Mine was another story. The contractor whom Alex hired was out of commission for months with a broken back. So I called around, but Palm Springs was in the middle of a real-estate boom that had no end in sight. Contractors were as scarce as real breasts in Los Angeles. I ended up dealing with drunks, drug addicts, thieves, or psychos—it looked like I was hiring men from the work-release program of San Quentin.

Unfortunately, I ended up paying many of these guys just to get rid of them. As Alex warned, they all knew they could put a mechanic's lien on my house, preventing me from doing anything with it. So now I was down to one contractor: Edwin. Edwin was polite, careful, and he did beautiful work. He was just slower than a Department of Motor Vehicles employee. And there was one other drawback: He moved into a pup tent he pitched in the backyard and proceeded to live there, showering naked using my garden hose on the side of the house. You just couldn't get good help nowadays.

I climbed over more debris, pushed aside the temporary plywood sheet that masqueraded as my front door, and was greeted with a round of excited barking and animated jumping from Knucklehead. Knucklehead was my Aussiedoodle, a "hybrid" the woman at the animal shelter said. Mutt is more like it—part Australian shepherd and part standard poodle. But he was adorable. At nine months, he sat 30 inches high already, his tongue lolling as usual out of the side of his mouth, which made him even more adorable. Knucklehead wasn't the brightest bulb in the chandelier, but between his sheepdog hair that seemed to be in a perpetual blown-back position and his cockeyed tongue, I couldn't help but love him. But like I said, he wasn't the sharpest knife in the drawer. Once, when I took him to the Palm Springs Bark Park to run and play with other dogs, he got so into chasing a favorite wire-hair terrier named Asta, Knucklehead ran right into a lamppost when Asta faked a right, then lurched left. Knucklehead wasn't hurt, but it validated my choice of names for him. So, like my house, Knucklehead was a metaphor for my life: askew, confused, always under construction, but lurching forward. To where, I don't know. Completion, I hoped.

I gave Knucklehead a huge hug, which got him barking

with joy and started his stubby tail vibrating with sheer excitement. Ah, unconditional love.

I crossed what vaguely appeared to be a living room, minced my way to what would someday be my kitchen counter, and picked up the phone and dialed Alex, my ex-husband.

"Alex Thorne here," the voice on the other end of the line said through a hailstorm of static. "AMANDA?"

"YES, IT'S ME!" I replied.

"YOU HAVE TO PEE?" Alex shouted. "I'LL CALL BACK WHEN YOU'VE FINISHED TINKLING."

"ALEX, LET ME CALL YOU BACK ON MY CELL. THE LINE IS STILL SCREWED UP."

I hung up, counted to twenty, and wondered if I'd hurt my hand if I punched it through the wall. Men did it all the time. So why not women? Plus, I was a second-degree brown belt in karate. So what if I broke a nail? I did push-ups on my knuckles to warm up before sparring. They weren't much to look at, anyway. I'd chewed my nails and fingers almost down the second joint. I picked up my cell phone and pressed the "1" button—speed dial for Alex (#1 . . . as if that wasn't a telling statement).

"Alex here. Is that you, Amanda?"

"Yes, it's me. A very tired, aggravated Amanda."

"So did you leave Judith's with a signed listing agreement?"

"Not quite. The only thing I left with was a feeling of pity," I sighed.

"Pity?"

"A pity that I didn't have a brick in my purse to hit her with."

"That bad, huh?"

"That chick needs to have her head rewired."

"Amanda, I don't want to say I told you so, but . . ."

11

"I should've known enough to listen to you, Alex . . . and the rest of the entire sentient world."

"It was a learning experience. Like I always say . . ."

". . . if all you learn about sticking your hand in the fire is not to do it again, it was a worthwhile experience," I jumped in, finishing Alex's sentence the way married people do when they've been married long enough—correction, were married. "But not all is lost. I have a listing appointment this afternoon at Caliente Sands. Of course, I'm one of four agents being interviewed, and one of them is Mary Dodge, the Dragon Queen of Palm Springs real estate."

"Now, Amanda, you know what I told you. You have just as much chance of getting it as any other agent. You just have to keep your confidence up."

"Easy for you to say. You were born with it," I said. And it was the truth. "You weren't raised Catholic, or had a bizarre, Lithuanian Old-Country grandmother move in with you for three years and taunt you with tales of wolves dragging village children into the woods and eating them, leaving only the bones behind. No, your parents were the coolest parents on the planet; your mom painting her expressionist paintings and practicing yoga while your dad was raking in the money from some patent your grandfather owned for toilets."

"Gravity backflow valves. The patent was for gravity back-flow valves."

"Close," I added.

"And my mother was a *minimalist* sculptor and painter. So what does that have to do with making me confident?"

I was aghast. "Everything! At least your parents let you develop and experiment. Mine were always looking for ways to make me feel guilty about something I'd done—or not done."

"You're not going to start with the Communion wafer thing again, are you?"

The *Communion wafer thing* that Alex had so easily dis-missed was an incident that took place when I was nine that was so mortifying, it still haunts me to this day with feelings of crushing guilt and overwhelming inadequacy.

It was a stormy Sunday in April and I was preparing to re-ceive my First Communion. When I say it was stormy, I am being kind. The lightning and thunder was deafening, the rain poured, and for a few minutes, we received an inch of hail. A tragic foreshadowing, to be sure.

For months before this auspicious day, the nuns had been instructing us on the history, the purpose, and above all, the *se-riousness* of the Act of Communion. Of course, being nuns, the serious nature was accompanied by a story so sick and twisted that if told today, the story would lead to numerous lawsuits and the local Department of Social Services being called in.

The story went like this. A little Catholic girl in Mexico, or some untraceable South American country, was likewise pre-paring for her First Communion. As a good student, she real-ized that the Communion host, through the miracle of transformation by the priest during mass, changed the taste-less bread wafer into the actual body of Christ. Cannibalism, to be sure. Now, little Maria put two and two together and fig-ured that if she didn't swallow the host, but spit it instead into a handkerchief and took the host home, it would be a power-ful talisman to grant her self-indulgent wishes like having food on the table and a doll to play with instead of a dead rat or a stick. Well, no sooner than nefarious Little Maria carried out her evil plan, than on her way home the host began to bleed profusely, pouring out gallons of incriminating blood on her, her bedroom, and the dirt floors of her proud, but ramshackle house. In horror, Maria grabbed the host and prepared to run back to the church to return it to the priest and confess her sins. Now, as in all stories calculated to instill terror and compliance through guilt, the ending was not happy for Little Maria. Depending on which nun told the story, Maria was either hit by lightning, torn apart by wild monkeys, or disappeared into a deep crack in the earth that opened under her tiny feet. No matter, the point was that questioning authority or possessing a free will was met with dire consequences.

With this cheerful backdrop, I made my way down the aisle of St. Benedict's Church toward the priest, terror making my heart pound like a jackhammer and my mouth dry up. I passed my mother and grandmother, my mother releasing a tiny flutter of a smile to encourage me on, but my grandmother's expression had only one interpretation: Don't fuck up, you ungrateful child, or God will come down on you ten times harder than I already do. Any confidence that was left in me before this moment whooshed out of me like the air out of a tired whoopee cushion. I thought about turning and running out of the church, but knew that despite my grandmother's advanced years, Merciless Martha could still summon amazing speed when she wanted to. So I headed down to the railing and kneeled next to the other terrified girls and boys, waiting for the priest to deposit the large wafer on my tongue when prompted. Before I knew it, Father Brown was standing in front of me. I opened my mouth and stuck my tongue out to receive the wafer from the priest, but because my mouth was so dry, the wafer got stuck on the back of my tongue as I tried to swallow it, causing me to cough the host out onto the priest's robe, where it stuck for a moment before falling on the floor.

Father Brown tried to minimize the incident, picking up the host and pocketing it discreetly in a handkerchief. But Martha, who was prone to Old-World theatrics, let out a wail that sounded like a cougar passing kidney stones. To add insult to injury, Martha left her seat, interrupted the Communion service, and crawled up the aisle to the spot where the host had fallen, kissing the spot fervently, then kneeling there and looking up to heaven while reverently hitting her fist to her chest over and over again.

Somehow, I managed to survive the day; but as I lay awake for hours that night, scanning the room for rabid monkeys or Satan himself, I felt a strange leaking sensation below my waist. Throwing back the covers and pulling down my pajamas, I was horrified to discover my crotch soaked with blood. Clearly, God was making me bleed to death for my sin, and true to form, He wasn't waiting around to get started. Had I received proper sex education, having my first period wouldn't have been a big deal, but my parents took an old-fashioned approach to learning about the facts of life: They preferred that I learn them in the streets like everyone else. So, to say the least, I was completely naïve when it came to knowing how my body operated, and I did the only thing a clueless, guilt-racked female of nine years old could do when discovering that God had fatally wounded me: I screamed hysterically. This was followed by more hysterics until my mother had discerned what was happening, but Martha, upon arriving at the scene, threw more gasoline on the fire by reciting the rosary and invoking in Lithuanian for God to do something horrible to me.

I won't go into detail how, but for weeks Martha managed to find dozens of pictures of the Devil and slipped them under my pillow, into my folded socks, my bookbag—anywhere she could punish me further. The point is, the damage was done. For the rest of my life, when something went wrong and I was in the vicinity, I would feel that I had some hand in it. Self-confidence wasn't an option when you felt like the walking wounded. This is one of the many, many reasons I fell in love with Alexander Thorne. He was always building me up, always pointing out my talents and encouraging me to do the most with them. He also worked night and day to get me to stop beating up on myself for just being human and making the mistakes humans do. How could I not love a man like that?

Since we're on the topic of beating myself up, I will take this opportunity to describe how I look. After all, I have lived in this body with this face and this mind for forty years, so no one is as highly qualified to describe myself. Of course, the danger in this line of thinking is that the one person most uniquely qualified to fool oneself is, well, oneself. How many of us motor through life with air bags built into the dashboards of our lives, ready to inflate at a moment's notice to protect us from a head-on collision with something or someone who reminds us that what we think we are is not always what is really there. That said, I have no such air bags. Mine were deployed so many times as a kid, they've ceased to function. So, by reason of deduction, I am seeing me as I really am: like Kathleen Turner punched in the nose. Yes, I'm six-feet one-inch tall (thank you, Goddess, for one redeeming, modelesque feature), with naturally dirty blond hair, average build, which I've molded into an athletic slimness with a regimen of cycling and hiking and occasional weightlifting in an underutilized bedroom, but the fact remains that I look like someone punched Kathleen Turner in the nose. And if you think I'm imagining this, I've had scores of people who described me this way. Most of them, of course, have made such a description behind my back or what they've thought was out of earshot, but my mother, once I explained to her who Kathleen Turner was and she watched *Accidental Tourist* and *Romancing the Stone* (but not *Body Heat* or *Serial Mom*, both of which she turned off after only twenty minutes), proudly proclaimed it to anyone who cared to listen.

"Doesn't she look like a movie star?" she would prod from complete strangers in shopping malls, grocery stores, or family gatherings. "Kathleen Turner . . . like someone punched Kathleen Turner in the nose."

To my mother, this was a compliment. A backhanded one, but a compliment nonetheless. She had defied centuries of genetic shortcomings and produced a bona fide movie star. I remember a particularly insane conversation we had in a woman's clothing store years ago. She had once again given me her standard introduction that would have been better suited for a drunken Friar's Club roast.

"Mom, I wish you wouldn't mention the punched-in-the-nose part so often."

"Oh, for gosh sakes, Amanda, you're always complaining that I never give you a compliment and the moment I give you one, you tell me not to."

"If I looked like Elizabeth Taylor but had clubfoot, you'd tell everyone: 'Look, everyone, she's my little star, Elizabeth Taylor . . . never mind the clubfoot.'"

"What's wrong with that, Amanda? If you had been born with clubfoot, I don't think I should be standing there spouting off about my gorgeous little star without mentioning a birth defect that everyone could plainly see. I'd be lying if I didn't tell the truth."

"Mom, you don't always have to spell out everything for people. They have eyes . . . and manners that keep them from harping on things like clubfoot. You know, you go through life like the Pope, always telling everyone else in the world what they're doing wrong while his own priests are sticking their hands down the pants of nine-year-old parishioners."

Anything that contradicted my mother's tragic view of life usually produced an icy stare and ended the conversation for the time being. Alex, always the perennial Pollyanna, mentioned the Kathleen Turner connection, while skirting the nose issue. Why not? Alex was born gorgeous. But in contrast to my mother, Alex saw only the good in me, halting my attempts at self-immolation. Reason number 438 for marrying Alex: He saw in me what no one else could, least of all myself. He was such an expert in seeing the good in everything, he made me think twice about having a nose job. He told me that if I felt strongly about it, then to go ahead and do it. But, as he always said to me, I love you just the way you are. Plus, he would always say he loved my nose. Although it was clearly Lithuanian, he described it as Prussian—an aristocratic term if I ever heard one.

"Well, Amanda, I'm sure you'll get the listing," Alex said, shaking me out of my flashback.

"I really need this listing. I need to prove that I can go out and get crème de la crème listings on my own."

"You got plenty of them in Michigan," Alex reminded me.

"Yes, but that was there. I need to be taken seriously here in Palm Springs, now that my divorce sabbatical is over. It's time to go back to work."

"I wouldn't put so much pressure on yourself, Amanda."

"That's all I do, Alex. You know that."

"And you do it better than just about anyone."

"You're damn straight," I replied, conscious of the phrase I just blurted out.

Alex laughed. "Do you realize what you just said?"

"Yes, it was already out of my mouth before I knew I said it."

"Amanda, I wouldn't worry about getting every top-notch listing. Look at some of the agents in your office. Take Babette, for instance. She's worked in your office for two years now and she hasn't brought in one sale."

"Yes, but she brings in those boobs of hers . . . the ones that arrive half-a-minute before she does. That's why they keep her," I conceded.

"Well, that and the money she pays to keep her desk space that she never uses."

"Touché, Alex." Alex had hit upon another reason real estate offices tolerate keeping part-time agents under their wings. These laggards pay monthly fees for renting desk space, and having phone service and Internet connections.

"Alex, I have to go get ready for my listing presentation. If I'm going to blow Mary Dodge out of the water, I've got to rehearse my presentation."

"Go to it, Amanda. Knock 'em dead."

I knew that Alex was wishing me the best when he uttered this. But in hindsight, I wish he had let things go with a simple "good luck."

CHAPTER 2

Help Wanted: Retarded Baboons Apply Within

I rushed around my chaotic house, making a mental checklist of all the things I needed to bring to my listing presentation. Computer with oversize display, check. PowerPoint presentation loaded on computer, check. Leave-behind folder containing PowerPoint presentation for client, check. Brochure, check. Cell phone, check. Driving directions to client's house, check. Digital camera to take pictures of house, check. Breath mints, check.

I loaded all my equipment onto my flight-attendant roll-on baggage cart and dragged everything out to my freshly washed and waxed Toyota Land Cruiser. A Realtor's car is as important as the clothes he or she wears. In the beginning, I clung to the mistaken belief that by driving an economical Toyota Camry, I would be trumpeting to my clients that I was a practical, down-to-earth kind of woman who was frugal and no-nonsense—like sensible shoes.

"People don't want frugality, Amanda," Alex said when we started dating long ago. "Clients want to think they're on board with a winner, an agent who is doing enough business to afford high car payments. They want to be impressed. They want their neighbors to be impressed. They're not going to feel confident if you drive up in a Toyota Camry, even if it is in black." So I gave in and traded the Camry for a tricked-out Toyota Land Cruiser—just like Alex's. Alex had another car that he saved for special occasions: a restored 1968 Land Rover in mint green. But that was Alex.

My Land Cruiser conveyed enough success without being too pretentious, but the main message it gave was its outdoor appeal, which suggested weekends cross-country skiing or hiking in semi-rugged outbacks—a person in control of their lives and the elements. The only point I refused to change in my transition from car to SUV was my EVE WAS FRAMED bumper sticker. Despite Alex's warning to remain politically inert, I needed to hold on to some part of my feminist side.

I drove the three miles to my listing presentation, passing the scores of construction workers and landscapers busy trying to make the ostentatious Caliente Sands development look like it had been there for years, complete with water-hogging grass lawns, partially mature trees, and a scattering of desert shrubs that made some lilting concession that we did, indeed, live in a desert. I pulled my car down to the end of the cul-de-sac and parked right in front of 2666 Boulder Drive.

I pulled up to the house, unloaded my arsenal of presentation materials and equipment, rolled the artillery up to the front door, and rang the doorbell. Perfect. I was on time to the second, I thought, checking my watch. Noon, on the dot. A second later, my cell phone beeped three times, confirming that I was exactly on time. I took a deep breath, then let it out calmly. I was ready. I was woman, hear me roar.

From somewhere deep inside the house, a voice yelled, "Come on in, the door's open."

I rolled Desert Storm inside the empty house, wondering where I was going to set up my killer presentation. I had made hundreds of listing presentations when I worked with Alex, but for some reason, I was really, really nervous.

I heard Mr. Sandoval, the owner/investor, rummaging in a far-off bedroom. "I'll be right there," the voice said.

I continued to unpack my computer, turn it on, and unload all the leave-behinds into a pile when Mr. Sandoval entered the room and stood, towering over me. I rose to my full six feet one inch and shook my client's hand with a firm grip, pumping it like I was trying to extract water from rusty pump.

"I'm Amanda Thorne, from Apex Realty. I'll have my presentation materials all ready in just a minute, then we can make a run-through of what I—and the substantial resources of my company (I handed him the company brochure)—can do to help sell your house."

"Don't bother unpacking your stuff," he said.

My jaw dropped to the floor along with my fragile confidence. "But, Mr. Sandoval, if you just let me show you what . . ."

"You've got the listing," he said, turning and heading off toward a pile of mail on the granite kitchen countertop.

I stood frozen, wondering if I had heard him correctly, suffered a stroke, and was just imagining this, or whether he was playing a joke on me.

"You're giving me the listing . . . just like that?" I asked.

"Yeah, just give me the paperwork to sign, then you can get out of here."

"But . . . what . . ." I stammered. "You mean you have that much confidence in my talents as a real estate . . . ?"

"Listen, Amanda, don't get all full of yourself. I'm giving you the listing because the other agents didn't show, or did show up and were drunk."

"Drunk?"

Mr. Sandoval looked at me like an exasperated Peace Corps volunteer trying to explain irrigation to a technologically backward native.

"One got hit by a bus and couldn't make it—he's alive, but

at Desert Medical Center in a body cast. The other was stinking of bourbon or whisky or something and 'taw-gged lick dis,'" he slurred, mimicking a drunken real-estate agent. "And Mary Dodge, Her Highness, didn't show . . . not even a phone call. So you get the listing by default."

"Wow, well, thank you, Mr. Sandoval. I know that you won't be disappointed in your choice of me."

Mr. Sandoval raised his face from the pile of mail he'd been staring at. "Ms. Thorne, I didn't exactly choose you. Like I said, you won by default. In this kind of seller's market, I could hire a retarded baboon to sell my house and he'd probably have a contract on this fucking joint in two days with multiple offers."

At this point, I could've fired back at this surly asshole, but I decided to swallow my pride, thank the prick, and get the paperwork signed and leave. After all, the house was 4,700 square feet and could be listed at $1.1 million.

"I'll stage the house at my own expense," I added as I was packing up.

"Good, I'm not paying for you to put furniture in this house," Sandoval added. "As I said, an orangutan could sell this house."

"A retarded baboon was the phrase I believe you used earlier. I just think your house needs to stand out from all the other me-too houses in this development."

"Yeah, whatever. Just don't try and charge me anything extra," Sandoval grumbled. "Six percent commission is highway robbery. You're lucky the other agents didn't show up. I know I could get one of them to take five."

I had finished packing and was on my way out the door when the real baboon spoke again.

"Hey, you . . . turn around."

Wearily, I did as ordered, wondering if prostitution or working for Donald Trump was any worse.

"Did anyone ever tell you that you look like that Kathleen Turner chick?"

I sighed. "All the time . . . unfortunately."

Mr. Sandoval was one of a breed of investors who get rich in hot markets by buying houses before they're completed and selling them quickly while the going's good. These investors usually wear cheap suits and sport combover hairdos, their tobacco-stained hands covered by gold rings. Their hairy chests are topped off with a gold chain or two. Mr. Sandoval fitted this description to a T—the only thing missing was the saliva-wet cigar between his lips that had been chomped on for days on end. But despite his complete offensiveness to all other carbon-based life-forms, he had one thing that I needed: a listing. The house was huge, new, modern, and was filled with over-the-top conveniences. He didn't care what I did as long as I brought him an offer on 2666 Boulder Drive. And as an investor with multiple properties for sale, he wasn't going to be in my hair all the time. He had too many other irons in the fire to get involved in all the petty details like flyers, ads, or what hours and days I would hold open houses. In other words, this listing would be an easy one.

Time, of course, would prove me wrong.

CHAPTER 3

What You Don't Know Won't Hurt You . . . Much

Meeting your neighbors can be an experience filled with hope and new beginnings, of endless possibilities of friendships that would form and last a lifetime. Mine was not such an experience.

The first neighbor I met was Regina Belle. Or, more correctly, Regina met me. Okay, assaulted me. I was taking some envelopes out of the mailbox when I heard the soft tones of Regina behind me.

"SO WHEN THE FUCK ARE YOU GUNNA SAY HELLO?"

I turned to see a woman of about 70, no 75, no maybe 80 . . . It was difficult to tell.

"So you're the one who bought the house?" said the woman who was wearing a T-shirt that proclaimed, THANK GOD FOR VIAGRA. "Hi, I'm Regina, your neighbor. Regina Belle. I was wondering when you were going to fuckin' say hello!"

I had gone out to my mailbox to pick up my first load of mail since I moved in. I was desperate to meet new friends, so I thrust my hand out eagerly. "I'm Amanda."

"Boy are we glad to see you!" she exclaimed, wiping imaginary sweat from her brow. "Whew, when the neighbors saw the Sold sign out front, we almost had a party!"

I didn't like the sound of this—as a Realtor *or* as a recent home buyer. Sellers love to think that if they don't mention a problem with the house they're selling, it will go unnoticed forever. That is, until something caves in, catches fire, or leaks. Or, in this case, the one thing that almost always happens: a nosy neighbor, eager to show the newcomer that he or she knows everything that's going on, spills the whole story on the unsuspecting buyer. "You should've seen the sewage flowing out the front door . . ." is one that buyers hear all too often. Runner-up to that one in terms of scariness is: "The owner did all the remodeling himself. The framing, the stucco, the electrical, the plumbing! And imagine, he wasn't even a licensed contractor!" Of course, the most frightening ends with something like this: ". . . and when the SWAT team finally broke down the door, one of the officers slipped on the blood inside and broke his back!"

What I was about to hear wasn't quite as horrific as that, but it wasn't pretty.

"Oh, for fuck's sake, Leonard, the previous owner, was a crystal-meth head. Crazy as a loon near the end. His mom gave him all those beautiful antiques and he put them out on the lawn. The sprinklers just ruined everything."

"Out on the lawn?" I asked with total disbelief.

"He moved everything from the house out onto the lawn and lived outside . . . furniture and all. He claimed that the CIA was listening to the thoughts in his head by using the house's electrical system. That's why he knocked all those holes in the walls . . . to pull the wiring out of the walls."

This wasn't the Welcome Wagon I wanted. It was more of a drive-by shooting.

"No wiring?" I pleaded.

"Oh, there's *some* wiring in the house. After all, he had to have some electricity in the house. The air conditioning was running all the time. . . . Of course, he left the doors and windows open all the time," Regina stated as if this were normal—air conditioning the yard.

"Miss Belle . . ."

"Call me Regina."

"Regina . . . I'm sure you must be mistaken. I had the house inspected before I bought it."

"By whom?" Regina asked.

"Lance Hogarth."

"Ah, there's your problem, Amanda. He was as crooked as Highway 74. You must be new here."

"I am. Sort of."

"He left town a few days ago. Along with several builders and contractors who, I hear, are going to be under indictment."

"Indictment?"

"They had this big scam going on. Billing for services never performed, getting loans over the amount of the worth of the house and pocketing the difference, dumping fucked-up houses on unsuspecting buyers . . ." she said, waving her hand from my head to toe, proclaiming me rightly as the dumpee of such a house.

"I don't know what to say." And indeed, I didn't. By purchasing The Curse, I wanted to prove to myself—and Alex—that I could make money on my own. I could remodel houses, flip them, and make money. I could stand tall. I was powerful. I was a force to be reckoned with.

Now I stood there as waves of humiliation washed over me, the power draining from my body as I watched helplessly. I felt like I had just purchased a parcel of Florida swampland from a guy on a New York City street corner.

"C'mon, honey, you look like you could use a drink."

I was going to say something about the fact that it wasn't

quite 11:30 in the morning, but then I told myself that this was California. People lived differently here.

As Regina pulled me along to her front door, I had a chance to get a closer look at Regina. Her odometer definitely had some major mileage on it. She tried to cover it up with pancake makeup slathered on so thick, you felt that you could lift it off her face in one piece, starting just below the right jaw. It did the trick if you were standing thirty feet away and had cataracts that made your eyes look like they had been stuffed with cotton balls. She even plucked her eyebrows, a custom I associated with women who wove scarves into their pineapple-upside-down-cake beehive hairdos from the early sixties. Everything about Regina seemed to be of another era. Her clothes, jewelry, hairdo. Perhaps she slept in a giant Tupperware container, sealing herself inside every night, burping out the air from the present and preserving herself in a bygone era.

She broke her grip on my arm and opened the door to her house, beckoning me inside.

The interior was like Regina herself: unaltered by time, and uncorrupted by it. As my eyes scanned the sunny yellow living room, it, too, seemed stuck in time, like a car idling endlessly. Nothing from the present day seemed to have penetrated this lair, no sense that time had passed. There was no flat-screen TV, no cordless phones, not even a remote control lying around to suggest that the second millennium had come and gone.

"Sit down and I'll make you a sidewinder," Regina said gleefully.

I didn't even know what a sidewinder was, but I decided it was best to be a good neighbor and take whatever was given to me.

Regina proceeded to pour a splash, a glug, and a deluge of liquor from no less than seven different bottles into a cocktail mixer, followed by a few cubes of ice, which incidentally came from an ice bucket that was filled with ice at 11:30 in the afternoon. I notice these things.

"Tony Curtis taught me how to make a sidewinder," she said, agitating the shaker with such force I feared that Regina's head would come loose and fall to the floor.

"I was an extra in *Some Like It Hot* and he had his eyes on my ass from day one. Well, during a break in filming, he gets me into his dressing room and asks me if I want a sidewinder. 'A sidewinder,' I said, 'sure,' thinking it was some kinda code word for his cock. Well, seeing that I wanted to get someplace in the pictures, I said, sure. For years, I'd been fucking Gable and Errol Flynn for free, but enough was enough. I figured that if I was going to pay the toll, so to speak, I was going to drive the road. So you can imagine my disappointment when Tony heads over to me holding a cocktail shaker and two glasses!"

My first reaction to Regina's potty mouth was pure shock. Besides the T-shirt, she looked quite well-bred. This is what made her cursing so surprising at first encounter. It was like watching your water faucet gush water, then—all of a sudden—see a lizard crawl out from the tap. My initial shock was overwhelmed by the fact that my new neighbor had rubbed elbows with the rich and famous. Or, quite possibly, genitals.

"I hear you're a Realtor, sweetie?" Regina asked, handing me a drink as tall as the ass on a Texas cowboy.

"Yes," I replied.

"Right. Who isn't in Palm Springs?" Regina chuckled. "Hey, I heard a good Realtor joke. This woman gets pulled over for speeding, see. When the cop comes up to her window to ask for identification, the woman realizes that she left her purse at home. The cop says he still needs to see some form of ID. So the woman reaches into her glove compartment and pulls out her real-estate license and shows it to the cop. He tosses it back at her, and says, "Everyone has one of those in California. I need something more specific."

I forced out a small, but polite laugh.

"Well," Regina continued, "it's a lot funnier if you're hammered."

I guessed it was my turn now. "So, Regina, I take it you worked in Hollywood at one time?"

"The Golden Age," she exclaimed.

"Well, that must have been exciting."

"Oh, honey, those were the days . . . when stars were stars. Hepburn, Bacall, Davis, Grant. None of these flash in the pans like Streep or Close."

I was about to remind Regina that, to date, Meryl Streep and Glenn Close had probably made as many pictures as some of the greats. Plus, Streep and Close were members of my personal Academy of Those Who Can Do No Wrong. They were strong women—on and off stage. They stood their ground and succeeded in a man's world, and kept succeeding—even when they became "women of a certain age." I looked up to them, and greedily devoured their antics in magazines and the newspapers. Like the time Glenn Close stood up to a bunch of evangelicals causing trouble in her daughter's school system over tarot cards.

Regina took another ladylike sip of her drink. "So, Roberto tells me you're a gay divorcee."

I grinned as I caught her double entendre. This cookie may look like she lives in another era, but her gossip-loving ears were firmly rooted in the present. I had the suspicion that little went on in this town without Regina knowing about it. Or Roberto, my hairdresser.

"I assume, Regina, when you say Roberto, you mean Roberto Castro . . . the hairdresser?"

"Yes, I go to him too. Everyone does. Roberto told me you came here with your husband to sell real estate, and then it turns out he likes packin' fudge more then pussy and you two get divorced."

"That's pretty much the story," I admitted.

"Oh, honey, never tell a hairdresser anything you don't want getting around. I know from personal experience. I once told Roberto that I had sex with my second husband dressed as a rubber nun and before you knew it, everyone in town knew about it."

"A rubber nun?" I *had* to ask.

"Oh, honey," she said, laying a hand on mine, "I've done *much* worse. Much."

"I once had sex with my husband in a suit."

"Amanda, you whore!" Regina said, laughing.

"Well, at the time, I thought it was pretty wild. He was smoking a cigar, and I was dressed in a corset, stiletto heels, and sheer nylons. I did feel like a whore."

"Try dressing like Ilsa, she-wolf of the SS, and then try and tell yourself you're not a trollop."

"You're kidding!"

"No, I am not," Regina replied, then took a large gulp of her highball.

"Well, we do a lot of crazy things when we're young," I replied.

"Young, that was last week, honey!"

"Gee, I feel like such a prude."

"Don't worry, dear, you still have a lot of time to try new things."

I decided to come clean. After all, from what I had just learned from Regina, I'm sure my marital story paled in comparison to anything she had lived. "Well, yes, I moved here with my husband, Alex, and he decided to come out of the closet," I confessed, then took a swig of my sidewinder, raising it in front of my eyes in a toast to Regina and the secrets we were about to share.

"Oh, honey, you talk like you're the first one to marry a gay man. Judy Garland married one, and Liza's still marrying 'em. Hell, I married one myself!" Regina boasted.

"You did?"

"Yep, third one. Franklin Garfield."

"So let me guess . . . you had no idea when you married him."

"Hell no," Regina replied with utter certainty. "I married him because he *was* gay!"

My eyes narrowed as I sat forward in my chair. This was something I had to hear.

"And may I ask why?"

"The same reason you probably did. He was kind, caring, smart, knew how to dress, conduct himself, and he was dynamite in bed—the usual things a woman is looking for."

I was astounded. "So you knew from day one?"

"Sweetie, he worked in the wardrobe department at RKO . . . with Travis Banton, for God's sake."

To most people, the name Travis Banton would've meant nothing. But since both Alex and I were big fans of the classic black-and-whites of Hollywood, we not only knew who Travis Banton was, but we could name the stars who insisted on his artistry to make them look fabulous on-screen. Take the outfit and gloves Marlene Dietrich wore in the escape sequence in *Desire*. Alex and I were the perfect couple: fag and fag hag.

But I wanted to get back to the matter at hand: Here was the first woman I had encountered since my divorce who had married a gay man. Purposely. I wanted to get to the big answer, the why, in an attempt to better understand why I did what I did.

"So, Regina, did you end up divorcing at some point?"

"No, dear, he died six years into our marriage. A light fell on him and killed him during a run-through."

"Regina, that's terrible!"

"Yeah, well, I miss the son of a bitch. Best husband I ever had!"

"So you were married after that?"

"Three more times," Regina said proudly. "I marry 'em and I bury 'em."

(Regina had obviously discovered the secret of eternal life: Devour your mate after coupling. Not such a bad idea, really.)

"They all died?"

"Nearly all. One had a heart attack. One drove his car off a cliff."

"Off a cliff?"

"Yeah, no big deal. He was a real Don Yawn."

"Don't you mean Don Juan? He cheated on you?"

"No. *Yawn*. He was a real dud in bed."

"So another had a heat attack?"

"Yup."

"Wow," I uttered, "you put the Kennedys' bad luck to shame—to have so many tragic incidences."

"Incidences?" Regina huffed. "Sweetie, there was a lot of drinking in those days. Lots of people fell off barstools and died, drove off cliffs, or more ingloriously, drank themselves to death. Nowadays, the stars write books about it and make a million dollars. But back then, you didn't talk about it—you just did it. Everyone was pretty much plastered a lot of the time."

"So, Regina, can I ask you a personal question? I know we just met, but I have to ask this."

"Shoot, sweetie."

"So you never felt embarrassed about marrying a gay man?"

"No, never."

"Never?"

"Never."

"And you never felt foolish, knowing that other people looked at you, knowing that your husband was gay, and yet here you were with this man, pretending to play the role of man and wife?"

"Nope. Now it's my turn to ask you a question, Amanda."

"Go ahead."

"Did you ever feel embarrassed or foolish about being with this Alex?"

"Well, no . . . not really. I was in love with him."

"Then why did you ask me those questions?" Regina said, smiling with an all-knowing smile.

"You know, Regina, that's what I'd like to know."

We continued to chat for some time about gay husbands, living in Palm Springs, and the general shortage of good, available men nowadays. I looked at my watch and realized that, unfortunately, I had to go and be responsible and work for a living.

"Me too," Regina confided. "I've got a curtain call at six o'clock."

"Curtain call?"

"I'm on the stage."

I was confused. "I didn't realize there *was* a stage in Palm Springs."

"Oh, yes, dear. *The Follies*. You haven't seen it?"

"Oh, yes, I've heard about it, but I've never seen it."

"It's a musical/burlesque review. All the actors are over fifty-five. I'm seventy-six. Mamie is eighty-one. We tell jokes, we sing, we dance, we wear great costumes, we've got great sets. Here," she said, getting up from her chair and then disappearing into her kitchen. She returned with two tickets, which she held out to me.

"Here, take 'em, come see the show. It's a real hoot."

"I've heard about it but have never been."

"Well, good. Now you have no excuse for not going."

Palm Springs surprised me again. It was like the desert around us. The average tourist looked out over the vast untamed desert and saw nothing but sand and dead things. But Palm Springs, and everything around it, was teeming with life... more than I had ever imagined.

Regina and I eventually parted, but as I negotiated the hazardous minefield that was my future front yard, I caught myself smiling. Regina, though she was a little odd, was the first person besides Alex with whom I had made a real connection. Oh sure, Alex and I met a lot of people in the year since we had become residents of Palm Springs, but I never really felt like I could confide in them. Or expect them to understand me. But Regina, she cut right to the chase when it came to my marriage and subsequent divorce. The real clincher was when she got me to confess that my time with Alex had been the best of my life. Actually, it wasn't much of a confession—it was more of an acknowledgment.

"Then I am advising you never to forget that," Regina said earlier, shaking a liver-spotted finger in my face. "Never forget."

But I often did. Let me correct that: I usually did. Despite all the good things about myself and my life, I had trouble acknowledging them. I knew the culprits: My self-esteem had been short-circuited by my negative grandmother, mother, church, and a handful of baleful teachers who had obviously received their teaching degrees from Taliban bomb makers.

I managed to amble home under the slowly lifting haze of

the sidewinder, stepping over nails, pieces of plywood, and dried buckets of drywall mud. I eventually found my phone again (which seemed to move from room to room under its own power) and put in a call to my stager, Ronald. Alex and I had used him several times to put some life into empty houses we had to sell; he was reasonable, and he could fill a place practically the next day. Since the house borrowed heavily from the mid-century modern Alexander houses that made Palm Springs so desirable in recent years, Ronald said the staging was a no-brainer. A George Nelson surfboard coffee table, a Saarinen tulip dining set, blah, blah, blah. I would let him in later this afternoon at Boulder Drive; then he'd take his measurements, draw his plans, and take his pictures. He would have the furniture in place by the end of tomorrow. Perfect. Things were going smoothly. I liked when things ran smoothly, when order was reigning, keeping everything in its proper place. I felt comforted, safe, and happy. Life was good.

CHAPTER 4

Never Wear Prada to Meet the Devil

The next day, Ronald arrived with a trailer full of furniture, rugs, pictures, pottery, and all the accoutrements needed to help the decoratively challenged envision what a house could look like when it was filled with furnishings that actually coordinated with each other. Within three hours, 2666 Boulder Drive looked damn good, considering the walls were to remain the requisite slightly-off-white-but-not-too-much-to-offend-anyone eggshell. Once Ronald had left, I did a last-minute runaround of the place just to make sure everything was perfect for tomorrow's agent caravan. On Wednesday, the agents of the Palm Springs Board of Realtors arrived in droves by car or bus (yes, some firms actually had their own busses that ferried their agents from house to house) and would buzz through this house like locusts, grab flyers and anything complimentary, then head off to the next location. My time slot was for 9 A.M. to 11:30 A.M., which was good. The agents would be fresh and not yet be sick of seeing another poorly decorated, overpriced house.

Satisfied, I checked the house once more, giving in to my anal-compulsive side, and tested each window latch and door lock, locked the front door, and left the key in the electronic Supra keybox so that any other agent who wanted to see the house before tomorrow morning could. All they had to do is enter their code, point their electronic key at the keybox, and voilà! The key would pop out, it would record that agent's visit, and they could see the property any time of the day or night.

I drove home, then watched a documentary on Agatha Christie, followed by a program on the life cycle of dolphins. I slept that night with dreams of the Queen of Crime herself spouting blasts of air through a blowhole in the back of her neck while she clapped her flippers and demanded more kippers.

The next morning, I awoke, had a leisurely breakfast, showered, read the newspaper, dressed for success, and decided to get to my house 45 minutes early to spruce it up and get ready for its first showing. I got into my Land Cruiser, checked to see if I had my Supra key, briefcase, and trays of croissants, scones, and other breakfast goodies, and closed the door, slamming the door on my skirt. Damn. I opened the door to release my skirt, only to reveal a huge foot-long grease stain where the door had sunk its teeth into it. There wasn't enough time to change. Maybe I could just turn it around backwards and stand behind a kitchen counter. Great. Just great. The only thing I needed now was for my car not to start, I thought to myself. I turned the key in the ignition . . . and nothing. I tried it again . . . and nothing. Once again. Nothing. I pumped the gas pedal a few times and waited, then tried the starter again. Nothing. Of all the fuckin' days for my battery to die! And for Edwin to be out looking for countertops. Shit, shit, shit, shit, shit! Thinking fast, I ran into the house, desperately trying to find the phone book. I flung open drawers, closets, tore at piles of clothes, and still no phone book. I called directory assistance and asked for the name of a cab company, jotted the phone number down, and called. The phone rang and rang while I nervously looked at the minutes tick away on my watch. A tired old voice finally answered the phone, sounding like the owner had a mouthful of sand.

"Yello."

"Ah, I need a cab right away," I pleaded.

"Where are you located, missy? What city?"

"Palm Springs. Central."

"Can't help you there, sweetie. We're in La Quinta."

I hung up. Now why the fuck would a company call itself the Coachella Valley Cab Company and only handle rides in La Quinta? I called back directory assistance and got the operator to give me three cab companies with the name Palm Springs in it. Calling around, I discovered that all the cabs were already reserved the day before by people needing to get to the airport first thing in the morning. They could pick me up in an hour, but I needed one right away.

I whipped out my cell phone and dialed Alex but got his voice mail. Damn, damn, damn, damn! I ran out to the street to look in Regina's driveway to see if her ever-present powder blue American four-door land yacht was sitting there, ready to launch, but it was gone. Nowhere to be found.

I thought about taking a bus or hitching a ride, but decided against both courses of action. First, I didn't even know where the nearest bus stop was or how often they ran, and second, there was a lot a surrounding desert to be buried in, so hitch-hiking was out of the question. As I stood there in my cracked and stained concrete driveway, my eyes followed a particularly large fissure in the pavement into the garage where I spotted the solution to my problems: my fancy-pants road cycle. I figured that I could lock the heels of my pumps into the pedals (which only accepted a special racing shoe with clips) and I could be there in less than 15 minutes. Fuck the food. I threw my handbag over my shoulder, hopped on the bike, and began

pedaling away, amazed and very self-satisfied at my resource-
fulness. After six blocks, however, I heard a sickening crack
and looked down to see the heel on my right shoe hanging by
a small strip of leather like a fractured limb. I hit the brakes
and came to an instant stop, forgetting that my left heel was
still wedged in the pedal, causing me to topple over onto the
side of the road. Fuck! Even though plenty of cars zipped by
and could clearly see my predicament, not one of them
stopped to lend me a hand. Not one. I sat there motionless,
trying to reassess the situation in my mind, then attempted to
get up, only to discover that my hair was tangled in a cholla
cactus. I knew enough from hiking in the desert not to touch
the cholla needles, since they stuck to just about anything that
brushed up against it. Fingers, hair, clothes—anything. So I
stood there on the side of the road, straddling my bike in a
business suit, one and a half heels, with my hair securely
wrapped around the limb of a cactus, wondering what to do
next. "FUCK!" I screamed.

In times like these, the common person would panic. But
since I had attended several outdoor survival training schools
with Alex, I stopped, rested, assessed, and created a plan. Or
was I supposed to stop, drop, and roll? First, I would try and
untangle my hair from the cactus carefully, then use my comb
to remove the fine needles that had lodged there. Easier said
than done. There was so little distance between the cactus
and my head, I couldn't get back far enough to see which way
to start unwinding my hair. I tried to unwind to the left, but
met resistance after an inch, so I reversed my course and tried
to unwind to the right. This wasn't much better. Then a
thought occurred to me—a horrid thought. I had a pair of scissors in my purse. This was the last thing I wanted to do, but
even worse was the idea that if I didn't free myself soon, my
close quarters with the cholla could mean getting the needles

in my eyes, so it looked like I was going to have to play hair-dresser. Holding myself stiller than a mime with rigor mortis, I made small jumping motions with my shoulder, which caused my handbag to take small leaps down my arm until it could be reached with my left hand, which had far more freedom of movement than the right. I clicked the purse open, rummaged around inside until I managed to stab myself in my index finger with the sharp scissors. Another "FUCK!" Taking the scissors in my left hand, I moved the scissors from the base of my hair slowly outward until I could feel the sharp spines of the cactus, then cut, and repeated the procedure, and cut and repeated until I was free. The blood from my stabbed finger had undoubtedly seeped into my hair.

I got back onto the bike and did what any normal, warm-blooded woman would have done in the circumstances: I took out a compact and looked at my face and hair in the mirror. Then I did the only other logical thing: I cried. And cried. And cried. It wasn't just the needles in my hair, face, and scalp; my running mascara; my dirty face and bloody hair that looked like it was styled by Stevie Wonder that made the tears come gushing out. It was everything. I was trying so hard to get over my divorce, the feeling of being so foolish, of trying to be independent and making a go of things myself and being a success, and now it seemed that everything was still blowing up in my face. There just was no letting up. The Fates were against me, and they were perfectly intent on kicking me while I was down.

I took one more look in the mirror and suddenly realized that there was now another face in the reflection that I hadn't noticed before. It was Amanda Thorne, who transformed herself into a successful real-estate agent in the tony city of Bloomfield Hills, Michigan, bought a mid-century home designed by Brayton Thorne—Alex's grandfather—a woman who bagged the most eligible bachelor (forgetting the gay part) in the office, who traveled to places on earth people in my hometown of Waterford only dreamed about, and moved clear across the country to Palm Springs and hit the ground running. The divorce, my cursed house, the car not starting—these were just temporary setbacks. I had survived these kinds of things before and I will survive them again. So I picked myself up, brushed myself off, got on my bike, and pedaled like a person who had nothing to lose and everything to gain.

The rest of my trip went off with no more accidents. When I arrived at the house, my worst fear was waiting there to face me: over 50 agents who were just arriving in busses and their own cars to see my listing. Some were starting to leave.

I hopped off my bike and tried to keep my head held high as I walked the bike to the front door, hobbling like a person born with two left feet. Scrape, clunk, scrape, clunk—I walked like Marie Antoinette to the guillotine. I felt that if I kept my dignity, the other Realtors would be amazed at how composed I was, despite the fact that I looked like I had just barely won a death match with a very pissed-off eagle.

I opened my purse to retrieve my Supra key, tossing away several twigs that had made their way into my bag. I calmly entered my personal identification number and pressed the Enter key, pointing the electronic key at the lockbox on the door. The box chirped a tiny chorus of beeps, and I heard the slide-out tray lock release and promptly plopped the key into my hand. Okay, fine, I could do this, I told myself. Once these people saw Ronald's mastery of décor and the over-the-top luxury of the home, they would forget all about my appearance, and ooh and aah and be dazzled and race to pull out their cell phones to call their clients to make an immediate offer on 2666 Boulder Drive.

My vision was shattered when I opened the door to the house. Inside, it looked like Snoop Dogg and his entourage had stayed overnight in the place. Tables were overturned, one cracked in half, sofa cushions were scattered all over the floor, fabulous fifties highball glasses were smashed to bits everywhere you looked. This was not good. I pushed the door open slowly, and as it opened wider, the scene revealed even more damage, followed by what was clearly a dead man lying on the carpet, the uncomfortable-looking sprawl of his body telling the whole story.

Oh shit!

I had never seen a dead person before. Let me modify that. Being raised in a Catholic household with a legion of elderly relatives who died almost on a daily basis during my child-hood, I had seen more dead bodies than a New York City coro-ner. But I had never seen one that was the result of violence committed by a person or persons unknown. And apparently, neither had most of the agents who brought up the rear be-hind me, since no one had screamed yet. The scene was so surreal, and people were so stunned that no one said a thing, but they kept close at my heels like frightened characters in a comedy murder movie. I approached the corpse and, to my surprise, found that his mouth was open and improbably filled with something no one would ever have suspected: rocks. Yes, rocks. There were so many of the grape-sized stones crammed in the victim's mouth, they forced his cheeks out like a chip-munk's storing nuts for the winter. Then, like a dull cliché, a woman agent who entered the house saw the body, let out a blood-curling scream, and ran from the house like a cadre of demons were in hot pursuit of her, just inches behind, snap-ping at the heels of her cheap shoes.

The other agents kept looking at the body, then at me, then

back to the body. So, since nature abhors a vacuum, I chose to fill it.

"The furnishings and the body are negotiable in the house's price," I said, not realizing that a joke right now was probably not the best idea. But I couldn't help it. Whenever I got into a tense situation, my way of dealing with the tension was to let loose a joke.

"OH MY GOD, THAT'S DOC WINTERS, THE EN-VIRNOMENTALIST!" a woman agent in a too-short skirt exclaimed. "Oh dear," she said, lowering her voice. "This isn't good at all. He's been a thorn in the side of developers and Realtors for years, and now he's been murdered. This isn't good at all."

I was somewhat new to the desert, but I had read all about Mr. Winters's efforts to stop development in the Chino Cone area, a triangular slice of land leading uphill to the Palm Springs aerial tramway. As one of the last large tracts of land in Palm Springs, this area held special interest for builders since this land had a panoramic view of almost the entire valley from its elevated position high above the desert floor. Developers and city leaders made the case that what Palm Springs needed was high-end housing with well-heeled residents in order to attract upscale businesses to the moribund downtown. The other half of city residents felt that they'd rather look up at the granite foothills and craggy peaks instead of hundreds of McMansions. I, of course, weighed in on the side of controlling suburban sprawl, making mine—and Alex's—the lone voices in the local real-estate business. I did my best to keep my opinions on the matter my little secret.

Now we had a body on our hands, and this was not going to stay a secret.

"I've called 911," someone said. "They're on their way."

"Doc Winters," another voice said. "Dead. Good! The bastard. A real prick."

I turned to see who was speaking ill of the dead. An agent in a cheap Hawaiian shirt (Why do people have to wear rayon Hawaiian shirts in the desert?) with a red face and harvest gold hair was looking down at Doc with a sneering smile on his face.

"Excuse me," I said, rising to my full six-foot one-inch height. "A man here is dead, and I think we could have a little respect."

Mr. Red Face continued, "If there weren't so many witnesses standing here, I'd give the ol' Doc a swift kick in the ass. That fuckin' rock hugger is—was—holding the whole town ransom. He cares more about a bunch of goddamn lizards than he does about houses and jobs. Now that someone's had the guts to do the job, he's out of the way and maybe this city can get on with moving forward."

The crowd of agents fell eerily silent. Most of them registered shock at the coarseness of Mr. Redface's tirade, but I also detected that some of them quietly agreed with the cheap Hawaiian shirt.

I tried to hold my tongue, but I could do so no longer.

"Listen, you—I-don't-know-what-your-name-is, but why do we have to stand by and let others turn Palm Springs into another Los Angeles or Phoenix? I would think that by preserving our mountain views, we would make the houses that already exist here worth more. Plus, think supply and demand. Restricting the amount of houses built would increase the value of what's already here," I said to a crowd of blank, unyielding faces. I might as well have been talking to a group of simians.

Mr. Redface was about to open his fat, little face when the

scream of sirens broke the confrontational atmosphere of the room.

Since I had seen a lot of crime programs on television, I decided to be the sensible one and suggest that we don't let anyone else into the house until the police arrived. I also suggested that we move away from the body and stand off to the side so as not to contaminate the crime scene.

"Who's she all of a sudden?" Redface had to chime in again. "Fuckin' Angela Landberry?"

"That's Lansbury," I corrected. True, a corpse was lying at my feet, but I was going to be damned if I was going to let a misinformed idiot with hair the color of a 1960s stove run roughshod over everything.

A police car screamed to a halt in front of the house, scattering agents right and left. Two officers, male and female, entered the house and seeing a dozen or so agents standing there, herded us all outside and took statements from all of us, most of them differing wildly from each other, even though the gist of what happened was that I walked inside and found a body. The rest merely entered the house and stared at the body. Simple. The body just laid there. But from what I was overhearing, it sounded like a pitched battle had ensued. And shots had been fired. Several, in fact. Throughout all of this, I did notice one curious but unmistakable thing: The other Realtors were shaking their heads and gabbing with just each other. And when I began to pace around to let off a little steam, the agents parted and let me through. I felt like a shark swimming through a school of fish. It never dawned on me until now that some—maybe all of these people—thought I was in some way connected to this murder. Or an even more frightening thought, that I had killed Doc Winters myself. I was considering the dire effect this incident could have on my career when I heard my name being called behind me.

"Mrs. Thorne?"

I turned to see a man in a suit coming toward me. A very handsome man. In a situation like this, I don't think I would have noticed his looks or anything about him, but I was struck by his ice-blue eyes. Like a Siberian husky's, except that both of his were the same color. And his hair was my favorite color: jet-black hair with small strands of distinguished gray placed perfectly for effect. Very Cary Grant.

"Yes, I'm Amanda. Amanda Thorne."

"Mrs. Thorne, I'm Detective Ken Becker, Palm Springs Police. I'm told that you have the listing for this house?"

"Yes, this is its first showing . . . off to a great start, huh?"

The detective managed a small laugh.

"Mrs. Thorne . . .

"Amanda, please."

"Amanda. Would you tell me exactly what happened when you came to the house?"

"Well, my car wouldn't start, so I ended up riding here on my bicycle. When I—"

"Your car wouldn't start?" Detective Becker interrupted. "Is your car an older model?"

"No, it's only a year old, that's the damnest thing about it. I just had the thing tuned up."

"Interesting. Could I go see your car after we finish here?"

"Sure," I said. "Oh, I get it. You think someone tampered with it, don't you?"

"Perhaps."

"That's funny. I never considered that possibility until now. Of course, I never expected to find a body in my open house, either."

He asked me to describe in detail everything that happened today, right up to and including how I opened the door to the house and found the body. When I finished, he fell silent, staring at his notes, then began flipping back and forth through the notebook he had been jotting in. Back and forth, back and forth, circling or underlining important facts with a very expensive ink pen. Standing there with nothing to do, I found myself looking over the detective, summing him up for a possible date. Here I was giving testimony to a murder investigation, and I found myself getting turned on by this officer standing in front of me. Normally, I would've been shocked by my thinking, but I chalked up my reaction as pure horniness—plain and simple. After all, it *had* been a long time. And secondly, I loved a man in uniform—even though he wasn't wearing one now (and probably hadn't in years since having been promoted to what I presumed was a detective). But I knew for sure that he had one at home in a closet, expertly cleaned and pressed and hanging on a cedar hanger. And I just bet that he looked damn sexy in it too. Okay, okay, Amanda, now slow down. Before we go too far, let's make sure he's not gay first. You've made that mistake once before . . . better not do it again. Plus, remember, you're in Palm Springs now. Your chance of the detective being straight is barely 50/50.

The moustache is very sexy, but it's trimmed so impeccably, so precisely, I'm going to have to chalk it up to being gay. (Why do so many gay men have moustaches? To hide the stretch marks. Alex told me that one last week.)

Hair, neatly trimmed. Cropped short. Gay. Although, he is a cop, of sorts. They like to wear their hair short—an authority thing. Okay, we'll call that one a toss-up.

Look at the shoes. Sleek, fairly expensive. Not cutting edge, but they are up with the times. I'm going to have to put this one solidly in the column of gay. Straight men seem to have a gene missing when it comes to picking out great shoes. But these are highly questionable. I would think that a police detective would wear something sensible, comfortable. Something you could crouch in the mud wearing without worrying about how they'd stand up. But these look like they've never touched the ground. Plus, these are definitely not from Florsheim.

On to the personal products now. I leaned ever so slightly toward our dear detective and took a camouflaged sniff. My nostrils barely fluttered.

"Allergies?" the detective suggested.

Jesus, this guy doesn't miss a thing. "Oh, yes, a touch," I replied.

"Happens this time of the year," the detective replied. "They scalp the lawns here."

"Scalp?"

"They dry out the summer grass, the Bermuda, then shave it down to a fraction of an inch. Tons of dust go up in the air during the process. Then they throw down cow manure and winter rye seed so the grass looks green all winter."

"It sounds like a lot of work, and a lot of pollution."

The detective looked up and stole what I was sure was a glance at me. He didn't think I was looking directly at him when he got his look, but his eyes met mine, and held just a nanosecond too long, I thought.

"The grass that handles the heat of summer goes dormant here in the winter. The snowbirds want to come here and see green lawns all winter. So that's what they get," he added.

This was weird. Here we were talking about dead grass and I swear to God there was a whole body language conversation taking place, just under the surface of the banal. I continued my evaluation of Becker's personal care products. I couldn't sense any rarified fragrances, so the detective earned a point in the hetero column.

Two points in the homo column and perhaps one in the hetero. Total them all, and still you didn't ever know for sure.

And even if you were good at noticing all the telltale signs, you were still no better than before. It got more confusing all the time. The gay men were getting butcher. They've been wearing their hair shorter on top and more cropped on the sides. Some are even out-butching the Marines. (Of course, as many are getting older and receding hairlines come into play, shorter hair isn't an option.) They've been slapping on the muscles at a faster rate than straight men. And I've noticed gay men wearing fatigues and big black boots more and more. Straight men are starting to look downright feminine.

And if that isn't confusing enough, we heterosexual women have to deal with the latest innovation in the sex evolution: the metrosexual. It's the straight woman's dream come true. A man who is sensitive, caring, knows how to groom and dress himself, and enjoys fucking women. But the trouble is, these men are so close to being gay, that instead of being confident and deliriously happy with them, I always feel that if I were to land one, I'd always be looking over my shoulder to see if my boyfriend was stealing glances at other men. Like they had one foot in the closet and the other outside. Never in, never out. And me, always wondering, never trusting. Some relationship.

Before I drove myself mad, I decided that I should stop beating around the bush and find some more direct way of determining if I was barking up the right tree.

"So what does your wife think about your line of work, bodies and all?" I asked, realizing that this wasn't the smoothest way of getting my answers. This guy, after all, was very perceptive.

"There is no Mrs. Becker," he replied, very businesslike. "I'm divorced," Becker added.

"Oh, me too," I gushed. There's hope, I thought to myself. I was just about to probe a little more when I saw a sight that made my blood run cold: a TV news van. The van had barely stopped moving when a news crew, headed by a blond Barbie-wannabe, sprang out of the van and broke into a gallop toward the detective and me. I asked Ken if I could have his jacket.

"You cold?"

"No," I pleaded, "I don't want them to catch me looking like this!"

As he handed me his sport jacket, he said, "You know you're going to look like a probable suspect with this over your head?"

"I'd rather look like I killed a family of sixteen than have the local news crew catch me looking like this," I admitted, throwing his jacket over my head.

Ken led me down the sidewalk to his car, where, like a gentleman, he opened the door to my side, and I slipped into the passenger seat, but not before clunking my head against the roof rather loudly, just about a half inch above my left eye. Fuck!

Ken closed my door, then a moment later, opened his and slipped in beside me. He started the car, and as he threw his vehicle in gear, I suddenly remembered my beloved and very expensive Specialized carbon-graphite road cycle propped up against the house where I left it before this whole mess began. I tossed off the jacket just in time to see both a TV camera crew and a photographer looming at my window with her camera, who, I might add, managed to get plenty of perp shots and footage of me before the car sped away.

"Shit!" Ken exclaimed as the car neared the end of the street and turned onto the main artery that would take us out of Caliente Sands. "I'm so sorry about that, Amanda."

"You did your best, Ken. I didn't even see the photographer sneak up. She came out of nowhere."

"Let me call back to the crew and have them drop off your bike when they come to take a look at your car."

We rode to The Curse pretty much in silence. Me, I was too stunned to say anything, and Detective Becker was lost in thought. When we arrived at my house, I got out of the car, and Ken began to run back over questions that he had been mulling around in his head.

"So let me get this straight. No one had been in the house besides you when you opened the door this morning?"

"The entire cast of *Cats* could've been in there since I put the lockbox on yesterday."

"Explain how this thing works. I know that you punch in a code into that handheld device there and you point it at the keybox, and it opens and gives you the keys to the house, but is there any way of knowing who's been in the house?"

"Absolutely. All I have to do is go online and I can tell you the name of the agents who have been in and out of 2666 Boulder Drive."

"I would appreciate if you would do that, but tell me first— is there any way of making your electronic key look like someone else's?"

"What do you mean?"

"Suppose I had one of those handheld electronic keys like you have there. Could I enter someone else's code with my key so the keybox would think I was another agent?"

"I don't know for sure, but I wouldn't think so. When you get your key, it has just one code that corresponds to it. The local board of Realtors are the only people who can change it. You'd have to go into their offices and switch it, but then again, each key has one specific code. So when I go to a house with a lockbox, enter my code and aim it at the lockbox, the lockbox opens it and knows that the person who got the house keys is Amanda Thorne."

"So what if I stole your electronic box there?"

"It wouldn't do you much good. You don't know my code," I remarked, showing the detective my code in the electronic display window.

"I could guess."

"You've got four numbers in any combination—you could be there all night trying. When you enter the wrong code, it takes a while for the key to tell you've got it wrong. It searches and searches, realizing that your code doesn't match your device, then it buzzes and tells you access is denied. Plus, you have to update this bloody thing every night by putting it in a cradle, and it either calls through a phone line or it updates via your computer's Internet connection."

"I see. Amanda, would you go into the house and get me a list of anyone who's been in that house since you put the lock-box on? I'm going to wait here for my crew to arrive."

I made my way into The Curse, past Edwin who was jack-hammering into the cement slab foundation, and sat down at my computer. Normally, most people upon arriving home to find a contractor burrowing into their house's foundation would ask what's wrong, how much this was going to cost, and how long this would take. Me, I was getting used to living with Hell House. I didn't even ask anymore.

I sat down at my computer and went online. In a few minutes, I had the list of agents who had entered the house between the time that I put the keybox on the front door and the time that I entered it this fateful morning. There were only two persons on the list: Cathy Paige and Ed Jensen. Not knowing who these agents were, I went on the Desert Area Multiple Listing Service and did an agent search. According to the MLS, Cathy worked for Dodge & Dodge Realty, headed by none other than the queen of Palm Springs real estate: Mary Dodge. This was an interesting turn of events. Ed worked for Desert, Inc. I noticed something else that raised my eyebrows. I printed out my results and took them outside to Detective Backer.

"Here you go, Detective, here's your list of suspects."

He took the list, read the names, and looked up at me.

"Just two names?"

"I'm surprised that there was even one."

"How's that?"

"Well, I only put the keybox on the door yesterday afternoon. Late. That's not a lot of time for someone to locate the property on the Internet, see that the place is open for showing, and go get in a car and drive out and see it."

Ken was formulating a question in his head. "But you had 2666 Boulder Drive on your Multiple Listing Service before that?"

"Yes, but only a day before. As soon as you have the signed paperwork in your hand for a listing, you have to put it in the MLS ASAP. If you don't, you get fined by the board. It's called a pocket listing."

"And what's so bad about a pocket listing?"

"It's not in the best interests of a client. I means you're holding back a house off the market because you are lining up a possible buyer of your own to make an offer on it."

Ken was clearly getting into the intricacies of real estate. "And that's bad, having a built-in buyer?"

"No, it's good for the agent because he or she can handle both ends of the deal—seller and buyer—and earn both commissions. Three percent and three percent. Six percent total. Multiply that times, say, five hundred thousand or even a million dollars and you can see where it adds up."

"Yeah, but it still sounds like a good deal for the agent and the buyer. You get a big commission and the seller gets an offer on his house. Everybody's happy."

"You forgot one thing. In a pocket listing, the seller's house isn't really on the open market. It's really in a closed market of just one buyer. The buyer makes an offer, the seller is happy to get an instant offer, and the house is never out there in front of other buyers."

Ken's face lit up like he discovered the grand unification theory. "Buyers who, in a crazy market like this one is, might bid even more, starting a bidding war for the property, which could ultimately earn even more for the seller."

I reached over to the detective and pressed my finger into his forehead.

"Congratulations, you just earned a gold star in real estate. That's why the board and the MLS don't allow pocket listings—it could be bad for the seller. Does this have any bearing on the case?"

"Pocket listings?" Ken answered. "None whatsoever. But it is fascinating to learn behind-the-scenes information like this."

"Yeah, this is the kind of action-packed excitement that attracted me to the business."

Becker took another look at the information I had printed for him and I could almost see a giant lightbulb appear over his head.

"Wait a minute! What's today?"

"The twenty-fourth."

"So this Cathy Paige showed your house to a client *at seven-eighteen A.M. this morning*?"

"That's what caught my attention when I first saw it back in the house. I don't know any agent who's that much of a go-getter. Not even in this market. But even weirder, Ed Jensen came in before her at six-fifteen. That's really suspicious. I guess that's a weird statement coming from me, a possible murder suspect. And that's what I am, right? A murder suspect?"

"Yes, everyone who had access to the victim is a suspect."

"That's funny," I remarked. "I've never been a murder suspect before."

"There's a first time for everything."

Eventually, the crime unit arrived at my house and set out to examine my car. A man and a woman went over it like two extraterrestrials examining an automobile for the first time, their latex-gloved hands floating over the surface of things, applying a little fingerprint dust here and putting small bits of things into plastic bag. What was next? A probe up the muffler of my car?

When they popped the hood of my car, the male examiner finally spoke. "There's your problem," he said, holding up a battery cable with a pen. "The wire's been clipped clear through."

Detective Becker, who up until now had said nothing, was intrigued.

"Bruce," he said to the man holding my battery cable, "can you tell what kind of instrument was used to cut the cable?"

"Something sharp, like wire cutters. Definitely not garden shears or anything with blunt, heavy blades. The cut is pretty clean, there's no crushing around the cut."

"Thanks, Bruce. Amanda, do you lock your car at night?"

A long hesitation on my part. "Uh . . ." I had been busted.

"So whomever did this had no trouble popping the latch on your car hood."

"Sorry."

"Nothing to be sorry about. But let's keep your car locked from now on. I wouldn't want anything to happen to you," Ken said, shooting a glance to me.

"Why, Ken," I said, "you sound like you are beginning to care about me."

"I care about you, and everyone else in this town. It's my job, ma'am," he replied, tipping an imaginary hat in my direction.

I couldn't help it, but my eyes darted to Ken's crotch again, at about the same time Ken looked up at me and caught me in the act.

He pointed up at his face with the end of his pen. "I'm up here, Amanda."

Busted again.

"So what's with the jackhammering in the house. You got mice?" No mention of the crotch.

"Oh, that? That's Edwin."

"Edwin?"

The way he asked, it sounded for a minute like he was disappointed that there was someone else in my life.

"My live-in contractor."

"Oh."

"You know how rare they are. This one's a little crazy, but he's good. So he's living in the backyard, in a tent . . ."

"In a tent? A Bedouin?" This revelation produced a wry smile on the detective's face. "Are you really that hard up for a contractor?"

I looked at Ken and asked, "Have you tried to do any re-modeling lately?"

"Not really."

"Well, let me tell you, they're harder to find than a condom in a nunnery. You don't look a gift horse in the mouth these days. You take what you can get. Plus, he doesn't talk much."

The detective whipped out his notebook again and began writing. "How long has Edwin worked for you?"

"Mr. Becker, you don't think Edwin had anything to do with this whole mess, do you?"

"I have to check out every possibility. Could I speak to him?"

"Sure, though I doubt you'll get much out of him. He keeps pretty much to himself."

Ken Becker went off and questioned Edwin, asking him primarily if he had seen or heard anything during the night, but he came up short. Edwin slept deeply and soundly the night before. No sound of wire cutters or garden shears disturbed his slumber.

Another hour and the detective had wrapped up his investigation with me. I, naturally, hated to see him go. I wanted to talk more, to see what kind of music he listened to, what he liked to read, what he did on weekends, what he looked like naked. But I just let him walk away, get into this car, and drive away. And I just stood there. The man that got away. Physically, I was attracted to him, but was my mind telling me to cool it? Was it once bitten, twice shy?

And there I was left standing there in my driveway, a recent divorcee, a murder suspect . . . with bad hair.

CHAPTER 5

The Hairdresser Is Always the First to Know

The bag of frozen peas I held on my head brought the egg-sized lump down to the size of a large, angry grape, but before I could go out in public again, I had to do something about my hair. It was so lopsided that I had to either walk around leaning heavily to the left, or I needed an emergency appointment with Roberto, hairdresser to the rich and annoying.

As luck would have it, one of his client's Botox treatments had resulted in a severe case of temporary eyelid droop, so much so that Mrs. Dorn couldn't keep her eyes open enough to drive downtown to get another layer of shellac applied to her hair (according to Roberto). You had to be careful what you said around Roberto.

An hour and a half later, I entered Roberto's salon just as he was finishing up blow-drying a client's hair. When he saw me, he actually screamed and dropped the dryer and comb, covering his mouth in horror.

"OH MY GOD! OH MY GOD! SOMEBODY BEAT YOU!"

"Roberto . . ."

"YOU HUSBAND! YOU TELL ME VERE HE IZ, I GO BEAT HIM UP!"

"It's not what it looks like . . ." I tried again.

"OH JESS, YOU TRY AND PROTECT HIM, BUT YOU MUST NOT."

"Remember, Roberto, my husband is gay. We're divorced."

"He is gay, yes. Oh good, then even I can beat him up," Roberto said, punctuating the word *beat* with his rattail comb.

"I wouldn't do that, Roberto. He's got a fifth-degree black belt in Isshinryu karate. He could punch through your ribcage and come out the other side."

"Really?" Roberto replied, raising his eyes in a suggestive manner. It was clear that Roberto liked things rough, if you know what I mean. "Ees he single? Do you think Alex would like Roberto?"

"Roberto!"

"So who do theze to you?"

"A cactus, my purse scissors, and the roof of a cop car—in that order."

"I dunt understand."

"I fell off my bike."

"Your bike? It must be very tall bike!"

"Roberto, I'll tell you all about it when you finish with your client."

Roberto turned back to his client, whom he had plainly forgotten in all the excitement. "Yes, I finish you, Missus Houston, then I make you the next bee-you-ti-ful woman in the world."

I headed back toward the receptionist and took a seat. Roberto was a man who loved drama and clearly admitted to it. He blamed it on being Brazilian, but I think somewhere deep in his DNA resided a protein that caused him to see drama where there was little, or to create it where there was none. When he finished with Mrs. Houston, he grabbed my hand and practically flung me into his chair.

"Okay, I figure out what to do and you talk."

Roberto circled my head slowly, like a mongoose sizing up a cobra. Where to strike, where to strike first?

Roberto held out his hand. "Wait, before you start, I'm going to cut you short. But dun't worry, I'll give you some sleek, heavily layered zuper short trusses. You look joost like Sharon Stone!"

I looked at Roberto's reflection in the mirror. "I'm not sure I want to resemble a woman made famous for ice-picking her victims to death . . . not right now."

Roberto started cutting, then after 30 seconds of silence, he started laughing uncontrollably. Years of breathing hairspray fumes had made his brain a tad slow on the uptake.

"I geet it . . . Basic EEnstink . . . You are so funny!"

I watched as my dirty-blond hair started falling onto the floor in clumps, like my head had decided to call an early autumn. Roberto wound my hair around his fingers and snipped like a brain surgeon, let go, then attacked from new angles, his scissors launching another strike from behind. Snip, clip-clip. Snip.

So while I started the transformation from Amanda Thorne to Sharon Stone, I told my story to Roberto, who snipped away, listened intently, or covered his mouth in horror—depending on where I was in the story.

"I know who did theeze. Mary Dodge!" he proclaimed. Again, a stabbing motion with his rattail comb.

Roberto's comment struck me with such force, I rose up in the chair a few inches and turned around to face him.

"That's funny that you should mention her, Roberto. Someone from her firm was in my house just this morning, a short time before the murder."

Roberto shrugged and raised his eyebrows as if to say, "You see!"

David James

"C'mon, Roberto, spill it. What do you know . . . and how do you know it?"

"Everyone tell Roberto everything. De hairdresser ees the virst to know."

"I see. So what do you know?"

Roberto took a deep breath, as if the story he was about to tell required large amounts of oxygen.

"Whell, whone of my clientz eez Helen Hatcher. People they call her The Hatchet, wheech I do not theenk is very nice, but anyway, Helen, she hate Mary Dodge. She sayz Mary she buys land up in the hills. It is a beeg secret. She sayz Mary ees probably going to put up a big house jhust for her so she can look down on us pions."

"Pions?"

"Jes, pions!"

"Roberto, pions are subatomic particles. Maybe you mean peons?"

I got the rattail comb pointed at me for another correct answer. "Jess, pee-ons. Helen, she also sayz that Mary Dodge give lots of money to ecology so she can look like she love animals and the land, but all she want to do is meek money and she no care if she pave over evertheeng."

"So Helen told you all this? Interesting. So I guess Mary is not a client of yours?"

"No, she drag her raccoon hair over to dat whore, Nikki Bertoli, who know how to color hair like she ees blind."

A little professional jealousy.

"So Mary Dodge is buying up land around the Chino Cone, but no one knows about it?"

"Like I say, a beeg secret. She don't want anybody to know theeze. She buy for herself and for others."

Roberto continued to prattle on and on, telling me how he drives down to Oceanside, California, to pick up Marines from nearby Camp Pendleton. ("The treeck is to pay for zem, meals, drinks because zey get such sheetty pay.") Then he launched into a one-sided conversation about some wealthy woman from Indian Wells who wanted Roberto to dye her snatch to match her Bichon Frise. Yes, her furburger.

As I listened to Roberto, it dawned on me how easy it was to get information from people. For the most part, it was like venereal disease: Most everyone was willing to pass it around without having the tiniest inkling that they were doing it. It was possible that I could do a little investigating and find the murderer myself, and show Palm Springs that I had nothing to do with Doc Winter's death. *Or get killed in the process*, the other little voice in my head said. I hated that other little voice.

After an hour of snipping and clipping, followed by tales of what it took to pick up a horny Marine, I was done. And to be perfectly honest, it was terrific. Because I had cut portions of my hair so short to escape the cactus, Roberto cut my hair even shorter, gave it some highlights, and I was transformed into a mature, city sophisticate. I was getting tired of the longer hair, anyway. After all, I was in my forties now. It was time.

After leaving the salon, I made a stop at my real-estate firm and talked to my broker. I was expecting more scorn or outright avoidance, but all I got was a wave of sympathy. It felt nice. Everyone wanted to know, in the following order: (1) Was I scared when I came upon the body? (2) What did I do when I saw it? (3) That's quite a lump on your head. (4) And gee, who did your hair? (I work in a very gay office.)

After all the hullabaloo died down, I went to my mailbox up near the reception desk to excavate the mountains of flyers and brochures that reproduced endlessly in my mail slot, hawking everything from overpriced architectural monstrosities to discounts on plastic surgery (guaranteed to make you look your best and land more sales)—anything that could be even remotely attached to real estate. There was no shame when you became a Realtor—it was open season for junk mail.

At the front desk sat Margie Blackwell. Amidst the maelstrom of frantic calls from buyers and sellers, escrow officers seeking impossible information, and contractors squawking about not being paid, Margie was an island of calm in a stormy sea of crises that were mostly self-created or self-imagined. Margie had seen millions of dollars come and go, residents move into Palm Springs and later leave, condos go up and, occasionally, fall down. Nothing was going to unsettle her. Not earthquakes. Not floods. Not a plague of locusts or a rain of toads or a tidal wave of snakes. Margie, a sprite 38 years, sat at her post, year after year, wearing her trademark fishnet stockings and Minnie Mouse pumps, her red-painted nails flying over the keyboard of her computer, answering the telephone with the calm dexterity of a brain surgeon. But what really endeared her to me was the way she handled all the drama that accompanied her post as the nerve center of a very nervous profession. She was a virtuoso of the insincere. Clients who got arrogant or condescending with her on the phone would receive such an outpouring of sympathy, followed by a promise to "get right on it," that the listener on the other end of the line wouldn't know if he or she was being ridiculed or not. Years and years of practicing and refining her act had made her the Queen of Smarminess. She diffused anger and hostility with confusion, surliness with sickening kindness. I loved her.

I was shuffling through my mail, dumping the majority of it in the trash, when the phone rang on Margie's desk.

"Apex Palm Springs. . . . Do I know about that house we have for sale over in Palm Springs?" Margie asked. "Could you narrow it down just a bit . . . We have quite a few houses for sale in Palm Springs . . . Uh-huh, so you don't remember the street or the agent's name . . . and no house number . . . It's near a golf course. Sir, everything in Palm Springs is near a golf course . . . Sure. I'll have that information for you in just a minute. Can I put you on hold for a minute?"

She put the caller on hold and looked up at me from her desk. "Amanda, would you hand me my crystal ball so I can find the house this jerk is looking for?"

Margie was thumbing through the company's book of listings, being careful not to break her obscenely long nails. She reminded me about tonight's cocktail party.

"Another one?" I replied, looking over a flyer sporting a photo of an agent with tremendously large, teased blond hair and an obscenely large crucifix around the agent's neck on a gold chain. And this agent was a man. No wonder Realtors had the reputation of used car salesmen.

"Oh, sweetie, this isn't just another cocktail party. Marcus Featherman is having one at one of his listings in Aqua."

"And I should be impressed why?" I replied, throwing another termite-detection brochure into the trash.

"Marcus always has the best booze, hors d'oeuvres, and jazz group in the desert."

"I see."

"And the best men," Margie added.

"Are any of them straight?"

"Oh, yes, sweetie. Some of the most eligible bachelors in the Coachella Valley will be there," Margie added, finally turning back to her caller on hold. "Marcus is queerer than a three-dollar bill, but the guys he gets to come to his parties . . . woof! Marcus has a thing for gorgeous straight men—just like me. Does that make me a gay man? Last year, I heard that Ben Affleck came to his Christmas party."

I paused my mail purge. Let's see . . . I could stay home, backed into the only room in my house that was habitable—my bedroom—and watch Seasons 1 and 2 of *Sex and the City* on DVD, or go to what might be a fabulous party in a subdivision of overblown mega-homes that held out the promise of a potential date and the possibility of ending my too-long period of sexual abstinence. Believe it or not, I actually weighed the plusses and minuses of seeing Carrie Bradshaw again throw a Filet-o-Fish at Mr. Big. But in the end, I convinced myself that it was time to get out and get back into circulation. I needed to get a life.

CHAPTER 6

And the Roof Caved In

That night, I took a long soak in the tub, lighting candles and listening to calming music while I picked out my outfit to wear, mentally constructing the perfect, killer outfit. I settled on a skintight, knee-length black leather skirt from Thierry Mugler (a Christmas present from Alex one year). Alex called it the Bondage Skirt because it was covered with a dozen straps and metal fasteners . . . and it was skintight. I paired the skirt with a white silk blouse, pearls, and stiletto patent-leather CFM (come-fuck-me) pumps. That should do the trick. This would get me noticed as I studied myself in the mirror before departing. I would be the most glamorous woman there—or the best-dressed fag hag. In either case, I was bound to be surrounded by gorgeous men. A few more makeup touch-ups to hide the knot on my head, and I was off.

I got in my car and drove through south Palm Canyon to Aqua. Aqua was a new breed of developments here in Palm Springs. Modern was the name of the game, but the other key operative word here was cavernous. Like the West Nile mosquito virus, the McMansion had arrived in the desert. Great sheets of uninterrupted glass were poised under tilted, intersecting planes of metal walls and roofs large enough to land a plane on. These structures sat defiantly on the desert floor, facing the stupendous San Jacinto mountain range with a fuck-you attitude. Built mainly for childless or gay couples, the homes were terrifying behemoths that perfectly echoed the current American mantra: Nothing succeeds like excess. They had refrigerators big enough to store a cow in, walk-in showers that could accommodate an entire Ecuadorian soccer team, and living rooms you could shoot skeet in—the American dream.

I pulled up at the valet stand, left my car in the hands of a very attractive valet, and vamped my way past the thousands—and I mean thousands—of votive candles in frosted glass holders that lined the ground all the way to the front door. I entered the house and true to what Margie had promised, the music was a very sophisticated jazz, the finger foods that sailed by on chrome trays looked fabulous, and the men, well, they were as succulent as the food being offered. Now, if what I've just described sounds more like a nightclub than an open house to sell an expensive property, you win the prize for your perceptiveness. These kinds of cocktail parties rarely ever sold houses. Their real intention was for the listing agent to impress the hell out of their clients and other agents. And for this purpose, they worked like a charm.

I slinked my way over toward the open bar and ordered a martini—slinked, mind you—there was no other way to move in this dress than to slink. That's why Alex bought it. He said there was nothing more beautiful than a beautiful woman, beautifully dressed, and in motion. The red-carpet arrival of the Academy Awards was his favorite part—to see the women arrive with their husbands or paramours. After the walk down the carpet, he usually went into another room to read. "Not much worth watching now," he would say, and pad off to the bedroom to pick up a novel of his favorite crime writer, Kinky Friedman. Of course, now that I think back, I wonder if Alex was picturing himself in one of the actresses' gowns. Naw. Of all the time Alex was married to me, he never once displayed any leaning toward cross-dressing.

The waiter made my martini exactly as I had ordered: shaken, not stirred. I took a sip and immediately spotted Alex coming in the door of the house. I should have run right up to him, but something made me fade back into the gargantuan furniture and watch Alex from afar. I couldn't figure out why I did this. Was it to see if he came with another man? Or to see if he was going to cozy up to someone in attendance? I watched for a while, and while he was his usual sociable self, I detected no sexual sparks flying, no knowing glances or up-raised eyebrows. Nope. Alex was still the loner. It was one of the things about him that really turned me on. He was so in-dependent. So sure of taking the different path. So sure of himself. For a person like me with the confidence of Kafka, his assurance was intoxicating.

I still remember the day Alex walked into our real-estate of-fice in Bloomfield Hills, Michigan. It was a cold, rainy day in October. Alex was introduced to the staff during our Tuesday morning meeting, and you couldn't help but stare at him. He was striking. He stood six foot one (my regulation height for sexy men), was dressed impeccably in a dark blue, pin-striped suit (another sexy plus) of exquisite tailoring, with eyes so icy blue, you felt you could swim in their crystal-clear depths. Al-though he was quite young, he shaved his head not because his hair was thinning prematurely, but because he knew he looked better with his head treated that way. And he was quite right. Plus, he had what I felt was the most perfectly shaped head in the world. In Michigan, men desperately held on to their hair, wearing it either too long for the times if they had it, or, if they didn't, clutching on to a few loyal strands and whip-ping it up into a combover that would only fool Helen Keller.

But it wasn't his looks that made him seem so formidable. He just projected an air of overwhelming confidence. He looked kind but formidable at the same time. It was quite extraordinary.

I wasn't the only one who was affected. It seemed every woman in the office (and a few men, I found out after the fact) wanted Alex in the worst way. From then on, the bras were worn tighter, desserts were routinely skipped, and local tanning booths experienced an onslaught of new customers.

As for me, I felt that there wasn't much of a chance, since I wasn't the flashy type of woman a guy like Alex would naturally go for. I had made up my mind that he went after the Teutonic warrior, Brigitte Nielsen type of woman. You know the kind. They wore breastplates instead of bras, could kill a man with a piece of chewing gum, and could change their panty hose while doing seventy-five miles an hour on a twisting country road without missing a curve. I might have been naturally blonde, but similarities between me and an Amazonian woman ended there.

Don't get me wrong, I was no skanky ho. I stood six-feet one-inch tall, had typically blond hair, thanks to my Lithuanian ancestors, a spattering of freckles across my skin and face, sky-blue eyes, and a good set of teeth. In a sea of thirty-one flavors of Baskin-Robbins, I was solidly vanilla.

I pretty much went about my own business while Alex went about his, which, by the way, was phenomenal. In just six months, he managed to surpass the top producer in our firm. Best of all, as frightened agents scrambled to catch up with Alex, he did the unthinkable: He took time off. He'd go off rock climbing in Needles, California. Motorcycling over the Alps. Or hiking on the Torres del Paine in Chile. Always something exotic. This guy didn't go to Disney World.

He fascinated me more than any other person I have ever met. Or ever will.

So it just so happened that I was out hiking early one Saturday morning, thinking about cosmic decay, when the skies opened up and the rain came pouring down with a vengeance. Instead of running the mile or so back to my car, I walked back with a slow resignation, knowing that my clothing held more water than the marsh I was coming upon, when lo and behold, I spotted Alex standing in the middle of the marsh wearing knee-high Wellington rubber boots, smoking a cigar under the protection of a very large umbrella, and smiling contentedly between each puff. His eyes were closed.

I stood watching him from the banks of the marsh, not knowing what to say. I just stood there for an eternity and a half, just observing Alex as the rain continued to fall. He looked so peaceful, I hated to disturb him, but eventually I did. I wanted him to know that I was the kind of person to visit a place like this, that we both had so much in common. That, and the fact that I would make a perfect wife for him.

"Are you okay?" I yelled out to him, my voice drowned by the falling rain.

Nothing.

"Are you okay, Alex?" I asked more timidly this time.

"I'm fine, Amanda. I heard you the first time."

Desperate to keep my tenuous connection with Alex, I tried to connect again, to show sympathy, that we were kindred souls.

"Are you meditating?" I asked.

"I *was*."

Oh. I was too desperate. I was annoying him. I blew my chance because I couldn't shut up. "I'm sorry."

"Don't be," was his reply. "You're probably wondering what

I'm doing, standing here in the rain in rubber wellies, smoking a cigar?"

"Well, the thought had entered my mind."

"Because I *can*. There . . . the rule of my life. Now you have me figured out. There's no more than that."

My heart began racing. He spoke to me . . . at length! I waited for him to continue, but he merely stood there, slowly puffing great clouds of lavender-tinted smoke out into the rain. It seemed that our conversation, such that it was, had ended. I walked away from the marsh slowly, hoping Alex would call me back, but he didn't.

When I reached my car, I climbed in and just sat there in the early morning light, just listening to the rain and the sound of my quickened breath.

Just as I was about to turn the key in the ignition and drive away, I saw Alex's form appear over a small hill and slowly make its way to my car. He knelt down next to my window and tapped on it with a tenderness that surprised me—he always seemed so forceful.

I rolled down the window and stared at him, waiting for him to say something.

He started first. "Hello."

"Hi," I replied.

This was followed by the longest—and most pregnant—silence in the history of the world. The minutes passed, the rain tumbled down, and still, nothing was said. After eternity passed into oblivion and the clock of the universe ticked by an eon, Alex stood up, reached into my car, and took hold of my hand. He coaxed it gently out into the rain and raised it to his lips, where he kissed my hand.

"There's one just like it at the end of my other arm," I said.

"You just always have to crack a joke, don't you?" Alex remarked.

"It helps to defuse uncomfortable situations."

"This situation is uncomfortable?"

"My *life* is uncomfortable. I'd give anything to feel good in my own skin."

Alex snorted a good laugh. "Why so?"

"You weren't raised Catholic, were you?"

"No, my folks raised me as a pagan."

"Well, no wonder you seem so well adjusted."

"Is it all that bad?"

"It is when you were brought up with a Lithuanian grand-mother who thought Stalin was after her and had a mother who is clearly insane."

"But aren't all mothers insane? I mean, to take on the respon-sibility of raising children and putting up with a husband. . . . What's the old saying, 'You don't have to be crazy, but it helps.' "

"No, my mother *is* insane."

"I see. Amanda, may I cut to the chase?"

"Yes, Alex." My heart started pounding like a woofer at a heavy metal concert.

"Amanda, will you be . . . I mean, will you . . ." Alex trailed off, leaving me at the edge of a cliff.

"Yes!?"

"Amanda . . ."

"Yes?" Oh my God, he barely knew me and he was about to ask for my hand in marriage. I knew what my answer would be—yes, of course—but this was all so sudden. I wanted to marry him, but now that the event was staring me in the face, I found myself wishing that I had a little more time . . . you know, to have a buildup.

"Okay, here goes. Will you team up with me?"

You could have knocked me over with a feather. "You what?"

"I want you to be my business partner."

Boy, did I read that situation wrong. I was halfway down the aisle with him in a Vera Wang when my procession came to a screeching halt.

"Your partner?" I asked. "Do you always kiss the hand of people you're about to ask to team up with you?"

"No, only those that I'm interested in romantically. Otherwise, I'd be sexually harassing you. I'm just being continental."

After that, we teamed up, dated, then eventually married. His apartness, his desire to march to the beat of his own drummer was what fascinated me about him. It still does.

I watched Alex and he looked around at the house, chatted briefly with a few people, then headed outside to the pool without noticing me.

As I took another sip of my martini, I heard a sneering voice over my shoulder.

"Amanda, I saw your little appearance on the news at noon today! I didn't know that Stevie Wonder was cutting your hair. What happened to Roberto?"

The comment came from none other than Andrew MacCallister, Scottish agent and all-around cunt. Yes, you heard me right. A cunt. Like the warning colors of a venomous coral snake or the rattling tail of a diamondback pit viper, the first signs that you're heading for trouble can be seen from afar. His shocking-white, full Santa Claus beard is meticulously trimmed, giving his face the appearance that it's resting in a benevolent, white cloud. The benevolence ends there. He's over 6 feet 5 inches tall—a height that he uses to full advantage to intimidate his clients. If that's not enough, his clothing is the final, thumb-in-your-face warning. It's not his occasional kilt or immaculately tailored pants, his customary button-down shirts, or even the ascot that he wears in cooler weather that signals that this man is a 100 percent, bona fide cunt. It's his signature footwear that gives it all away: black, embroidered velvet slippers with a skull-and-crossbones motif on the instep stitched with real gold thread. Custom-made in England. Sun or rain, the cool of winter or blazing heat of July, McCallister always has on his slippers of death.

You'd think that his toxic personality would make him about as welcome as a tell-all hooker at a televangelist convention, but it had quite the opposite effect. Andrew found that certain clients wanted to be abused and humiliated. Others signed on the dotted line with MacCallister because he would play hardball on their behalf. He had a well-deserved reputation of reducing weaker agents to tears. And he got away with it because he would restrain his acerbic comments and concentrate on finding the tiniest technicality overlooked by an agent that he would blow up into a matter of gross negligence, making the Realtor look like a fool in front of his client.

Andrew harbored hatred toward all carbon-based life-forms, but he had a very special bone to pick with me. Alex and I had a run-in with him a year ago where his client lost out on a bidding war on a house that, once the sale closed, tripled in value in a matter of four months. The lost deal cost Andrew over $30,000 in commissions, and his client, hundreds of thousands more. And Andrew never forgot it. Tonight, he was out for blood—mine.

"Andrew, how good to see you," I muttered while taking a sip of my martini and looking away. Rule number one: Don't argue with a borderline personality. It only throws gasoline on the fire.

"Amanda, you've cut your hair since they found that dead man in your listing this morning!" I noticed that he had raised his voice so that all could hear of my misfortune. "Your TV appearance was really special. It looked more like you had a lawn service as your stylist."

I gave him a withering look, but he wasn't going to let me go.

"And that outfit, Amanda . . . I never get tired of seeing you in it." Andrew lobbed the statement at me like a fragmentation grenade.

Andrew was about to release another poisonous line at me when he went down like he had been shot. He wasn't hurt—enough—but his ego was about to take a bruising. The plate of food he had been carrying in one hand was now all over the front of his ruffled white shirt.

"Goddamnit," he hissed, "a grape! Someone dropped a grape and hadn't the manners to pick it up! What a bunch of low-class morons!"

Just as I was about to laugh, I noticed Alex standing silently about thirty feet away, popping a grape or two in his mouth. You had to love this guy.

"Thank you for the rescue, Alex," I said as I walked over to him.

"You're welcome, Amanda."

"I wanted to haul off and clobber him one, but I restrained myself."

"A fork into the back of your hand?"

"No, I was afraid I'd break a nail . . . and you know how hard it is for me to get them to grow to any length at all. Rock climbing really does a number on them."

"Chewing on them doesn't help, either. Amanda, I'm so sorry about what happened. And by the way, why didn't you call me about this?"

"Alex, I called your office today, but they said you were up in Joshua Tree on a sale. A big one?"

Alex knitted his eyebrows. "Was what a big one?"

"Your sale!"

"Oh, that. Yes, one-point-nine million."

"I didn't know there was that kind of money up in the higher desert."

"Oh yeah. There are a lot of artists, recording industry people, New Age, metaphysical types, and a few reclusive movie stars buying up property there."

"Leave it to you to sniff out where the money is going next, Alex. You've always had that ability to guess the future."

"Okay, okay . . . enough about me. So tell me what happened today."

I related the entire sequence of events while Alex listened intently, silently nodding his head from time to time, as if he were compiling all the facts, sorting them, and preparing to spit them out in a startling conclusion. When I finished my story, I waited for him to respond. I could see that his little gray cells were furiously processing the information, trying to see the answer in the fog of details.

No answer came. He turned his head ever so slightly, as if to physically change the subject.

"So how are you, though, Amanda? You must be pretty shook up."

"Naw, not me. At least not in the scared sense. There's just this overarching feeling of shame."

"Well, you were raised Catholic. What do you want?"

"Not that, Alex. I just feel that I have to clear my name."

"Of what?"

"Of the fact that of all the houses for sale in Palm Springs, someone chose mine to murder someone in."

"But *you* didn't murder him."

"I know that, but you know the old Lithuanian saying: The strong perfume hides the foul stench."

"What does that have to do with the murder of Doc?"

"Oh, right . . . wrong saying. What I meant to say was, Stand in a manure-filled field and you, too, will soon attract flies."

"Did your grandmother tell you that . . . Martha the Merciless?"

"Yes, but she once claimed that she saw the Virgin Mary in a jar of pickled pig's feet, so her credibility is a little shaky. Plus, she used to collect strange-looking mushrooms from deep forests and cook them."

"So your point is . . . ?"

"My point is that other agents are going to think that I wasn't chosen just by accident . . . that I had something, however small, to do with Doc's death . . . no matter how absurd that would be."

"So what do you propose to do about it?"

"Clear my name."

"By doing what?"

"By finding out who murdered Doc Winters."

"And how will you do that?" Alex asked, staring right into my eyes like my mother seeking an answer to the question of who ate the last piece of lemon pie.

"I'll do a little investigating on my own. I realized today how easy it is to get information out of people, especially in the real-estate business. People are just aching to talk. My hairdresser, Roberto, gave me an earful of good information just this afternoon."

"Amanda, he's a hairdresser. People treat them like psychiatrists. And for the most part, they are the same . . . only cheaper . . . and you come out looking better than you went in. Anyway, you will do no such thing, Amanda. You don't know who did this. To murder a prominent environmentalist in broad daylight is pretty ballsy. You don't know what someone might do to a person like you who goes sticking her nose where it doesn't belong."

"Oh, Alex," I remarked, taking his hand. "I'm a big girl . . . I can take care of myself!" I added, patting his hand to reassure him. "Let's go outside."

As I turned to leave with Alex, everything on the drinks table started following me, as if I were holding a large magnet that attracted only liquor and the glasses it was put into. For a second, I thought we were having an earthquake, but there was no noise, no rumbling. Dozens of bottles and pyramids of highball glasses and champagne flutes came crashing at our feet while every eye within a forty-mile radius turned to see what all the commotion was about.

When the crashing, which seemed to go on forever, finally subsided, I looked down to see the tablecloth had latched itself under one of the buckles on my bondage skirt. Jerry Lewis couldn't have pulled a better stunt.

There was an eerie silence, which, in my deserved guilt, I felt inclined to break.

"Boy, one martini and you can't take me anywhere!"

Alex and I promptly put some distance between us and the drinks table that was now mostly on the floor, and stepped outside to enjoy the beautiful night sky of the desert. My move wasn't just to minimize embarrassment, it was for protection. Realtors, being huge alcoholics, would be furious that I had destroyed almost all of the booze at the party. They might be forced to drink, God forbid, water.

"Amanda," Alex started in a tone that suggested he was about to propose. "Amanda, how about I come back to Apex and we hook up as business partners again?"

I just about leaped out of my panty hose.

"Well, I don't know about . . ." I started, not wanting to

sound too eager, even though it was the best news I'd heard since Regina said she's been having hot sex through her seventies. "Okay."

"I don't want to push . . ."

"Alex, are your ears full of sand? I said okay."

"Really?" Alex seemed truly surprised.

"Yes, really! Alex, did you really think I was going to turn you down? We may be divorced, but we're soul mates. In fact, we're so attuned to each other, you knew what my answer was going to be before you even asked your question. Am I right?"

"Well, yes, but I just didn't want to appear too eager—just like you were thinking a moment ago."

It was uncanny. In our brief marriage, Alex and I soon discovered that we usually knew what the other was thinking at any given moment and could often complete each other's sentences. As I was thinking this, I looked at Alex and could sense that he was, ironically, thinking the exact same thought.

I reached out and held Alex's hands in mine and looked deeply into his beautiful blue eyes. "Alex, why couldn't I have been born with a cock?"

"Had you been, luck would have it that I would've been born with a vagina."

We both broke down into stifled laughs.

"Oh, hell," I relented. "If you're handed lemons . . ."

"Squeeze it and make it into a cocktail."

"Better than lemonade. So, Alex, how's the new gay life going? Have you found anyone special?" It sounded so weird asking this, but it had to be thrown out into the limelight at some point. It was time to start acting like a divorced woman who's still friends with her ex-husband.

"No, no one at all."

"Alex, I'm shocked. I would have thought you'd have guys waiting to swoop down on you the moment you were free."

"They have been," he replied.

"Oh," I said, dripping with despair.

"But I don't want most of them," he said with a wry smile. "It's just that the men here are so . . . so . . . faggoty."

"Faggoty? Could you define that term?"

"Uhm, how do I say it? Ah, I've got it: The glitz is the substance."

"That's from Shakespeare, isn't it? *Twelfth Night*?"

"No, the *Merchant of Penis*."

"Hey, Alex, that would be a great name for a gay porn film. We could produce a whole new series of sophisticated porn based on the works of Shakespeare! We follow *Merchant of Penis* with *Tite-Ass Andronicus*!"

"Followed by *Winter's Tail*, *A Midsummer's Night Wet Dream*, and *Rimming of the Shrew*."

"That's good, Alex. We wouldn't even have the change the names for *As You Like It*, *Two Gentlemen of Verona*, and *Measure for Measure*!" I added, extending my hand from my crotch out to twelve inches each time I pronounced the word *measure*.

"We'll make a million. Now, where were we?"

"Trouble finding suitable soul mates."

"Amanda, I'm not even shooting that high. I'd settle for a fuckbuddy who can say something intelligent."

"You encourage them to talk?! There's your first mistake."

"I know, I know. Either they open their mouth and I have to hear all about the new couch they just bought or . . . or a purse falls out."

"That can really ruin it. You cruise someone and instead of Darth Vader, the sound that comes out when you walk up to them to make contact is more Paris Hilton. Or that's the least of your problems."

"Yes, like he leads you into his bedroom, and there in the

corner on a mannequin is a wedding dress that once belonged to his mother."

"Euuuu, yuk!" I replied. "Could he fit into it?"

"All it needed was a little taking in here and there," Alex said.

"Have people always been this insane, or are they just getting worse?"

"I think the human race has always been that way. People like you and I are just getting more adept at spotting it. But at the same time, yes, I think that everyone's coming unglued."

"Would you like to go get another martini?" I asked.

"Sure . . . maybe we can suck some vodka and olives off the floor."

"It wouldn't be the first time. Remember that party in Berlin?"

"Oh, Amanda, I think this is the beginning of a beautiful friendship."

CHAPTER 7

Curses, Foiled Again

The next morning, my phone rang at 8 A.M. It was a little early, but I expected that the police wanted me to come down to identify a suspect. Or tell me that the case was solved. Imagine my surprise when it was neither.

"Hello Amanda Thorne."

"This is Coyote Woman."

I assumed that I was talking to a human instead of a canine, so I proceeded carefully. "Yes, what can I do for you?"

"There was a murder in the house you have listed in Palm Springs yesterday."

"Yes, yes, there was."

"I know all about it."

"Have you talked to the police? They could use your information."

"Miss Thorne, I'm a psychic."

You predicted it?"

"No, no, I read about it in the newspaper. But I do have psychic powers. And this is why I am calling you."

"Okay," I said.

"You need to have your house cleansed."

"I'm having the carpets steamed on Wednesday."

"No, not cleaning. *Cleansing*."

"Okay. And I suppose you are the person to do it?"

"Absolutely, you can't leave something this important in the hands of an amateur."

"You're absolutely right, Mrs. Coyote, it would be tragic to leave this cleansing to someone who didn't use the proper eye of newt."

"Mrs. Thorne, this is a serious matter. If that house is not cleansed, the bad energy will prevent you from ever selling it. People will feel it the moment they step foot in the house. Doc Winters was a firm believer in higher consciousness. He was a frequent visitor to the Institute of Mentalphysics and the Integratron here in the high desert, and I'm sure that his spirit would want the bad energy removed from your listing."

I was about to dismiss Coyote Woman as a huckster who scoured the obituaries in search of profitable house-cleansing gigs, when the possible connection to Doc Winters was mentioned.

"Mrs. Coyote . . ."

"Barbara," came the correction.

"Barbara," I said into the receiver that I momentarily held away from my face as if it were an object of puzzling origin. "I agree that the house is in desperate need of a cleaning."

"*Cleansing,* Mrs. Thorne. This isn't Molly Maid service."

"Yes, of course, Barbara. When can I have this done? I'm eager to put this all behind me. For me and my client."

"Of course. I can drive down next Thursday. Midday is better since the energy will be at its peak then."

"Two o'clock?"

"Fine. I will see you then."

"Oh, before you go Coyote Woman, could I ask how much you charge for a cleansing? I'm new at this sort of thing," I said timidly. After all, I wanted to get some answers about Doc Winters, but I wasn't prepared to get hosed in order to get them. It's not that money was a big concern—it was the principle of the thing.

"Two hundred dollars," came the answer.

Nice gig, I thought.

"Okay, Barbara, we will see you at two P.M. next Thursday."

"We?"

"My business partner and I. Actually, my ex-husband."

"You still talk to each other?" Barbara asked.

"Well, yes. Why not?"

"I don't talk to mine. Of course, he wouldn't talk to me after I filled his behind with rock salt."

"You caught him in bed with another woman?"

"Bingo."

"You must be a good shot, to hit a running target."

"Oh, he wasn't running. I made him get out of bed and bend over and grasp his ankles. Then I pulled the trigger."

"You didn't hurt him too badly?"

"Just his pride. Okay, so he couldn't sit down for a month," Coyote Woman answered with pride I could hear over the telephone. "Okay, enough of that. Now, one last thing, Mrs. Thorne . . . I don't allow others in the house while I cleanse. And I can't perform this cleansing if you two don't believe in what I am attempting to do."

Since I planned to pump this broad for information, I decided to sound as humble as possible.

"Absolutely."

"And I don't take checks. Only cash."

"Certainly. I will see you next week."

I hung up, realizing that I would have to work on Alex beforehand, explaining that he would have to hide his disbelief in order to pump the gal for information. Alex, due to his extremely progressive upbringing, was allowed to choose his own faith—if any—based on what he concluded. (I loved his

87

parents.) And he concluded that he was an objective existentialist. In other words, Alex felt that the universe exists, and that it and nature and events just happen, not according to any god-influenced design. As humans, he reasons, we must strive to find meaning in our work and our relationships not with just humans, but with the earth and the universe itself. Alex had invented a religion based on his observation of the world and the universe around him—not on what others had told him to do.

My mother, while delighted that I was marrying "into money," as she termed it, was beside herself when she found out that not only was Alex not Catholic, but a proud atheist.

"When you mentioned you were going to marry in a civil ceremony, I thought it was because he was Lutheran or something. But an atheist! How can a person believe in nothing?! That old joke, about the atheist who died: He was all dressed up and had nowhere to go—that's what he wants to do when he dies? Just lie there?"

"He'll be unconscious, so what does it matter?"

"And what's going to happen to you? I suppose the next thing is that you'll be dressing in yellow robes and dancing around at airports, huh?"

"Mom, I'm not going to become a Hare Krishna. I will make up my own mind about what religion—if any—that I choose to join!"

"That's why I did my level best to raise you Catholic—where you don't get a choice, where for two thousand years people didn't question things. You just kept your mouth shut and did what the church told you to—even if it made no sense at all!"

That, in a nutshell, is my mother's take on the world. You keep your nose to the grindstone, don't ask any questions or have conflicting thoughts, you die, and go to heaven, where, presumably, it's just the same rigmarole all over again. For eternity. Hey, sign me up!

No sooner than I hung up on Coyote Woman, the phone rang again.

"Is this the real-estate agent Amanda Thorne?"

"Yes, it is. Who's calling?"

"Eagle Feather."

I half-expected a knock-knock joke, but when none manifested itself, I felt it was time to take another tack.

"Yes, Eagle Feather, what can I do for you?"

"I heard about the murder in the house you have listed for sale."

"And you think it needs to be cleansed and that you're the one to do it."

"That's uncanny!" exclaimed the voice on the other end of the line. "How did you know that?"

"I'm psychic," I confided snidely.

"Really? How long have you had the gift?"

"About fifteen minutes, give or take. Now, what can I help you with?"

"The house cleansing."

"Oh, yes, the cleansing. Well, to tell the truth, I just agreed to have a person by the name of Coyote Woman cleanse my house this Thursday."

I could hear a sharp intake of breath through the receiver. From the sound of it, I could tell that this was not welcome news to Eagle Feather.

"Coyote Woman?! Coyote Woman?! Okay, but don't say I didn't warn you."

"Why, what's wrong with Coyote Woman?"

"When we have our full-moon drummings to summon the spirits, her rhythm is all off."

"Well, we can't all be Buddy Rich."

"Who?" Eagle Feather asked.

"He was a great jazz drummer. He played with everyone from Tommy Dorsey to Louis Armstrong."

"Who?"

"Never mind," I said. "So Coyote Woman has no rhythm. Is that a good reason not to hire her?"

"She also has a bad aura."

"Really?" I challenged.

"Too much blue," Eagle Feather admitted.

"And her aura doesn't match her handbag."

I expected a strong response, but nothing. The comment seemed to sail right over her metaphysical head. For a person who claimed to have great insight into unseen worlds, she was quite blind to what was happening in this one . . . and definitely deaf to sarcasm.

Eagle Feather wasn't done trashing Coyote Woman yet. "She even uses store-bought sage to create her bundles for smudging. Can you imagine?!" she exclaimed, as if Coyote Woman ate Christian Baby Puffs for breakfast.

I didn't know what a smudging was and didn't want to know. I sensed that this conversation was going nowhere, so I felt that a hasty retreat was in order.

"Listen, Eagle Feather . . ."

"Margie. You can call me Margie."

"Margie, I've already agreed to a cleansing of my listing by Coyote Woman. If it doesn't work or she leaves some unsightly spirits behind or doesn't do windows, I'll give you a call."

"I have nothing more to say to you, except that you will regret your choice. Bad energy is nothing to play around with, because it can turn on you. We are dealing with forces larger and more powerful than anything that we can imagine, Miss Thorne. Good-bye."

"Eagle . . . Margie, I'm not really into all this stuff—" I was cut off.

"Miss Thorne, I curse you. Ei-bartu-do-ra-me-borga-chuleesa!"

I stood there holding the receiver for some time, thinking that I had just been cursed over a cell phone. I didn't pay it much attention at the time. After all, when you find a body in your listing, it's a tough act to follow.

CHAPTER 8

Think Before Putting Strange Things in Your Mouth

Alex phoned me at ten to inform me that he just transferred his license to my real-estate office, so he could start anytime. I had to go back to open 2666 Boulder Drive for the cleaners, set all the furniture back up, and take stock with my stager of everything that was damaged.

As it turned out, when I had the chance to enter my listing in body-free circumstances, more of the furnishings had taken a beating than I had realized. As Ronald stood in the living room where Doc had bought the farm, his eyes began to tear up; then he began to visibly shake.

"I know, I know, Ronald," I consoled. "I was pretty shook up when I saw Doc lying there."

"How could . . . how could . . . !" Ronald tried to spit out.

"Easy now," I whispered, patting him on the shoulder.

Ronald calmed himself enough to speak loudly, but clearly. "What kind of sicko could do such a thing to an Eames surfboard table! Vintage!" Ronald sputtered, pointing at the two broken pieces lying dejectedly on the floor.

"Look on the bright side, Ronald. Before, you had just *one* surfboard table . . . now you have *two* boogie board tables."

He flashed me a look that said, *We are not amused*.

"Maybe you can use them as side tables," I suggested, trying to find the silver lining in a dark cloud. "You just have to sand down the rough edges and—" I started to say, but Ronald raised his hand and held it facing me as a warning that I had already dug myself into a hole and that I should stop digging.

Next to the remains of the surfboard table lay pieces of glass from the vintage fifties highball glasses. Figuring that there was little that I could do to comfort my distraught but somewhat callous stager, I got down on my knees to pick up the shards of glass so that no one got injured from them. As I gathered them up in my hand, it struck me that something was wrong.

"Ronald, how many highball glasses did you have set up on this tray?"

"Six, why?"

"Are you sure?"

"Absolutely. It was tough enough finding a set of six to begin with. They're pretty rare."

"Ronald, I am so sorry about all this."

"Don't worry," he relented. "It goes with the territory. So why were you asking about the number of glasses?"

"Well, the glasses aren't tempered, so the broken pieces are quite large. And when you put them together, only four were broken."

Ronald looked puzzled. "Maybe the murderer took two into the kitchen or somewhere else in the house."

"Why?" I replied. "To share a nice bottle of Riesling before Doc died?"

"Maybe Doc was thirsty."

"Enough of the jokes, but I checked the house before you arrived. Everywhere. No glasses."

"That's strange. So you think the killer took the highball glasses?

"Yes, it looks like it," I conceded.

"But why? For value? They're not worth much as a pair. Wait. Maybe he had a partial collection of the same thing. Now he has a full set, thanks to me," Ronald conceded dejectedly.

"Well, maybe we can take comfort in the fact that they were probably painted in lead-based metallic paint. Pure poison."

I rose up and dumped the pieces of glass into a plastic garbage bag that I had put in the living room to hold the broken furnishings.

"That is strange. Very strange," I muttered.

Ronald threw a broken picture frame into the bag.

"Amanda, did the police tell you how Doc was killed?"

"No, and I don't think they're going to, either."

"Well, there doesn't seem to be any blood on the floor. That would rule out stabbing or shooting."

"No, there wasn't any blood. And I don't remember any marks around his throat; but then again, I wasn't exactly looking for signs of murder. But wait, I do remember the oddest thing: Doc's mouth was full of rocks."

"Rocks?" Ronald blurted out. "You mean, like pebbles?"

"Um, no, bigger. About the size of a grape. Dozens of them. His mouth looked like a senior citizen at a one-visit-only salad bar."

Ronald screwed up his face as he imagined what it would be like to have a mouth stuffed full of rocks.

"Do you think that someone force-fed Doc rocks until he choked on them?"

"I'm not sure."

"Sheesh, what a terrible way to die!"

"I suppose Doc might have been killed that way, but I imagine there wouldn't be a lot of people who would sit calmly by and let an attacker shove rocks into their mouths."

"Doc's killer must have drugged him."

"Not that I have a lot of experience in shoving rocks into my mouth, but I would think that even with a mouthful of rocks, you could still breathe by sucking air through all the cracks between the rocks."

"I can't say I've tried it, either, but it sounds plausible," Ronald suggested.

A strange idea came over me.

"I have an idea," I said excitedly, and made for the back door. I bent down into the flower bed and picked up a handful of granite rocks that had been placed there to cover the dirt and prettify everything.

I came back into the house and went into the kitchen, dumping the granite stones into the sink and running the hot water on them for some time. Ronald came into the kitchen to see what I was up to.

"Amanda, you didn't hit your head on a rock when you fell off your bike yesterday, did you?"

"Hit my head?"

"Yes, you're acting like a person who recently took a blow to the head."

"Ronald! I'm trying to get to the bottom of things. I want to confirm a theory. Here, help me dry these rocks with these paper towels."

"Amanda, you're not really going to put these rocks in your mouth, are you?" Ronald pleaded. "They're . . . dirty!"

I bent forward and looked Ronald square in the eyes.

"Ronald, I want you to look me straight in the eyes and tell me that you haven't had worse things in your mouth."

Ronald thought for a moment. "Fine, you win."

"Now," I said, pointing at the rocks, "these are about the same size as the ones I saw in Doc's mouth. I'm going to put them in one at a time . . ."

Ronald was clearly concerned—and I didn't blame him.

"Be careful of your dental work! I once cracked a crown on a body piercing."

I looked over at Ronald.

"Well, I did!" Ronald exclaimed.

I had placed the rocks carefully in my mouth one by one until I had reached the degree of fullness I had observed in Doc's mouth. I then concentrated on my breathing, the air hissing as I sucked it in past the granite obstacles lodged in my mouth. I heard the front door to the house open, and a few seconds later, Alex appeared in the doorway and froze there, unsure at first at what he was seeing.

Ronald turned to look at Alex like a man caught cheating with the wife of another man.

"Wis fisn't wot dis wooks wike," the stifled words huffed out of my full mouth.

Alex shrugged his shoulders. "She was like that as a child, Ronald. Always putting things in her mouth."

After we had extracted the granite from my mouth, the three of us stood around in the kitchen taking stock of things.

"I discovered one thing I hadn't thought of," I confided.

"And what was that?" Ronald asked.

Alex, always one step ahead of me, put his finger on his nose.

"Yeah, that's right. Doc could breathe through his nose. I didn't think of that at the time because I was so intent on the rocks-in-the-mouth angle." My eyes brightened. "Unless . . . unless the killer shoved the rocks into Doc's mouth so far, they became lodged in his windpipe and he suffocated."

Alex shook his head. "If that were true, then Doc's face and head would have been blue from lack of oxygen. It's called *cyanosis*. Was his face blue?"

"No," I replied with certainty. "That's why I married this guy in the first place, Ronald," I said, patting Alex on his shoulder. "He was just a veritable gold mine of ways to kill people. But getting back to the rocks . . . so it looks like unless the man who killed Doc Winters put a clothespin on his nose or held his nostrils closed, Doc didn't die from asphyxiation. So why the rocks?"

"Anger, revenge, or even a warning," Alex surmised. "Or just a red herring."

"Oh," I responded. "No, I don't think so. I think it was a warning."

Ronald looked surprised. "You mean, like, people who stand in the way of building in the Chino Cone beware—this could happen to you—you rock huggers?"

"Exactly," Alex said.

"Wow," I said. "Someone is really serious about this stuff. I know there's millions of dollars at stake here, but to kill someone for that?"

Alex gave big sigh. "People have killed for far less. In the movie *Fargo*, those losers killed all those people for a few dollars."

"True," Ronald added. "And when I get my hands on the person who destroyed that Eames table, I'll be doing the murdering."

"Ronald, I'm so sorry," I said. "If it's money you need . . ."

"Amanda, dahling, it's not the money—everything I stage with is insured, but just the thought that someone would break a vintage mid-century table like that without thinking . . . We're obviously dealing with a psychotic madman!"

Mid-century modernism, something that Palm Springs had in spades, was taken very seriously here. To some, it was something that you had to abide with, clashing with your Chip-and-Dip (Chippendale) furniture brought from the East Coast. To others, it was a holy relic, sacred and worthy of endless worship.

The cleaning staff arrived and I set them to work while Alex and I discussed what happened in greater detail. Ronald left to attend elsewhere to a sofa that a thoughtless open-house attendee had punctured with a high heel. Why a person would be standing on a couch in heels at an open house was beyond me. But in all my years of selling homes, I've just about seen it all while showing properties: people having sex, oblivious to the fact that I was standing there with clients; closets of single men filled with women's dresses, bustiers, and silk teddies; closets full of CIA-grade rifles and handguns; bricks of cocaine.

Alex asked me to give him a blow-by-blow description of what I saw and what I did yesterday.

"I know you told me this yesterday, but now that you're standing here, you might remember details that you forgot."

"Check. When I arrived, a swarm of agents were standing on the sidewalk and driveway, waiting to get in."

"You already forgot one detail, Amanda."

"And what was that?"

"You neglected to mention that there was a crew of land-scapers on the lawn three doors down, putting in plants and sprinkler systems."

"Now, how did you know that, Alex?"

"Because they're five doors down today."

"Yes, but how did you know they were there yesterday? You weren't here yesterday."

"Just look at the sod marks. The farther you go away from this place, the more faint the lines between the pieces of sod are. So, they've been going down the street from west to east. Any more questions?"

"Not now."

"Please continue, Amanda."

"Well, when I arrived, I hobbled up to the front door and opened it. . . ."

"Okay, stop right there. Was the door locked?"

I thought for a moment.

"Yes."

"Are you sure?" Alex interrogated.

"What is this, the Nuremberg Trials?"

"Amanda, I just don't want you to leave anything out."

"Now, wait a minute, does this mean you're going to support me in my investigation?"

"Yes."

"Well, forgive me for doubting you, but I seem to remember just yesterday that you warned me against trying to do this on my own."

"That's correct, but with my help, you won't be on your own. Why do you think I came back to Apex? It wasn't for the listings."

"Woo-hoo! So you're really in this case with me?!"

"Amanda, have you ever known me to shirk away from anything?"

"Well . . ."

"When I said I was going to bungee off that eight-hundred-foot-high bridge in New Zealand, I did it, didn't I?"

"Yes, yes, you did."

"And when I set out to climb Everest, didn't I go through with it?"

"Yes, but you didn't make the summit. You said it got windy or something."

"Yes, I chickened out from the one-hundred-and-five-mile-an-hour winds. But I made it to the South Col."

"You are correct."

"And when you asked me to sit through the entire Wagner Ring series with you, I went to the opera with you, didn't I?"

"Yes, even though you had the look on your face at the time that you would rather be holding the back of that anaconda's head like you did in South America."

"Getting bitten by the world's most powerful snake was preferable to sitting through several nights listening to opera from Hitler's favorite composer."

I threw my arms around Alex and gave him a hug.

"Thank you, thank you, thank you."

"You're welcome, Amanda. Now, where were we? Oh, yes, you unlocked the door."

"No one had gone in even though there was a Supra keybox on the front doorknob."

"And you know that because your keybox report only showed that Cathy Paige and Ed Jensen had entered 2666 earlier that morning?"

"That's right. So when I opened the door, the first thing I noticed was the mess."

"Anything peculiar about the way things were scattered? A pattern, maybe?"

"No, just a bunch of stuff smashed around Doc . . . as if all the fighting had gone on right at the sofa."

"Okay, so you opened the door and then what?"

"I came in and I think I walked toward the kitchen counter to put my purse down when I noticed a body lying there."

"Go on."

"I was shocked, but I wasn't scared. I mean, I had a whole cadre of agents behind me, and who could be more vicious than a bunch of real-estate agents?"

"Right. Then what?"

"At first, I thought the person on the floor had suffered a heart attack or stroke or something. But he was lying there awful still, so I had this sense that he was dead. So I got close and could see that he wasn't breathing . . . the chest was motionless. So, seeing that I couldn't do anything, I backed up because I knew the police would investigate and I didn't want to disturb the scene."

"So at that point, you believed Doc had been murdered?"

"I didn't know it was Doc until someone behind me shouted it out. My first thought was that he was some kind of homeless man who broke in, looking for a place to stay for the night, and that he drank himself to death.

"That's what you thought?"

"Of course. I mean, Doc is kinda scraggly. Well, I was hoping that it was a heart attack—I guess that didn't come out right—but something in my bones told me otherwise."

"Interesting."

"I mean, the mess looked like there was a fight or some kind of struggle. But I figured, maybe the guy had a heart attack and fell back on the furniture, then started grasping things in a desperate attempt at getting help. I wasn't really sure what had happened."

"Okay, then what?"

"As I got closer, I noticed the rocks in his mouth," I said.

"And what went through your mind as you saw the rocks?"

"I thought, gee, are those igneous or metamorphic rocks?"

Another smirk from Alex.

"Okay, next question. Were all the rocks in his mouth—I mean, were there any lying around on the floor like the killer couldn't fit them all in?"

A big lightbulb went off over my head.

"Oh, I see where you're going with this, Alex. In other words, was the rock thing planned, or did the killer hurriedly grab some rocks outside and shove them inside his mouth, which would probably leave some extras?"

"Exactly."

"No, Alex, they were all in. None were left on the floor. But . . .

but let me poke a possible hole in your theory, Alex. The cheeks can expand greatly, so unless the killer had picked up way too many rocks, it would be possible to fit all of them in. The mouth can expand to accommodate a great many things."

"Indeed, it can," Alex said with a sly wink.

I winked right back.

"So, Amanda, I think we can conclude that the killer had planned this rock gesture all along."

"As what, pray tell?"

"As a message—a warning."

"You mean, like, 'Back off, rock huggers, don't stand in the way of us developing the Chino Cone area.'"

"Well, Doc was known for one thing lately—opposing the building of houses up in the Cone."

"Yeah," I sighed. "It's pretty much a no-brainer. So what do we do next?"

"I think a visit to Cathy Paige is in order. Followed by one to Ed Jensen."

Alex took out his cell phone and checked it to see if he had any messages.

"Alex?"

"Yes?"

"I know that a man was killed here and all that, but . . . but . . ."

". . . this is kinda fun?" Alex finished.

"Yeah, kinda fun. Exciting, really. Just like the old days, huh?" I suggested.

Alex gave me a glance that spoke volumes.

"Yes, yes, it is . . . with one exception."

"And what is that?'

"When this whole thing is over, I don't think we'll start a photo scrapbook about it."

As I closed up Boulder Drive, Alex went to talk to the landscapers who were working a few doors down. He came back a few minutes later, hopped in the seat next to me, and started the engine.

"So what did you find out?"

"They all saw a woman in a red dress, wearing a hat. That's the only person they saw that morning."

"A red dress? And a hat? Who wears a hat nowadays?"

"My question is, if you were going to kill someone, assuming that the woman spotted that morning was the killer, would you wear a red dress? Hardly. I'd wear something dark, plain, and no hat."

"Exactly. Unless the women that the landscapers saw wasn't the killer."

"They said they only saw one person that morning," came Alex's reply.

"Hey, did they say what kind of hat she was wearing? Did it have a wide brim?"

"Funny you should say that. The guys said it was big. Like a sombrero . . . but not a sombrero, of course."

"Well, it just occurred to me that the killer would wear a hat to hide her identity. The bigger, the better. Did the guys say anything else?"

"Well, Spanish is the only language I don't speak well, so I used my smartphone and recorded what they saw."

"Very smart," I replied.

"Now, we just have to get someone to translate it."

"Roberto, my hairdresser. He can do it. He speaks Portuguese and Spanish. Alex, I think we should tell the police what we found out."

"They were way ahead of us. Detective Becker talked to them already. Now I think we need to pay a visit to Cathy Paige and see what she was doing in your listing that morning."

* * *

Alex placed a call to Cathy to set up a time that the both of us could see her. I listened to Alex talking with Cathy, with the conversation stalling and lurching like a Third World bus.

"... no, no one's saying that ... but it's important that we ... yes, we realize that ... no, that's not true ... but you've got to see Amanda's point ... yes, I see that ... but if you just ... I understand that ... yes ... okay, in an hour. Yes, thank you, Cathy."

Alex flipped his cell phone closed in his usual manner, like an expert gunslinger holstering a favorite Smith & Wesson, but with more force than usual.

"Jesus Christ, that woman is trying to hide something!"

"Jimmy Hoffa?"

"He's buried under the third row of the Bloomfield Hills First Baptist Church auditorium."

"That's what I always thought too. It went up at the same time Jimmy disappeared. You don't think she killed him, do you, Alex?"

"Jimmy Hoffa?"

"No, Doc Winters. Is this going to be that easy?"

"Discovering the killer on our first try? It's a nice thought, but life never seems to work out that easily, does it?"

"No, but it would be nice, wouldn't it," I said with no real conviction. "To have all this behind me—us. So we could go on with our lives."

"I guess so," Alex replied. "I guess so."

Alex's comment was followed by a pause so uncomfortable, I swear I could hear the second hand on my wristwatch ticking. Alex, always the one to break the silence, did so with his signature, German-accented, karate-chop word. "ZO! Vat next?" he asked, rubbing his hands.

Taking the clue, I dove in. "Let's go see Cathy."

CHAPTER 9

Vee Haf Ways of Making You Talk

An hour later, we pulled up into the parking lot of Dodge & Dodge Realty, the powerhouse of real-estate firms in Palm Springs. We walked past a profusion of bedding plants that had been hammered into blooming perfection, up sparkling-clean sidewalks, and through crystal-clear doors into the reception area. Mary was obviously the love child of Martha Stewart and Attila the Hun. On the wall behind the receptionist's desk was the glittering logo of Dodge & Dodge, a hulking brass vulture that stared down at visitors, treating them as just so much roadkill. Okay, maybe it was just a very mean-looking eagle.

The receptionist announced us, and before she could hang up the phone, Cathy Paige came careening around a corner, shook our hands like they were maracas, escorted us to a conference room, and shut the door behind her as she motioned for us to sit down.

"What can I do for you two?" Cathy chirped happily.

A little too happily, I thought, considering that, under the circumstances, she should have been a frightened mess. After all, I'm sure the police had already questioned her and considered her a possible suspect.

"Cathy," I started, "you do know why we're here, don't you?"

"It's about your listing, right? On Boulder Drive?"

"Y—e—s. You were in the house just an hour before Doc was murdered there."

"Oh, yes, I suppose that does look suspicious!" she blurted.

"Kinda," I said. "Only two people were in 2666 Boulder Drive between the time I left on Tuesday night and the time I showed it in the Multiple Listing Service on Wednesday morning."

"Yes," Cathy said, staring over my shoulder, out the window, down the street, and out to the Hawaiian islands. This girl was clearly under some terrific strain. "I was previewing your house that morning."

"At seven-eighteen A.M.?" I asked.

Still staring, Cathy continued, "I had a client who was looking for a house just like yours. And considering the hot market we're in, I didn't want someone to get the jump on it . . . so I got up early. Oh, and Mary was after me to preview it for her. She had a hot client too."

Seeing that Cathy wasn't going to tell us the truth about why she was in my listing, I decided to probe elsewhere. Alex, always the gentleman (and observer extraordinaire), sat back and let me continue my questioning.

"Cathy, I need to ask you if you saw anything strange the morning you entered the house—like someone standing around, or a car sitting there on the street that didn't seem to belong there."

Cathy's gaze returned to the room for the first time since she sat down. She was still avoiding looking directly at me, but at least she was looking in my general direction.

"Let's see, let's see . . . uh . . . no, not really. The streets were empty that hour of the morning. It was pretty early."

"Try hard, Cathy. Nothing?"

"No, I didn't see anyone around. Like I said, it was early."

"Cathy, was there anything out of the ordinary when you entered the house?"

Cathy searched the ceiling with her eyes, looking for an answer.

"Let's see," she said, her hands visibly shaking on the table. "I entered the house, looked around the living room, then went into the master bedroom, then the other three bedrooms, scanned the kitchen, opened the door to the garage, then I left. No, nothing out of the ordinary. Could I get you some coffee?"

"Sure," I replied. "Alex, how 'bout you?"

"Yes, I'll take a mug."

"Fine, I'll go get you two some," Cathy said, getting up so quickly the conference chair she was sitting in shot back against the glass wall on its roller wheels and came to a stop so loud, it was a miracle it didn't crack the glass from top to bottom. "Oops," she said, grasping the chair and marshalling it back to its position at the table. She darted out of the room. I was about to comment to Alex, when we could hear a teaspoon rattling against the side of a mug with such ferocity, it sounded like an alarm bell. He put his finger to his lips, suggesting that we hold our conversation for later. Just as soon as she had disappeared, Cathy swooped back into the room, holding two mugs of coffee that she slammed on the tables in front of Alex and me.

"Here's some cream and sugar, if you take it," she said, slamming down a small caddy filled with packets of sugar and nondairy creamer that jumped in their containers when they hit the table. Normally, Alex wouldn't touch "the fake stuff," but he seemed more enthralled with Cathy's nervous behavior than his tastebuds. "I wasn't sure about offering you our coffee," Cathy apologized. "The brand we've been buying lately has been so bitter."

I took a sip of my brew and found it to be fine. Alex smacked his lips in approval.

"I had the same problem when I was at the University of Michigan," Alex confessed. "Every batch was so bitter. So I complained at the shop where I bought my beans. The guy who ran the shop said he was getting the same complaints, but he couldn't figure out why his coffee was so bitter. It wasn't until I saw a cat walking through the shop and watched him climb over the open sacks of roasted coffee beans that it dawned on me. That, plus the comment from the owner that his cat's litter box was always empty, and the riddle was solved."

I started laughing, but Cathy seemed to be in a dream. Then Cathy burst out laughing as if the punch line had been delivered to her on a three-second delay.

Alex shot me a did-you-see-that look. I countered with a let's-get-out-of-here look.

"Cathy, thank you for taking the time to talk with us," I spouted, already half out of my chair. "If you remember any-thing—anything at all—call us. Here's my business card. Oh, one last thing, Cathy. Do you own a red dress?"

"No, I look terrible in red. Mary Dodge can wear red, though. She always wears red to a listing appointment. She says it's her lucky color."

"How about a hat?" Alex inquired.

"No, I can't say she does. I've never seen her in one."

"Again," I began, "thank you for taking the time to talk with us."

Cathy shot up like a rocket, then sprinted ahead of us, hold-ing the door open for us. We walked down the sidewalk again, past the flowers that had been shouted into blooming, and back to Alex's car. But before we could get in, a woman came down the sidewalk in a half-trot, nervously looking over her shoulder for a man wearing a hockey mask and carrying an ax.

"Amanda? Amanda Thorne?"

"Yes?"

"My name's Anne Clexton—I'm on Mary Dodge's team," she explained.

"Yes, Anne, what can I do for you? Oh, this is my partner, Alex Thorne."

"In life?"

"No . . . business. But we were married before."

"Oh, I'm sorry."

Alex chimed in, "Don't be, Anne. We're still the best of friends."

"That's very rare. You both are very lucky. Most breakups and divorces can be so nasty. So terribly nasty . . ."

"So, what can I help you with, Anne?" I interjected.

"Oh, yes, I couldn't help overhear that Cathy is connected in some way with the murder of Doc Winters in your listing?"

"Yes, I ran a report on the Supra keybox I had on the listing and Cathy was one of two people who entered my listing that morning."

Anne scanned the parking lot to see if anyone was within earshot. Satisfied, she pulled in closer to the two of us and lowered her voice. "Can we speak in confidence?" she asked.

"Sure," we both answered simultaneously.

"Well, Cathy has been acting strange lately."

"How so, Mrs. Clexton?" Alex asked.

"Jumpy as a cat. Dropping things, spilling things, forgetting things, losing things . . . always in motion. I'm really worried about her. I mentioned it to her, but she just brushes it off."

Oh boy, I thought, this was getting good. "Is this behavior something you've noticed in the last few days?" I probed, Alex catching my drift immediately.

"No, she's been like this for a few weeks now. But it was like, all of a sudden. It was like a light switch. One day she's herself, then the next"—Anne clicked her fingers for extra emphasis—"she's all jumpy and absentminded. Then after the police came to question her, whew, she was really acting wigged out."

Anne looked over her shoulder again, hearing a car pull into the parking lot, then turned back at us. She grabbed my hand dramatically.

"Amanda, you won't say anything about this to Cathy or Mary, will you? I'm just worried about Cathy. I've never seen her like this, and she and I have worked on this team for eighteen years."

I gave my still-captive hands a friendly shake to emphasize that I would keep my promise of confidentiality.

"You can count on us," I reassured her.

"That's what I was hoping!" Anne replied, then released my hands, turned and hurried up the walk, and was swallowed back into the building.

I turned to Alex.

"Would someone please tell me what just happened?"

"I'm not sure myself," Alex replied. "But if I do, I'll drop you a postcard."

Alex and I sat in the parking lot for a while with the air conditioning on and the windows up. We were both eager to compare notes.

"What the fuck is that Cathy on?" I asked.

"Offhand, I'm guessing Pop-Tarts and amphetamines."

"I'm surprised that the cops didn't pick her up already. She comes across as guilty as sin."

"Okay," Alex started. "Let's assume she killed Doc—what's the motive?"

"More speed?"

Alex chuckled.

"Motives are usually pretty straightforward . . . and they're always the same ones: money, revenge, or love—love that's gone bad."

"From what I've heard by asking around, Doc's never had a girlfriend," Alex said.

I let out a grunt. "I'm not surprised. From what I've seen of him, I think his personal hygiene scared the ladies off. It looks like you could pull a bird nest out of his beard."

"So what's Cathy's connection to Doc?"

"None that I know of. But then again, I don't know much about Cathy or Doc."

"Then I think we should investigate that angle. Cathy, after all, works on Mary Dodge's team, and Mary's one of the most successful real-estate agents in Palm Springs. She's a wealthy woman."

"So what's your point, Alex? That because Mary Dodge might want to get her hands on the land up there at the base of the mountain?"

Alex turned to look at me. "It seems like the natural thing to assume."

"So do you think she killed Doc for Mary? It just seems too bizarre!"

"But just think of it for a minute, Amanda. The biggest piece of land in Palm Springs available for development . . . looking down on the city by day and the city lights at night, towering mountains literally in your backyard . . . Wouldn't you like to have your hand in that deal? Maybe she promised to cut Cathy in for killing Doc."

"Yeah, but what about the electronic key? It leaves a clear trail," I said.

"I don't think Cathy is thinking very straight. She might not have considered the ramifications."

"Oh, c'mon, Alex. Cathy has been an agent for a long time. She knows that when she uses her electronic key, she leaves a big neon arrow pointed at herself."

"Okay, try this on for size. Maybe Mary steals Cathy's key . . . or better yet, she says she can't find her own key—she's misplaced it—and she borrows Cathy's key. She goes and kills Doc, then brings the key back like nothing happened. When Cathy finds out what happened at 2666, she's scared because she's going to be the number one suspect."

"Well, then, Alex, why wouldn't she just tell the cops that Mary borrowed her key that morning?"

"We don't know *what* Cathy told the cops. And we're unlikely to."

"Okay, but let's say we don't know. But if you were Mary Dodge, would you borrow the key, knowing that Cathy could very well blab the truth?" I posed.

"No, not unless I were sure that Cathy would take the fall like a loyal employee."

"Alex, do you really know that many employees who would set themselves up for a murder rap just because someone employs them?"

"No, so my favorite theory is that Mary knew the personal identification number for Cathy's electronic key, took the key, murdered Doc, then brought the key back without Cathy ever knowing it was gone. Cathy finds out it was her key that was used to gain access to Boulder Drive, she freaks out and clams up. She says, maybe, that she lost her key. Meanwhile . . . oh shit!"

"What?"

"Mary knows that she has to kill Cathy at some point . . . to shut her up permanently."

"Oh shit is right. Cathy could be in danger right now. Now, wait a minute, Alex, do you think Mary would do all that just to make another million dollars? Mary already is a wealthy woman. Why would she want more money? She's got more than she can use."

"Silly Amanda, when you have all the money in the world, you'd be surprised to learn what people would do to get their hands on just a little more of it. Money creates its own momentum."

"Touché, Alex."

"And people are willing to kill for it," Alex warned.

"Often, far less. There's the prestige, too, I guess."

"Of landing the largest sale of land in the last fifty years? You bet!"

The implications were, for the first time, really sinking in.

"Alex, you don't think we're getting in over our heads, do you?"

"Us? Naaaw! There's nothing we can't handle."

"I know that, but the reality is that someone was willing to kill for some land. And after you've killed once, I'm sure it gets easier the more you do it. Or at least the punishment stays the same."

"And what do you mean by that, Amanda?"

"Well, even if you're found guilty of multiple murders, the State of California can only execute you once."

"You have point there, my dear."

"Yeah, and a scary one at that," I replied.

Alex and I agreed that we should spend a few hours attending to the business of selling houses, but it was clear that the both of us were more excited about unmasking a killer than putting a four-bedroom house into escrow. But the bills must be paid. So I went back to the office to get Alex's cubicle ready, snagging him some hard-won office supplies and setting up his phone, and finally, submitting some paperwork to our escrow coordinator. Neither Alex nor I used our offices much when we lived in Michigan, but it came in handy when you needed somewhere to make a slew of long-distance calls. Alex, true to the way he commanded and controlled life like an orchestra conductor, had almost his entire business on his computer and cell phone. No fuss, no muss. The office was a place that he used merely to catch up on the latest news . . . inside information that he used for leverage, to alert clients to off-the-books deals, and to steer clear of troublesome sellers and buyers.

You can tell a lot about a real-estate office just by walking through one. An office full of agents sitting behind desks working on computers is a bad sign. Chances are, they're playing video games or surfing the Internet, or paying bills and balancing checkbooks. If it's empty, that's a good sign. That means most of the agents are busy showing properties or working out at the gym or getting their hair done. In any case, you've got a hardworking agent, or at least one who also spends time working on her looks—an undeniable asset in the mystical, magical art of selling houses. I used to poo-poo the idea that good-looking agents have a leg up in selling houses, but Alex convinced me otherwise. I wanted to think that personal traits, presentation skills, and your drive to succeed made all the difference. I used to believe in Santa Claus and the Easter Bunny too. But I've seen it with my own eyes. This doesn't mean that just merely being a bimbo or himbo means you can drive money to the bank—selling real estate is hard work. But . . . looks are important. And the old adage is true: In order to be successful, you must project an image of success. That's why the movers and shakers all drive expensive cars. Buyers and sellers reason that if a Realtor can afford to drive such cars, then he or she must sell a lot of homes, and consequently, make a lot of money in order to afford such an expensive car. In reality, it just means that some car company was willing to lend money to a person who just happens to sell homes.

I was going through some files of Alex's when I heard the familiar voice of Grant Smallwood.

"You're looking beautiful today," came the raspy baritone.

"Grant, don't you ever get tired of making insincere compliments?"

"Not really."

"But do they ever work on anybody?"

"Sometimes they do. Hey, I heard that Alex is coming back."

"Present tense. He is back."

"Great, great. Hey, Amanda, have I ever told you that your ex-husband is hot?"

"Only about one hundred times."

"Well, he is. I've fantasized about having sex with him a lot. And I mean a lot!"

"Thank you, Grant. It's nice to have confirmation that I have good taste in men . . . gay men, in particular."

"You do, you definitely do. I'll bet he has a huge dick."

I raised my head slowly to stare in Grant's face without saying a word. I mean, what could you say? It's not like he was sexually harassing me. Grant was one of those people who never stopped talking, said things that could easily bring on a lawsuit, and was clearly fascinated with everything he had ever uttered.

"Well, does he?" Grant continued.

One last trait in Grant that I failed to list: He was one of those types who pestered you until you relented. Or, if you refused to respond, he'd continue having a conversation all by himself. You weren't really necessary. That was the thing with narcissists: It's all about them.

Grant was not about to give up. "So you're not going to tell me?"

More filing.

"You know who else in the office has a horse dick?"

More filing.

"David Kress. You want to know how I know? Well, when Miss Thing isn't out showing houses, he's prowling around the steam room at my gym, swinging his Louisville Slugger back and forth like it's an elephant trunk. . . . It's that big," Grant exclaimed, holding his hands a good twelve inches apart, just in case I needed a visual aid. "That's how he got that staph infection that had him in bed for a week. And a month before that, he got that urinary tract infection, which totally baffles me since I can't figure out how an infection managed to swim all that way down a cock that long."

I paused before stuffing a bulging folder into its prescribed slot in the open file drawer.

"Grant, is there a point to this rambling?"

"No."

"Then off with you," I said, swishing him away with empty folder, "before someone drops a house on you."

"Then you don't want to tell me if your ex has a big dick?"

"Grant, can't you go smoke near a propane tank or something? I've got work to do."

"Okay, if you're not going to tell me . . ." he trailed off, as if I was supposed to feel guilty about not divulging the exact measurements of my former husband's penis.

"That's right, Grant. I am not."

"Your silence is my answer," Grant added smugly.

My cell phone rang as Grant walked away. It was Alex.

"Hey," I chirped into the receiver. "Grant and I were just talking about you."

"So do you have a knockout black dress?"

"Alex, look who you're talking to."

"I'm just asking."

"Of course I do. Several. Are you taking me somewhere special?" I guessed.

"Absolutely."

"Where there are people and music?"

"Right again."

"Heels or flats?"

"Neither . . . hiking boots instead."

"What!? What kind of place is this?"

"A funeral. I'll pick you up at nine-thirty tomorrow morning."

CHAPTER 10

Excuse Me, Is This Rattlesnake Taken?

I had to admit that as we pulled up on the street that led to Eagle Canyon to park, I was actually looking forward to this memorial service. In fact, I was sporting a discreet, but definite smile on my face. Don't misunderstand me, the fact that a prominent ecoactivist had been brutally murdered was sad—even sadder that this man had the temerity and lack of good graces to do it in one of my listings. But having been raised Catholic and having attended literally hundreds of Catholic funerals before I even reached the tender age of 12, I would have looked forward to a memorial service where bereaved family members immolated themselves in front of my eyes. Now it was a funeral in a canyon. At least it would be something new.

Funerals, you see, is one area where the Catholic Church really shines. Even though time has dulled some of the terror they've perfected over the years, they still knew how to work the emotions of a vulnerable crowd. The main theme was horror, followed by retribution, guilt, pomp, and then finished off by artery-clogging food, which, in turn, lead to more deaths and more funerals—the Catholic cycle of life. From the kneeling bench in front of the open casket where you could pray over the deceased to the clouds of incense that they broke out at the right moment, they had it down pat.

So as Alex and I made our way past the line of cars belonging to the attendees, I couldn't help but feel exhilarated. This gig couldn't make you feel any lower than a Catholic funeral. The bumper stickers affixed to the many cars that lined the street also gave me reason to smile: There was no doubt where these people stood, politically. DEFOLIATE THE BUSHES, said one. THERE'S A LOT OF DIRT UNDER EVERY BUSH, declared another. Following this one: A VILLAGE IN TEXAS IS MISSING ITS IDIOT. Clearly, Bush was not a favorite here. There were several LOVE YOUR MOTHER stickers with a picture of Earth, but the ones using sarcasm or double entendres really captured my heart. One ancient Volvo that looked as if it had been rolled in mud exclaimed, from left to right, VISUALIZE WORLD PEACE, VISUALIZE WHIRLED PEAS, VISUALIZE TURN SIGNALS. My favorite: WITCHES PARKING. ALL OTHERS WILL BE TOAD. I let out a brief but audible chuckle, causing several people making the trudge up into the canyon with us to shoot me a look so dirty, it would have to be scooped up in a plastic doggie poop bag and dumped into a trash can.

I had hiked into Eagle Canyon before, and found its amazing beauty even more stunning because it existed only a few hundred yards from a Volvo dealership off Highway 111. As we neared the spot where the memorial service was being held, I looked around for chairs but saw none. Goddamnit, I thought, I'm wearing DKNY, for heaven's sake. I did a quick scan of the area for a free rock to pull up and sit down upon, but all the good rocks were already taken.

"A word of caution," one woman who appeared to be entirely attired in white cheesecloth warned. "There's a *Crotalus atrox* over there behind that rock," she said, pointing with the cane she was resting her chin on.

"What did she say?" Alex inquired.

"Something about a girl named Alice," I whispered.

I trudged over toward the rock in question and came face-to-face with the first rattlesnake I had ever seen. I froze. Alex, who was only a foot or so behind me, froze also. The snake was coiled into a mass of aggression, its tail rattling like a maraca with Parkinson's.

"Good, Amanda. Stay still. Now, slowly back away, one foot at a time. Don't turn around, just face the snake and slide your foot slowly backward, first one . . . good . . . now the other . . . now the other one again . . .

As soon as I was safely out of range, I turned and walked in a daze back toward the bulk of the people. Feeling that it was my civic duty to inform everyone about the danger nearby, I made an announcement.

"Attention, attention everyone."

A sea of heads turned.

"There's a deadly rattlesnake behind that rock over there," I said, pointing.

The look I got in return was not one of concern for safety of the attendees, but one of "who is this chick with the drama-queen problem?"

Miffed, I went back toward the woman who almost sent me to my death.

"Why didn't you warn me there was a diamondback over there behind that rock?"

"I did," she answered casually. "In Latin."

"I don't speak full Latin—just pig, ifway uoyay nowkay hatway Iway eanmay."

No reaction. I noticed that the top of the cane this woman continued to rest her chin on was carved into the head of a snake, fangs bared.

"He wouldn't have harmed you. He's more afraid of you than you are of him," Snake Lady informed me.

"Don't be too sure of that. I almost spoiled my dress—thank God I'm wearing Depends."

"Close to fifty percent of all bites are dry . . . no venom," she continued like an irritating National Park Service employee.

"Well, I didn't want to test that theory."

"No theory . . . it's a fact."

"I see."

"Anyway, we're on his territory. He was here first. And his ancestors were here millions of years before us," Snake Lady instructed me.

Alex lightly grabbed my arm and led me away before I had a chance to retort. "We better go find a seat before the service begins."

Alex scanned the throngs who milled about, chatting, praying, lighting incense, smoking odd cigarettes, dancing to music that was not being played, while a circle of women sat on the ground, holding large drums snuggled in their laps. This memorial service was going to be a humdinger.

Before long, there was a hush that fell over the crowd as an amazingly tall woman with hair almost as long and flowing as the clothes she wore floated to the front of the crowd—literally. The way she walked, there was no discernable gait, like she was mounted on rubber wheels cleverly hidden under her diaphanous gowns. This woman obviously lived in a bad neighborhood, since it seemed that she wore every piece of jewelry she ever owned at once in an attempt to foil thieves breaking into her house. Her weakness for bracelets was apparent, with dozens of them encircling her arms. When she raised her hands upward to the sky in a supplication, then out

to the crowd, it sounded like a waiter with a trayful of silver-
ware had fallen down a flight of stairs.

"Welcome, welcome, *namaste*," the woman said, pressing
her palms together, bowing slightly. "We have come here to
celebrate and remember a life, a life of devotion to serving the
Earth Mother, the Giver of all Life. We will begin with a
prayer, led by a spiritual leader you probably all know, Coyote
Woman."

On cue, the drum section broke out into a cacophony of
synchronized pounding so deafening, I thought it unwise to
make so much noise in an active earthquake fault zone.

"Oh good," Alex whispered to me, "there's going to be a
sacrifice."

I smiled over at Alex. As Coyote Woman neared the front of
the congregation, the drum beats retreated into a soft, repeti-
tive thumping, giving Coyote some room to speak. Coyote
bowed her head, then fell into a deep, reverential silence.

"Oh great spirits of the Earth, Moon, and stars, we gather
here to summon you to bless us, to give us strength, and to
help us find those who have taken the life—but not the
spirit—of Doc Winters."

At this proclamation, I couldn't help but look around to see
what reactions there were. Some heads nodded, some still had
their eyes open, one puffed away on a joint, contentedly sending a stream of the smoke into the blue skies, and one woman,
who sat to our left, seemed visibly upset—so much so, I could
see her squirming with rage that made the packet of smolder-
ing leaves she held in her hand shake violently.

There couldn't have been a more diverse group of people
on the planet. While the majority of the people in attendance
clearly belonged to the Poligrip-hippie group, they by no
means owned the day. There were Gen-X environmentalists

wearing itchy wool knit caps and tie-dye T-shirts, Range-Rover-driving Sierra Club members, and up front in dead center was an incredibly chic woman wearing what I guessed to be unimaginatively expensive clothes and shoes; from where I stood, I could see the glint on her finger of what could be no less than a ten-carat diamond. Diversity was the name of the game here.

"Spirits of the East . . . West . . . North . . . and South, come down amongst us, let us feel your energy pass through us, and bind us together here today."

As most of the people around us bowed their heads in silence, I took a minute to study Coyote Woman. If you were going to be mystic, jewelry was the way to go. No doubt about it. Coyote Woman took a different tact than our emcee, however. Crystals were the operative word here. Lot and lots of crystals, hanging from neckchains, earlobes, attached to rings by tiny wires—the more, the better. Why a rock in crystal form was supposed to have mystical powers and a regular rock didn't struck me as mere prejudice. Just like people, I thought. The attractive ones were made of the same substance as the more common species, but it was the good-looking ones that got all the attention. Life, whether you're a rock or a person, is just unfair.

With the exception of all the crystals she wore, very little about Coyote Woman suggested anything mystical. In fact, she was rather plain. She looked like she could be anything from a Baptist minister's wife to a cashier at Walmart. This is what made the crystals that she wore seem so hokey. She came across like a psychic Roseanne Barr—the two just didn't go together. My prejudices demanded that she at least should look like a Coyote Woman. You know, seven-feet tall, weighing eighty-eight pounds, wearing a sari covered with mystical runes and symbols. She would speak as if from far away, which she was, living partly in this world, partly in a nether world of dead people and energy from wormholes in space caused by black holes. You know, the usual. This one had none of those characteristics. Forget the eighty-eight pounds . . . this Coyote Woman had a paunch. Too many jalapeño-jack cheese poppers at Applebee's, I guessed.

"Come upon us here, oh spirits of the desert, the mountains, and the valleys; come spirits of the tortoise, the serpents, lizards, ravens, hawks, owls, jackrabbits . . ."

"If she leaves out the dung beetles, I'm leaving," Alex slid out of the corner of his mouth, never taking his eyes off Coyote Woman. "They always get passed over."

". . . come, send us the strength of the universe flowing through us, around us . . ."

"AIIIEEEEHHHHHH!" The blood-curdling scream came from my left. The woman who sat with smoking leaves in her hands burst up from her seat like a harpy from hell, stormed up to Coyote Woman, and slapped her hard across the face while people looked on in horror.

For what seemed like an eternity, no one moved or said a thing. Then, two men in the front row got up and quietly escorted the attacker out of the canyon, with no resistance being offer by the deranged woman.

"Geez, this tops my grandfather's funeral, where my psychotic grandmother tried to crawl into the coffin with her husband," I whispered to Alex.

"She was that distraught?"

"No, she had just found out from a brother-in-law that her spouse had spent all their savings . . . left her penniless. She was trying to hit him, but she was short, so she had to hoist herself up on the edge of the casket to get a clear shot at him."

Alex looked at me as if I had told him that our family ate bugs.

"Noooooo!"

"I never told you about that one? I took a picture of her with my Brownie camera, but my mother tore it up when I got the prints back from the developer. She thought it was in bad taste."

"And climbing into a coffin to pummel your dead husband isn't?"

"Grandma was a little headstrong. Grandma once told me she killed a Cossack with her bare hands. . . . Well, to be precise, she claims she hit him in the head with an ax, which split his skull in two . . . just like a melon . . . she would say, cackling. Every time she sliced open a melon for us for breakfast, she would tell us that story, laughing as the melon parted under the blade of the knife and the two sections rolled around on the table. Sometimes she put the two halves back together in front of her face, then parted them suddenly to reveal her face. It's no wonder I would wake up screaming some nights."

"Are you sure your family name wasn't Manson?"

Coyote Woman, having had a short time to recompose herself, continued asking for energy from every conceivable planetary body, rock, animal, insect, and multicellular creature, then admonished us to feel the positive energy of the universe, which I felt was about the same as asking someone to visualize whirled peas.

Coyote Woman, the handprint of her attacker still visible on her left cheek, sat down and was replaced by a white boy with Rastafarian hair who launched into a tirade against developer Marvin Sultan as being responsible for the death of Doc Winters. This utterance was greeted with nods from many of those in attendance. The idea wasn't lost on me. Or anyone else in town, either. Marvin seemed the natural assassin, since he and Doc Winters were thorns in each other's proverbial sides. Doc had caused endless delays to Marvin's plans to develop a neighborhood in the Chino Cone. Doc's pièce de résistance was getting enough signatures to place the issue on the ballot in the November elections, just a few weeks away.

Marvin's troubles began long before he announced his plans for Marvin Gardens, his prize neighborhood of three-million-dollar-plus homes in the Cone. Marvin had a long history of being associated with heinous crimes that benefited him greatly. Besides razing a historic Richard Neutra home in Rancho Mirage in order to build a hideous tract mansion in its place, Marvin engineered a dastardly coup that gave his Bel Air home unfettered views of downtown Los Angeles, when previously it had limited vistas blocked by the trees on the property of one Edward J. Lamston, and his wife, Claire. By a mere coincidence, when the said neighbors were away in Barbados with their servants, a crew of gardeners chopped down all the trees that stood in Marvin's way. When the Lamstons found out about the deforestation of their property, the lumberjack gardeners defended their actions by claiming that they received a call from none other than Edward J. Lamston himself. Indeed, the police, when investigating the matter, looked on the cellular phone call log on the head gardener's phone, and lo and behold, the call had been placed from the Lamstons' home phone number. Stranger still, the payment for the gardeners' job was left in a potter's shed on the grounds—all $25,000 dollars of it—in cash. The papers had a field day with the incident, with the majority of its readers rightly coming to the conclusion that Marvin paid a telephone lineman to place a call from a neighborhood switching station to make it appear as if the call came from the Lamstons' home. Someone also opened locked gates to the Lamston estate, beckoning the gardeners in to do their dirty work.

In the end, the gardeners took the fall for the deed and

Marvin got off scot-free. Well, Marvin got his view, but most of Southern California had made up their minds about Marvin. In fact, readers voiced their opinions in countless letters to the editor pages, placing guilt squarely on Marvin, and with most making the logical change in his last name, from Sultan to Satan. The name stuck.

Our Rastafarian eulogizer went from castigating Marvin to calling for the abolition of all Humvees in Southern California. When our speaker mentioned Hummers, I recognized him immediately. He was none other than Lance Talbot, the head of the People's Army for the Liberation of the Earth, or P.A.L.E. for short. His organization spent their time liberating animals from testing labs, handcuffing themselves to trees in Northern California and Oregon, and throwing pies in the face of industry CEOs like Bill Gates of Microsoft and CEOs of oil firms. Mostly, P.A.L.E. got minor news coverage, but when thirty-six Hummers were torched at an Orange County car dealership in Newport Beach, the spotlight was directed at Lance and his cohorts—all of whom denied any involvement in the act. The police and the FBI built a flimsy case against the organization, but somehow, this ragtag group of eco-terrorists hired high-profile defending attorney David Stuart, called the Great White Shark because of the way he tore apart his prosecutor's cases, and the fact that his hair was a shocking white, even though he was just barely 43 years old. How a grass roots group like P.A.L.E came up with the money to hire Stuart is still a mystery, but soon after the case was dismissed, people began to realize that ecologists now had well-heeled friends in high places. This led me to scan our well-dressed mourner in the front row. The connection seemed to strengthen in my mind.

Our speaker was replaced by a succession of people, all pretty much spouting the same idea: that Doc was killed by real-estate developers, namely, Marvin Sultan. What I found interesting was the ferocity of the speakers. These were passionate people, people who were clearly angry and more than capable of committing just about any act to defend their beliefs. Would they kill for them? I wouldn't put it past them.

"I feel like a lamb amongst the wolves," Alex whispered to me.

I knew how he felt. Here we were, two real-estate agents, whose main income derived from selling land and houses. We both belonged to the Sierra Club and the Nature Conservancy and donated heavily, but some of the friends surrounding us might not think us so sympathetic to their causes. In actuality, both of us intended to vote against Marvin Gardens come that first Tuesday in November. Why not? The one thing that made Palm Springs so special was its small-town feel and its pristine mountains. If we didn't do something soon, Palm Springs would look like Phoenix.

Alex continued his train of thought, "Let's just keep the fact that we're Realtors our little secret, huh?"

"Good idea."

The last speaker was introduced as Monica Birdsong, Doc's "life partner." This was a surprise to me since I was told Doc didn't have girlfriends. Monica was not what I'd picture as the quintessential girlfriend of an activist environmentalist. This woman shaved her armpits. She wore tight spandex that wasn't stretched over bulging stomachs like sausage casings. And her hair was, well, big and brassy. And her tits were so rounded and prominent, they were like two flesh-colored grapefruits glued to her chest. Monica fell squarely into the category of bimbo. Hands down.

"I think I've developed a buzz from all the secondhand pot smoke." Alex pointed. "I'm seeing things."

"Do you see a bimbo?"

"Yes, I do. I don't get it," Alex remarked. "What's wrong with this picture?"

While we were sitting there in stunned amazement, Monica dropped another bomb: She opened her mouth. Not that what came out was any different that what we expected, but when we heard it, we were still stunned. Monica's voice fell somewhere between a terrified parrot being stomped to death and Betty Boop.

"My ears must still be pretty good. I would've bet that only dogs could hear her."

"Oh my God, I don't believe it," was all I could muster.

Monica, after thanking everyone for coming to remember the life of Doc Winters, said that there was little she could say. She then unfolded a piece of paper and told us all that she had written a poem that expressed her feelings. I wished I had brought a tape recorder, and after I heard her verse, I kicked myself that I hadn't.

Today, I'm sad,
When I should be glad,
Doc's spirit is free,
To soar among the breeze,
Oh birds, take care of him,
Let him spread his wings,
Like the dove
To fly, to see things
That I can only dream of.
So fly, fly away,
Across the mountains, across the sea,
I'll think of you each day,
As I watch the birds and sip, my coff-ee.

What I did next surprised even me. I starting snickering—I just couldn't help it. Monica was the classic bimbo reading a classic bimbo poem. In fact, Monica's verse was better than anything in Suzanne Somers's poem about bedwetting in her seminal book of poetry entitled *Touch Me*. I fought the waves that convulsed my body, but it was a lost cause. I decided to try and steer the snickers until they sounded a little like crying. Indeed, the tears were streaming down my face, but they came from the way Monica broke the word *coffee* for dramatic effect. Shakespeare would have been proud.

I was attracting some stares from our neighbors, so I hung my head and dabbed at my eyes with a tissue to give the effect of being devastated. From the moment Monica finished, the crowd fell eerily silent, which I chalked up to her poem. I couldn't look up, because if I saw Miss Birdsong again, standing there in her spandex, the floodgates would have turned into gales of laughter . . . there would be no stopping me. So I chose to keep my head down and try to make my shudders look like out-and-out crying. Just as I thought I had the situation under control, the chorus of drums thundered up again, causing me to laugh all over again.

And that was it. The memorial service was over. Not with a bang or a whimper, but with a guffaw. Alex stood up and surveyed the crowd.

"How did you keep from laughing all that time?" I asked Alex.

"I thought about dead kittens."

"Cheater."

"I've been watching the crowd and I think we should meet with one or two people."

"Monica?"

"Check . . . if you promise to behave yourself. Remember, think of dead kittens."

"I got it . . . something to make me sad. Me, I'd like to talk to Coyote Woman. I want to know if that crazy woman who slapped her is Eagle Feather. Come to think of it, since I'm going to have this woman cleanse my house of evil spirits, I think we need to know a little more about these cactus huggers."

"Just what I was thinking. And I want to know who that woman is with the million-dollar wardrobe."

"Why don't we split up, Alex? You hit the bimbo and I'll get the woman with the crystals. We'll meet back here at eleven hundred hours. Check?"

"Check. Watches synchronized."

Alex trundled off in search of his prey and I pounced on mine. As I approached Coyote Woman, she stepped back suddenly, raising her arms slightly. Coyote Woman was gun-shy, and rightly so.

"Coyote Woman?"

"Yes?" she replied, sounding halfway between a smile and a grimace.

"I'm Amanda Thorne . . . the Realtor . . . you called me the other day, offering your services to cleanse the evil spirits from the home where Doc was killed."

"Negative energy."

"Negative energy . . . right." I forgot that even psychics had to move with the times. Levitating tables and Ouija boards were a thing of the past. Today's modern psychic had to adapt New Age parallels to scientific principles in order not to be thought quaint. "I need your help. As soon as possible."

"We're scheduled for *next* Thursday."

"I need to see you sooner. Tomorrow, if that's possible."

"That will have to do, Miss Thorne. My schedule is very

busy. My services are *very much* in demand," she replied, tipping me off that she was going to play hardball on price. "I have four house cleansings, a full-moon drumbeat, and a highlighting to do on a lady in Yucca Valley."

"A highlighting? Is that some sort of spiritual illumination?"

"No, it's when you dye portions of a person's hair. I'm a hairdresser too."

"Cleansing hair and homes!"

"I just couldn't imagine doing a cleansing any earlier than next Thursday. . . ."

"I'll pay you six hundred if you manage to fit me in sooner."

"I'll be there tomorrow. Is ten A.M. fine?"

Alex was busting with information on the ride back to my house after the memorial service.

"So there's quite a mix of people opposing development in the Chino Cone. Environmental lawyers, old hippies, several heiresses, society women, even a coat-hanger mogul. And there's a whole rash of reasons why they're against building up there, from environmental to aesthetic to economic reasons. They're smart, they're political, and lots of them come from areas of the country that had strict limits on building and growth: Seattle; Portland; Boulder, Colorado; San Francisco. You see, in the past, the old city councils just rubber-stamped development and the developers just ran over the opposition. Now, the opposition is connected . . . all the way up to friends in the state capitol."

"Why do I feel like I'm standing between author Stephen King and a mound of coke?" I asked dryly.

"And someone's bound to get hurt."

"And you can be sure it ain't gonna be me."

CHAPTER 11

God Is Kinda Dead

I went home and organized some things around my house in a blind attempt to impose some sense of order in The Curse. I was putting a box full of photographs up on a high shelf when the bottom of the box burst open, spilling forty-odd years of photographs to the bottom of the closet. Shit!

I grabbed a photograph that had gotten lodged in between the vacuum cleaner and its hose attachments. It was a picture of Alex and I and my mom and dad, all mugging for the camera in my parents' backyard in Michigan a few weeks after our wedding.

Of course, they say that while you're marrying the man, you're dating the family too. In Alex's case, things couldn't be better. I fell in love with his family as much as I did with him. They were everything my family was not: funny, intelligent, able to communicate with each other and offer true emotional support, and best of all, essentially drama-less. Alex's dad, Martin, despite attempts to look uncaring about his looks, was still as handsome as he was in the college photographs that lined the fireplace mantel in their family room. Martin's ace in the hole was his silvery hair worn long for a man his age. The length of his hair caused him to be constantly pushing it back out of his eyes, like the captain of a sailing ship crossing the finish line of the America's Cup or a man who just yesterday finished testing his Lotus on the winding roads of Provence or the Amalfi coast.

Alex's mother, Zara, was too cool for words. Her name was the cool and impressive door that opened to the fascinating person who went on and on, room after astonishing room in the fascinating house that was Zara. Translated, her name meant "yellow desert flower" in an African dialect. Even cooler was the fact that she had spent much of her childhood in Kenya, playing next to her ultra-cool-before-her-time mother, Katkja. It was here that Zara learned to paint, had a mad affair with the rakish bon vivant Peter Beard, personally knew Karen Blixen, who wrote *Out of Africa*, and went on camera-only safaris and painted the animal life there in violent, colorful canvasses that littered their Bohemian home in Franklin, Michigan.

Alex had one sister, Cosima, whom I had never met until Alex and I wed. Cosima was wed to a wealthy German count and spent most of her time with Fritz at their home in Fiji, studying the native fish population when they weren't working on killer tans.

People like these didn't live in Michigan. They lived in Paris or Bombay and spent their time circumnavigating the globe, seeking to help the world or, at the very least, seeking to advance their creative talents through Zen meditation with Buddhists monks or clear their nasal passages through ancient yoga routines. How Alex's family managed to survive in Michigan was beyond me, but having a sizable income was a great part of the solution. Alex's grandfather had invented a water backflow valve that revolutionized irrigation and, through the patent he secured, allowed his descendants to live comfortably and indulge themselves in just about anything they fancied.

When Alex and I had been dating for a while, the dread of

his family eventually having to meet mine began to raise its ugly head. Alex had already met my family, which he did with absolute grace and decorum. The circumstances of that first meeting were as carefully orchestrated as a Met production of *Aida*. I spent weeks choosing the restaurant, agonizing in finding one that didn't reek of banal Midwestern suburbanism, yet one that wouldn't cause my father to squawk out loud when seeing the menu prices: "Thirteen dollars for a piece of cheese? What's it going to do, sleep with me?"

The meeting went as well as a Noel Coward play, with a host of social gaffes played out on the table like cards from a casino dealer on speed. But Alex, cool as if he had suddenly found himself staring into the face of a starved lion, spoke in a calm voice, backing away only where there was no option available. There was one exception, however.

My mother brought up the subject of religion, feeling that this was an appropriate topic for driving a wedge into what looked like a perfect exterior, a perfect match for her daughter and splitting Alex wide open to show all the ugliness she suspected festered beneath.

"So, Alex, what religion were you brought up in? You're Presbyterian, aren't you? I can always tell!" she gushed.

"No, Mrs. Kazulekis."

"Oh, please, Alex, call me Mildred. Then you're Methodist, aren't you? That's what you are, Methodist."

While Alex tried to avoid an answer that wouldn't set well with my mother—I had already warned him beforehand of her usual battle plans—my mother became increasingly worried as she worked her way down the list of religions she loathed, starting at the nondescript Presbyterians and working her way down to those she considered the left hand of Satan.

"No, not Methodist."

Like all games my mother played, this cat-and-mouse version would only end in a tragic explosion, the ground littered with shattered bodies and ambulances wailing.

"Baptist?" she said with a calculatedly perceptible moue of disgust.

"No," Alex replied with a little chuckle, trying to keep my mother at bay.

"You're not Jewish, are you?" she offered, scanning his shaved head to see if there was any sign of dark hair and reevaluating the size of his nose. People who live in glass houses, Mother.

"No, I'm not Jewish."

My mother stabbed a piece of perfectly squared filet mignon, delivered it daintily into her mouth, then chewed and swallowed. Now she was ready. She let loose her final volley.

"You do go to church, don't you?"

Alex, who was the perfect diplomat up to this point, decided to throw his cards on the table. Alex was very tolerant of fools, but when people challenged his beliefs—or his right not to have any where religion was concerned—he wasn't about to back down.

"Mrs. Kazulekis . . ."

"Mildred."

"Mildred, I don't believe in God."

"You don't believe in God?" Mildred countered. "Then what do you believe in?"

"Myself. Understanding myself and family, being kind and helpful to others, exploring this great planet."

"That sounds like a summer program at Outward Bound, Alex. What about your plans for eternity?"

"Mildred, I plan to spend it with my ashes spread across the Torres del Paine mountain peaks in Chile. And after four billion years when the Sun expands and incinerates the Earth, I, like everything left on what's left of Earth, will probably drift into space until we coalesce into another gas cloud that will condense into a star, and we'll start the whole process over again, until the universe expands and tears itself apart in what cosmologists think will ultimately happen in an event called the Big Rip."

This shut my mother up, mostly because she had only a vague idea of what Alex said, though she knew it had somehow been sarcastic—and definitely something to which the Pope wouldn't agree because it made people think. My father, always living in the shadow of his own life, stepped into the light with his own stalemate breaker.

"You know, this filet is really quite good, but I can grill a pretty decent steak myself on my own charcoal grill, after, of course, I have properly tendered the coals using my home-made charcoal chimney, made from a coffee can. Yes siree, a coffee can. Isn't that right, Mildred?" he cajoled my mother, nudging her in the arm in a lost effort to upright the conversation.

But, as usual, my mother was done with the subject. If her son-in-law was going to be an atheist and her daughter was completely uninterested in religion, then maybe there was hope for the grandson . . . and it would be a grand*son* . . . Boys always counted for more in Lithuanian families: They could clean stables, bring in the harvest, and fight off Cossacks— even though we lived in Michigan.

"So what about your children?"

"Mom, don't you think you're getting a little ahead of yourself with—" I tried to squeeze in.

"Shush," she said, holding up her hand to set the stage for what Alex was going to say.

"I don't have any."

"No, but when you do," Mom countered.

"What about them?" Alex toyed with her.

"What religion would you bring them up in?"

"I would let them choose, Mrs. Kazulekis. The way I see it, I think that if you have a child, it's better to let them make their own decisions once they're smart enough to make them. To bring a child up in a religion just because a parent wants them to be brought up that way seems dictator-ish. It's like telling a child you will think my way, feel the way I do. Like Thomas Jefferson, I believe in the inherent rights of man."

Alex had her there. Mildred was very firm in her Catholicism, but it was hard to argue with a Founding Father. Even if she knew no more than the fact that Thomas Jefferson ran around in what she considered drag and lived somewhere in Virginia, you didn't mess with core American values . . . whatever they were.

Alex, already running rings around Mildred, turned to my father in order to change the conversation.

"So, Mr. Kazulekis, tell me about this charcoal chimney you designed."

And that, as they say, was that.

I put the photograph that I had been reminiscing about down on a shelf and shut the door to the closet, leaving all those memories lying there for another day, another time.

The next morning, I stood outside the death house, waiting for Coyote Woman, er, Barbara to arrive. When she pulled up in a Dodge minivan that was encrusted with the dirt of countless centuries, I was somewhat surprised. I half expected her to be driving a Volkswagen beetle with a huge daisy painted on the side. Or maybe a panel van with dragon murals airbrushed onto the doors, just something other than a vehicle more associated with ferrying kids to and from school and Little League games. Her car ground to a halt on brake pads that were probably as thin as a politician's alibi, the grinding squeal was so high pitched, it opened a clogged sinus. The driver's side door opened with a haunted-house creaking, rebounded from the hinge's farthest reach, then slammed again on her flowing dress, the crystals sewn to the hem tinkling against the van's running board. Where did this woman get a dress like that? Was there some kind of Psychic Dress for Less store? I was paying how much for this?

"It's one of those days," Coyote Woman said as she finally emerged from her Indiana Jones Soccer Mom vehicle. "I had a premonition last night that this was going to be a rough day."

She approached me, cupping my outstretched hand in her hands as if she were trying to incubate it. No shaking of hands for this woman—it would probably disturb the healing powers in it. She turned back to her car and opened the back hatch of her wagon, the hinges creaking even worse than the driver's side door, perhaps forcing a pod of whales in California to beach themselves. ("Jesus Christ, what the fuck was that?!" they said in Whalese as they threw themselves on the sand in confusion.)

We talked a lot while she stood at the open hatchback of her car, me mostly chatting about my life and, of course, Alex. Lots of Alex, who, by the way, couldn't make it to the cleansing because of a burst water line in a house he had listed.

Coyote Woman wrestled with a plastic crate on wheels, extracting it from the womb of her car and dropping it on the pavement with a loud crash.

"There," she said satisfyingly, turning toward the house across the street in order to sum it up like an opponent in a sumo wrestling match. She closed her eyes and began to moan. "Oh, oh . . . the aura is very disturbed by the murder. We must put things right."

"Coyote Woman?"

"Yes."

"That's not my listing. The murder took place in *this*

house," I said, pointing in the opposite direction at the structure in front of us.

"I knew that," she said, trying to recover her mistake. "I was just commenting on the negative energy I was receiving from that house across the street."

"Yes, I know. That color's hideous."

"I was talking about energy given off by the house, not bad design. Although, now that you mention it, the trim color really sucks."

Figuring that this was only going to get sillier and sillier, I felt it was time to get down to business. I steered Coyote Woman toward the house, opened the door, and gestured to her to enter. I wanted for her to get her job done so I could pick her brain for information.

Coyote held out her hand dramatically. She fished a crystal the size of a small dove out of a pocket in her dress. She held the massive crystal in her hand and pointed it toward the house like a surface-to-air missile. She invoked a litany of words, most of which included "spirits" (fives times), "energy" (three times), "she-goddess" (two times), and "great horned toad" (?). She then closed her eyes while holding the crystal toward the house, presumably to wait for it to launch. She returned the crystal to her dress pocket and returned to the land of the living.

I decided to play along a little. It would be amusing and help to pass the time.

"Coyote Woman, could you tell me what kind of crystal that is?"

"It's a citrine. It's the only crystal that doesn't accumulate negative energy. In fact, it dissipates it."

"Wow," I responded with false interest. You'd think that a person with extrasensory powers could detect the disbelief even in my voice, but Barbara seemed clueless. "It must be very powerful."

"Miss Thorne, you just expressed a common misconception about crystals . . . which is why so many people report that they don't work."

Maybe they don't work because they're just rocks, I thought.

"Crystals don't have any power of their own. Even a lot of so-called psychics think that crystals emanate power."

More insincerity. "They don't?"

"No, crystals are like lenses that focus power from other sources."

"I see dead people," I whispered.

Coyote Woman rolled her eyes in exasperation. "Miss Thorne . . ."

"I'm sorry. I envision myself as sort of a comic."

"Then you need amazonite."

"Does it cure flatulence?"

"Miss Thorne!" Coyote Woman intoned like a frustrated fifth-grade teacher trying to lecture about fractions. "It clears creative blockages."

"And . . . ?"

"Then you could put your humor down on paper and make some money and wouldn't have to sell houses for a living."

Ouch—a psychic bitch-slap. I started to reevaluate my opinion about Coyote Woman's perceptiveness.

"So, as I was saying, crystals just focus energy from the elements or spirits through me and through the crystal. That's where the power of crystals come from . . . not from the crystal itself . . . although citrine is good for curing constipation."

I didn't want to think about how she used citrine for curing reluctant turds. Even more importantly, I was certainly glad Coyote Woman didn't ask me to hold that crystal. Like Harvey Milk, San Francisco's first openly gay mayor who is said to have said to evangelist Ruth Carter Stapleton when she shook his hand, "I'm surprised you shook it . . . You never know where it's been."

Coyote grabbed the handle of her rolling crate, and like a New Age flight attendant, made for the front door of my listing with me in tow. She stopped abruptly and turned around with an outstretched hand.

"No, you must not enter while I cleanse! This can be very dangerous. The negative energy must be purged from the house completely. Unprotected, the energy could enter you."

"Couldn't I hold a clove of garlic or a piece of Kryptonite?"

"Miss Thorne, you shouldn't make fun of these things. We are dealing with powers you can't begin to understand.

I relented. "Okay, okay, I will defer to the expert. I will wait here."

A quick nod from Coyote Woman's head: She was ready. She faced the house, raised her hands up to the sky and took a deep breath, held it for what seemed an eternity, then exhaled with the force of a tuba player between pursed lips. There was an uncomfortable moment of silence; then Coyote Woman corralled her crate on wheels and headed bumping over doormats and thresholds into the home. Coyote Woman left the front door open, supposedly to let the door hit the bad energy in the ass (or asses) when it exited, so I struggled to get a glimpse of what this crazy bitch was doing inside, but she must have caught on to my plan and moved her crate into the kitchen where I couldn't see her. I tried to act uninterested into her doings, but every once in a while, I would stand on my toes to peek into the windows.

Coyote Woman began with incantations, followed by clouds of sage that she burned and wafted around the house with what looked like the large wing of a bird, I swear to God. So much for being one with the earth. She walked from room to room, reciting strange, poetic incantations and waving huge fog banks of sage toward the front door, from which she finally emerged, standing on the front steps. She spread-eagled herself in front of the door. Oh, I got it . . . to barricade the spirits from reentering the house after she'd kicked their butts out. After holding this pose long enough for several neighbors walking their dogs to see and muse over, she reached into a pocket in her diaphanous dress and pulled out a handful of tiny rust-colored crystals, which she sprinkled liberally in front of the door.

I raised my eyebrows.

"Carnelian. It protects against fear, envy, and rage, and helps to banish sorrow from the emotional structure," she answered, no doubt quoting dutifully from the book *Using Crystals to Promote Good Energy and Healthy Bowel Movements*.

I just had to ask this question: "Coyote Woman, so if you chased out the bad—"

She corrected me with a hand raised to my lips. "Negative energy."

"Okay, negative energy, so where does it go now? Does it go into another house? Another person?"

"They wander the earth in search of new misfortunes."

"Can I ask you another question?"

A look of fear came over Coyote Woman. "The owl wing came from a roadkill. I didn't shoot it!" she blurted out. "I know they're a protected species!"

"No, not that. Who do you think killed Doc?"

"Marvin Sultan . . . no doubt about it . . . and the others."

"The others?"

"His financial backers in Orange County. And the Realtors."

"Realtors? Be careful, I'm one of them."

Coyote Woman gave me a reassuring smile. "You're not one of *them*. I can tell, you know, I'm—"

"A psychic. Yes, I know."

"I knew you were going to say that," Coyote Woman laughed. "Just a little psychic humor."

A little, I thought. No sooner than I had thought that, I worried that maybe she was even just a little psychic. She intercepted what I just thought. Shit. I searched her face for a sign of indignation. None. I was okay.

"It's obvious. Marvin wants to build four hundred overblown tract mansions on the one of the most sacred spots in Palm Springs. And the most beautiful: the Chino Cone. One of the main roads in north Palm Springs is called Vista Chino . . . view of China."

"Why is it called the Chino Cone. I get the cone part . . . it's triangular in shape. What part of that area resembles China?"

"There were a lot of alcoholics here in the past, what can I say?"

"And you think the Realtors are in on this?"

"Well, someone has to be an agent for Marvin buying up all this land."

"And do you have anyone in mind?"

"Mary Dodge."

"You didn't hesitate a second before you said that."

"I didn't have to. She's had her manicured hand in so many deals to build on the hillsides, against the hillsides . . . anywhere she can make big bucks. And speaking of bucks . . ." she drifted off, looking innocently skyward and around me, but holding out her hand ever so slightly.

"Oh, yes, how much was it again?" I asked.

"Six hundred . . . because it was a rush."

"Can I write you a check?"

This was met with a scowl, followed by a roll of the eyes heavenward. I knew she clearly stated she wanted cash. Okay, sue me. I wanted to write this off as a business expense and wanted a receipt. This was a legitimate deduction . . . if not just a little bit insane. I considered for a moment what tax-deductible category I would file this one under. Domicile exorcism? Psychic market-report consultation? I fished around in my purse, extracted my wallet, and started to make a check out for six hundred dollars to Barbara . . .

"Barbara?" I asked, looking up from my checkbook. "Your last name?"

"Coyote."

"Nooooo."

"Yes, I'm not kidding. It's Coyote," Barbara admitted with a laugh. "My husband's name."

"The one you shot in the ass with rock salt?"

"Yes, the very one. I kept it because it helps me in my work."

"And do you mind if I ask what was your maiden name?"

"Not at all. Paicopodopolis."

"Good idea sticking with Coyote. Can I ask you one more thing?" I ventured.

"I don't have a receipt, if that's what you were going to ask," Coyote Woman countered.

"No, not that. Do you sense that I'm in any danger, being wrapped up in this thing?"

"You will be if you go snooping around. Several people who made trouble for Marvin have disappeared over the years."

"So you sense that I was considering pursuing this thing a little further?"

"Listen, honey, I don't have to be psychic to see that you invited me out here to ask questions. You could care less whether I cleansed your listing or not."

I looked at her for a minute, surprised by her brashness. "Boy, you *are* good."

"I can do better than that. You better tell your ex-husband what you're planning to do. Something tells me he's not going to like you getting mixed up in this."

"He agreed to help me," I said, confessing.

"That's because he's still in love with you. And you're still in love with him. You don't have to be a psychic to see that."

When I pulled up in my driveway, I could see the curtains in Regina's front windows moved aside by a hand, then fall back to their perpetually half-closed position. Before I could even take my key out of the ignition, Regina's liver-spotted hand was excitedly knocking on my driver's side window. Today's T-shirt proclaimed, RIDDEN HARD AND PUT AWAY WET.

I got out of the car, wondering what Regina was so animated about.

"I have the most wonderful news!" she blurted out to me as I slid out of the car. "Doc Winters was poisoned!"

"Er, yes . . . that's great, Regina! I'm hoping you have more tragedies to tell me?"

"Nope, that's my big news," she gushed.

"Did you hear this on the news?"

"No, darlin. I got it through one of my sources."

"One of your sources, huh," I surmised. "This wouldn't happen to be that cop whose car I've seen parked around here in the middle of the night, would it?"

Regina kicked at the dirt while looking down coyly. "Maybe."

"So you fished it out of him in the throes of passion?"

"No, I got him all hot and horny and refused point-blank to have sex until he told me. And at his age, you don't have sex all that often, so I was holding him hostage. When you have 'em by the balls, their hearts and minds will follow."

"You have a T-shirt that says that."

"Yes, yes, I do."

"So he was poisoned? With what? Arsenic?"

"Nope."

"Strychnine?"

"Not even close."

"Cynanide?"

"No, I'll give you a clue—it's found in your backyard."

"Rattlesnakes?"

"No."

Scorpions?"

"No."

"Black widow spiders?"

"Unh-uh."

"But, Regina, that's what's in *my* backyard."

"Yes, I know, dear. You really have to break down and call an exterminator. You can't be friendly to the earth all the time!"

"Yes, but they were here first," I remarked, trying to be friends to all creatures great and small.

"Yes, but who's paying the mortgage and the taxes?"

"But I'm afraid the poisons will affect Edwin. He lives in my backyard."

"Honey, the poisons aren't going to affect Edwin."

"Yes, but I'm afraid they'll slow him down . . . he moves slow enough as it is. My house will never be finished."

"Let's get back to the poison," Regina said, nudging the conversation back into its groove. "You'll never guess what poisoned Doc."

"I give up . . . what?"

"Oleander."

"Oleander?"

"Yes . . . probably the most common plant in Palm Springs. Probably half the properties use it as a hedge or screening plant."

"I didn't even know it was poisonous."

"It sure is. The bark, leaves, flowers . . . all of it."

"So that means that someone had to feed Doc a bunch of oleander leaves in order to kill him . . . a fairly unlikely scenario since Doc probably knew his botany."

"Correct," Regina emphasized with an arthritic finger pointed at me. "Someone probably made a tea of the plant parts and served it to Doc."

"And probably mixed it with some other legitimate tea to mask the taste . . . not that anyone would know what oleander tea tasted like. Alive, at least. So whoever served the tea to Doc had to be either a friend or someone he trusted." I thought a minute, then something occurred to me. "So if he was poisoned, why the struggle? The furniture at my listing was knocked all over the place."

"Convulsions from the poison?"

"Probably," I replied. "So why go to all the trouble to poison Doc? Why not shoot him and bury him in the miles of untouched desert that surrounds us?"

Regina pointed at me again for drama—once an actress, always an actress. "Because someone wants to scare the environmentalists, the preservationists. And how do you do that? Easy, you use natural, botanical poisons. It's like a revenge . . . using nature against those trying to preserve it. Take that, you nature lovers! Here's a dose of your own medicine."

"Marvin Sultan!" I responded. "Boy, if I could tell you how many times people have offered his name as a potential killer."

"And Mary Dodge's?"

"Yes."

"She goes hand-in-hand with Marvin. In fact, she's had his schlong in her hand more than once. In her coochey too!"

"Noooo!" I exclaimed.

"Oh yeah! Maria Rodriguez's daughter, Suzanna, used to be Marvin's secretary in Los Angeles. She went into his office once, not even knowing he was there, and what does she see happening on Marvin's desk?"

"Mary Dodge is polishing Marvin Sultan's tent pole?"

"More. He's schtupping her and doesn't even stop when Maria's daughter walks in. He, of courses, finishes with Mary, then calls Suzanna on his cell phone and fires her for walking in on them. He doesn't even have the courtesy to walk out to Suzanna's desk and sack her. Just calls her on his cell phone."

"So, Regina, you think Mary and Marvin are our two suspects?"

"It sure looks like it."

We were both lost in thought for a moment. Regina spoke up.

"Or, people who are on board with Marvin. No offense intended, honey, but a lot of Realtors could stand to make a lot of money handling the sale of land to Marvin and other developers who will want to create neighborhoods right next to Marvin Gardens. I'm not so sure he isn't dealing with other agents behind Mary's back. He'd sell his own mother for a nickel."

"That much, huh?" I said.

CHAPTER 12

A Mean Transvestite Is Such a Drag

Besides the Palm Springs *Follies*, our little city is not known for its theater. But what it lacks in *Chorus Line*'s, *Evita*'s, and *Rent*'s, it makes up for in drag. Somewhat. The annual gay pride parade in Palm Springs is so full of drag, you can barely bat an eyelash without hitting a man in a dress. That being said, there is a shocking lack of world-class drag performances in a town so filled with gay men and women. Oh sure, we have Penny Slots from Las Vegas, Dee Ridgable, Ella Catraz, Jackie Oasis, and my favorite, Mildred Pierced. But where are the real stars?

Despite that, Alex dragged me to Cocka2's for a Sunday afternoon ritual: the 2-o'clock drag show. Alex had just ordered another gin and tonic for us as a drag queen named Winnie Bago brought the house down with a barnburner rendition of "Stain on My Pillow." As the stagehands were changing the bare-bones set for the next act, I decided that this was as good a time as ever to get in a quick pee.

I made my way through the crowd, jostled by inebriated gay men in Hawaiian shirts wearing leis. Drinks sloshed right and left, making a wet suit a wiser choice than shorts and T-shirt.

As I rounded the corner for the hallway to the women's restroom, a drag queen bumped into me. No, make that smashed into me. I looked into the face of the drag queen and instead of coming face-to-face with a happy trannie, I met up with a full grimace. A man wearing heavy facial makeup was scowling at me with a homicidal expression. It was more horrible than my worst clown nightmare.

The throngs in the background yelled and laughed to an ear-splitting roar, but time just stopped as the psycho-trannie continued to stare at me. Was he planning to kill me? Or waiting for me to apologize for him slamming into me? As we stood in a Mexican standoff with too much makeup, I looked at his hairy chest that he didn't bother to shave and noticed the strangest charm hanging on a gold chain that struggled to unbury itself from its hirsute thicket. The amulet was in the shape of a gold pig head with devil horns.

Eventually, one of us blinked and I headed back to join Alex. A new performer had entered the stage. Straight from her "very limited engagement" in Las Vegas at the Drag Strip Lounge on Vegas's famous semicircular gay-bar street, the Fruit Loop, was Miss Anthropy, who, true to her name, began politely but systematically dismantling the customers in the manner of Dame Edith Everage.

"I just ran into . . . well, he ran into me . . . the saddest drag queen I ever met. The meanest too. I thought all drag queens were out to spread laughter and criminal dress sense."

"I thought that too. But you haven't seen Miss Anthropy yet. I heard she's like going to see Blue Man Group."

"And why's that?"

"You definitely don't want to sit in the front row."

"Uh . . . let's move to the back of the bar."

"Good idea," Alex replied.

Alex and I watched the rest of the show from a safe distance, danced for twenty minutes or so, chatted with a few friends, then left Cocka2's. It was just like old times. Okay, maybe not exactly the same. When Alex and I were married, we were never once under suspicion of murder.

On Monday, I went into the office to do a little research. Being a Realtor, it was easy to find out a lot of things without ever leaving my desk at work. I found all the Assessor Parcel Numbers of the lots up in the Chino Cone, the area Doc was trying to protect. Then I went on the tax rolls and found out who owned the various parcels of land, and how many times they've changed owners and at what prices. And lo and behold, an amusing little pattern started turning up. All the various parcels of land up in the Cone belonged to various people until just recently. Even more interesting was the fact that just one entity owned a great deal of them now: Everest & Peak Properties, Ltd. Even more shocking was the fact that Mary Dodge handled the bulk of those sales.

So who was Everest & Peak?

I placed a call to Jimmy, my know-all lawyer friend who knew about as much as went on in this town as Regina—he just had more of a business slant than Regina.

". . . Marvin came up with that name because he tried to climb Mt. Everest a few years back. The old fuck was out of shape, had never climbed anything higher than the social ladder, and had a fear of heights, but when you have millions of dollars, you can pay some unfortunate son-of-a-bitch guide who needs the money to push your fat carcass up the world's tallest mountain, even if it kills everyone in your climbing team—which he did. Two Sherpas died when Marvin sent them down a tricky slope to pick up his satellite telephone, which he had dropped. The guy never made it past the second base camp, thousands of feet short, but he goes and names his partnership after Everest like he made it to the top. Does that give you some idea of this guy's character?"

"So he's kinda like Nixon, Hitler, and Donald Trump all rolled into one?"

"Right. Maybe throw in a little Mussolini . . . the guy's a porker. Amanda?"

"Yes, Jimmy?"

"Why do you want to know all this? You got a big deal going on with him? Watch yourself . . . when you deal with this guy, Marvin is the only one who wins."

"I'm not dealing with him," I answered back.

"Amanda, I hope you're not snooping around him, trying to tie him into this land grab, are you?"

"No, certainly not . . . well, kinda, well, maybe just a little."

"Amanda, this isn't Nancy Drew here. This guy may be a laughingstock behind his back, but there have been more than a few people who dared to make trouble for him and disappeared."

"So why don't the cops arrest him?"

"Habeas corpus," Gary replied. "No corpse, no case . . . like Jimmy Hoffa."

I spent hours on the Internet digging up more information on Marvin Sultan, and there was a lot of dirt to be dug up. There were Web sites galore, news articles, bulletin boards— you name it. And they all said the same thing: Marvin was a blood-sucking jackal who was ruthless in the extreme. If Marvin wanted a shopping mall, condo development, or boat marina in a certain place at a certain time, he almost always got it—no matter what the locals wanted. Was I getting myself in over my head? I had a third-degree brown belt in Isshinryu karate, and I could run fast, almost endlessly. And I could scream loud enough to shatter windows or wield a stiletto pump like a ninja nunchuck. Surely, I could protect myself.

But before I approached Mary Dodge, I selected a much

easier target: Cathy Paige. I had a lot more questions to ask now that I knew what was going on with Mary Dodge. I called Cathy and invited her to lunch, feeling that if I got her off the Dodger's turf, she might feel more comfortable about opening up. Plus, I didn't want Mary to see me coming into the office to talk to Cathy again. I phoned Alex to let him know my plans.

"So you don't want me there?" Alex responded to my intentions.

"Alex, I think if there was just one person, it wouldn't be like an inquisition."

"The Spanish?"

"Which no one ever expects."

"Where are you taking her?"

"Spenser's . . . I thought the garden would be nice today, plus I've requested a table way in the back . . . away from everyone else."

"Good thinking. You have your questions all written out?"

"Yup."

"Would you ask a question for me?"

"Sure, anything."

"Ask her if Mary Dodge is a cyborg."

"She's not a cyborg, Alex."

"How can you be so sure?"

"Because cyborgs don't need breast implants, nor do they need to have their faces lifted. Just new batteries now and then."

I arrived at Spencer's and asked for a table way in the back of the garden. In keeping with the clandestine nature of this lunch, I was wearing my Jackie O face-engulfing sunglasses for complete anonymity. Cathy arrived shortly after I did, threading her way through the sea of chairs, swooshing back and forth like an Olympic skier on a slalom course. Anne Clexton was right. This was one nervous cat. Cathy flung herself into her seat, then folded her hands in her lap like a schoolgirl being grilled by the Mother Superior about how black shoe polish got onto the toilet seat that Sister Mary sat on that morning. (Okay, so I still feel guilty about that.)

"Thank you so much for joining me, Cathy."

"Oh, my pleasure."

"Cathy, the reason I'm asking you these questions is because I need to clear my name, so to speak. It's a personal thing. So I need your help in answering a few questions."

"It seems that's all I've been doing lately."

"The police?"

"Detective Becker. He's been calling me like twenty times a day. 'What exactly did you see when you entered the house? Did you see anything suspicious? Did you see anyone outside? Was the door locked?' Questions, questions, questions!"

"So everything was normal when you toured the home?"

"Uh . . . yes. Yes, it was."

A nanosecond of hesitation, followed by an epiphany on my part. While you'd think that an in-depth knowledge of poisons was something right up my alley with a spooky grandmother like I had, it occurred to me that if Cathy saw nothing out of the ordinary when she previewed the home, then Doc had to enter the home after Cathy, be served oleander-poisoned tea, the poison had to have time to take effect, Doc had to go through the death throes and smash up the place, give the killer time to remove any clues, and exit the house in plenty of time before any agent got to the house for the caravan, which started at 9:00 A.M. Something didn't add up.

"Cathy, I did a little investigating and found out that Mary Dodge is acting as agent for Marvin Sultan, who has bought up just about every piece of saleable land in the Chino Cone."

"Are you sure?" Cathy feigned.

"I'm quite sure. And I'm sure the police are way ahead of me."

I could see that Cathy was mulling this all over.

"Amanda, could we order lunch first? I'm just starving!"

"Sure, sure, Cathy. My treat."

I watched Cathy as her eyes darted back and forth across the menu like an electronic Ping-Pong game. She wasn't giving the slightest bit of attention to the entrées. She was clearly shaken by the possibility that the law and I were closing in on her, and that her story was about to come unraveled like a cheap sweater. She ordered a salad and a glass of chardonnay. I followed suit.

Then, in the background, Mary Dodge came into view. I thought you had to strike the ground with a hickory branch to summon her, but she merely walked into the restaurant, saw me with Cathy, and took her seat, coincidentally facing me with an unobstructed view.

"Cathy, can I be frank?"

"Okay, I'll be Cathy and you be Frank," she said with a nervous giggle.

"Did Mary put you up to this?"

"Put me up to . . . ?" she said, playing dumb.

"Put you up in the Presidential Suite at Caesar's Palace. C'mon, Cathy, you know what I meant. Did she ask you to go to my listing for her?"

"No, no . . . It's like I told you. I had a client I wanted to preview the property for . . . and I wanted to be first. I had a client that your home would be perfect for."

Keep pushing, Amanda, keep pushing . . . she's on the run.

"And would you mind telling me who that client was?"

Another moment of hesitation. Too long of a moment.

"Er . . . Jack Ellis."

"Cathy, come clean with me. I know for a fact that Jack just closed on a house that Mary Dodge sold him three weeks ago . . . 457 Miramar Road. Patty Pearson had the listing."

"He wants another house . . . for investment purposes," Cathy shot back.

"Cathy, I'm friends with Patty. She told me about this deal because she was having so much trouble getting him to qualify for a loan. He doesn't have money for a second."

The salads arrived.

Cathy got up suddenly, knocking over her chair in the process. "On second thought, I'm not hungry, Amanda. I'm sorry about lunch," she said, rushing out of the restaurant crying, but not so quickly that she didn't get a faceful of Mary Dodge, who stared at Cathy with a look of horror on her face. Then like a ripple across a pond filled with a mat of green algae, Mary's look was back to normal, or what was normal for her.

I could tell that she was looking at me from time to time, but mostly, she laughed and smiled at her client. I knew it was a client because it was a well-known fact that Mary didn't have any friends. Apparently, she had screwed them all. Or eaten them.

Whether she laughed or smiled or listened, Mary always had a pained look that formed the substrata beneath her surface emotions.

Cool as a cucumber, I picked up my salad that the waiter had placed in a Styrofoam clamshell and stood up to leave, when déjà vu happened all over again. The tablecloth and a half-dozen dishes and glasses decided to follow me on my way out of the restaurant and cascaded onto the patio flagstones.

"You know, I've got to start wearing skirts with buttons," I said to the diners who stared at me with looks of shock on their faces.

A few minutes later, while waiting for the valet to retrieve my car, my cell phone rang. As I struggled to open my cell phone and hit the Answer button, my salad container opened unexpectedly and the contents spilled to the ground. Well, only after hitting most of my leg and soaking my shoes.

"Amanda Thorne."

"Hi, this is Denise Flaherty with Sonora Realty. I just showed a client your listing at 2666 Boulder Drive."

"Oh, why thank you so much, Denise."

"Well, Amanda, you probably won't thank me when you hear what happened."

Thoughts slammed through my head—none of them good. Another body? A rattlesnake in the kitchen? Four feet of water in the home?

"Well, we were coming out of the front door and my client slipped on a bunch of colorful rocks that were spread outside the door. He's suing you and the owner."

The curse of Eagle Feather Margie struck again.

I went home and showered. Then I placed a call to Alex.

". . . so Mary Dodge came into Spenser's while Cathy was running out, huh? Maybe you better sleep at my house tonight," Alex said.

"Oh, for Pete's sake, Alex, you think that Mary Dodge is going to kill me because she saw me with Cathy?"

"Amanda, you know I still love you very much. You are still my soul mate, the closest person in the world to me. Would you please do just this one thing for me? Just tonight?"

"Okay, but just for one night."

"I'd feel safer with you staying with me."

"But you forget that I have Edwin at my house."

"Yes, Amanda, if Mary or one of Marvin's henchmen come to kill you, he can turn the hose on them . . . that is, if the plumbing works."

"Hey, don't make fun of my house. Mine will be done a lot sooner than yours, seeing that you started four months after I did. And when I'm luxuriating in mine, you can come visit me and I'll let you flush the toilets and you can marvel over my indoor plumbing."

"All the same, I'd feel better if you came over."

"Only if you have electricity."

"I do. The cell phone reception sucks, though."

"I'll be there. What time?"

"Make it seven. I'll cook."

"Oh, Alex, not on that little hibachi! Do you still have that?"

"I *have* a stove, Amanda. See you then."

I hung up, thrilled. This was my first chance to see his house. We had both made a pact that neither of us would see each other's house before it was finished, but in light of the current situation, it looked like Alex was willing to make an exception.

Even more thrilling than seeing what Alex was planning was the chance to snoop into what his life was like now that he was single. And gay—almost forgot that part. Were there signs of lovers coming and going? A misplaced sock here, a jockstrap or condom there? Was he alone? Did he hole up in his house, reading poetry, or did he just sit on his porch, smoking a cigar? Did he think about me? A little? A lot?

I sucked in a gasp, fighting back the tears that threatened to gush out from my eyes. My phone rang.

"Alex, I am not going to tell you again, Carrot Top and I are just friends . . ."

"Miss Thorne?"

It was not Alex.

"This is Detective Becker. I was just talking with Cathy Paige and she told me about lunch. She's very upset. And so am I."

"About the Carrot Top thing? Don't worry, it's purely platonic. And I just can't move to Vegas to be with him. My career's here."

"You're quite the comedian, aren't you?"

"I try."

"Miss Thorne, let's get back to lunch, can we?"

"Good, I'm famished. All I had was a small salad."

"I don't want you questioning witnesses in this case. And I don't want you snooping around. Whoever did this isn't kidding around. They're killing those who get in the way."

"I'm just trying to clear my name."

"I'm a detective. Let me do the clearing for you. Plus, it would be a shame to have you get hurt. Leave the detective work up to me."

"Okay, then can I at least help?"

"No."

"Pretty please with sugar on it?"

"No, Miss Thorne, this isn't a game. I don't want anything happening to you."

"Why, detective, I'm beginning to think you . . . care for my concern."

"I do. It's not just for your concern . . . I'd hate for the world to lose such a great comic mind . . . then we'd be left with Adam Sandler, and you know what that means for the future of comedy."

My heart raced. Cute and funny. And I was detecting a definite softness for me.

"Can I funnel information to you, then?"

"If you have material facts, then, yes, you can call me with them. But I don't want you going around talking to people. You don't know who you could be talking to."

"Okay, did you know that Mary Dodge, Her Highness of real estate, has been buying up land for Marvin Sultan up in the Chino Cone. Plus all the land that borders it?" I stated proudly, like a secret witness in the trial of the century. Aha! Gotcha!

"I'm way ahead of you, Miss Thorne."

"Amanda, please."

"Okay, Amanda Please."

"So you know all about Mary Dodge?"

"I do my homework."

"Okay, so you don't think something's funny when she—or Cathy Paige—went into my listing at seven-thirty in the morning?"

"Seven-eighteen. That's what your electronic key report said."

I whistled. "Like a steel trap!"

"What?"

"Your mind."

"Miss Thorne, I can't really comment on the case, but I would like to interview you again."

"Down at the station?"

"No, over dinner."

"I'd love to. When?"

"Tomorrow, if you're free. Seven-thirty?"

"Not seven-eighteen?"

"Whatever time you want."

"Seven-thirty, then. Where?"

"Pesca."

"Fabulous. I'll be there."

I hung up the phone, thrilled twice in less than twenty minutes. I entered the appointment into my cell phone. Then made a mental note to myself: Don't wear bondage skirt to dinner tomorrow. Something plain. Maybe jeans this time. With a zipper fly. Nothing that will catch.

CHAPTER 13

Come Into My Parlor Said the Spider to the Fly

I arrived at Alex's house at 7:00, tight skirt on, tall heels, flowing blouse, and enough fake pearl necklaces to choke a horse. I was clearly out to show Alex that I wasn't the devastated person that I really was. I was cool, confident, powerful, immensely happy.

I grabbed my overnight bag from the back seat of my car and headed up the driveway, my heels clicking on the broom-finished concrete. The landscaping seemed to be upside down, with irrigation pipes stacked near his garage and dozens of potted plants lined up like soldiers on the side of the garage. I rang the doorbell, a European doorbell if I ever heard one. More of a tone you'd hear in an airport in Berlin than in an American home. No Westminster chimes for Alex.

A few seconds later, the door pivoted open (Alex had a thing for doors that pivoted instead of those that opened on banal hinges) and Alex stood there, our signature vegan martini in hand: three different cucumber-infused vodkas, rosemary syrup, and an olive speared by a sprig of rosemary—more food than drink. Even more tempting was Alex, who had dressed up for the occasion. It was funny, here we were, two divorcees, trying to impress the hell out of each other, even now. Why? To seduce each other? Maybe, or at least I was trying to? Or to show that we were getting on with our respective lives in the most fabulous way possible?

"Cheers," he said, as he handed the glass to me and took my bag. "Come in."

I followed him in as the door pivoted closed behind me. I was stunned. His place was finished.

"How the fuck did you mange this?"

"I hired contractors who knew what they were doing. Plus, I offered the construction manager an extra $15,000 if he finished by the twentieth."

"Well, I am impressed." And I was. While I found that it is not true that all gay men have impeccable taste, Alex had it in spades.

His house was unlike many of the other hard-edge modern reconstructions using terrazzo floors, glossy walls, and an oh-so-tasteful splattering of orange or lime green as a nod to the mid-century pedigree most Palm Springs houses had. Alex's was a study in highly masculine browns, woods, soft travertine, and bronzed metals. His home embraced the outside pool and entertaining areas, but cuddled you in sensuous luxury while you were safely inside. Very tactile, his house was Alex in the flesh—chiseled and confident on the outside, and cuddly, warm, and protecting when you got close to the interior.

I was so jealous.

He showed me around. All-new furniture. Sleek as an Armani dress. Some pieces of old art that he had taken with him, and more than a few new pieces. No pictures of nude men—a dull cliché in a city as gay as Palm Springs. A photograph of cowboy boots taken toe-on with a fish-eye lens, seven-feet wide by two-feet high. They seemed to leap out at you, kicking you in the face. Perfect Alex. Unexpected and provocative. Over on a hallway wall was my favorite photograph he had collected before we were married: a two-foot female child mannequin dressed in traditional German alpine garb, crying hysterically, tears running in torrents down over the plastic cheeks. (My mother, when she saw this photograph in his home back in Bloomfield Hills, Michigan, begged me not to marry Alex. "I don't want to find parts of you in Ziplock bags all around town." Of course, seeing this photograph made me want to marry Alex all the more.)

He showed me the guest bedroom, throwing my overnight bag on the mink bedspread (politically correct—it was made of old mink stoles picked up at yard sales by a company in Los Angeles that made such bedspreads, so it was recycled).

Then he showed me his bedroom. There was an uncomfortable moment between us as I stood in the pivoting doorway, my eyes searching a place I had once occupied, emotionally and physically. The low bed was immaculately made and covered in soft, earth-toned linens, backed on the wall and acting as a headboard was a wall of square panels covered in ultrasuede that reached to the ceiling, making the bedroom feel more monumental that it could have otherwise been with thirteen-foot ceilings. And there, on his bedside table, perfectly lit by a low-voltage halogen pinpoint spotlight, was his photograph of me, taken just before we were married. There were no other photographs—just mine.

I turned quickly away, a single tear squeezing out from the corner of my eye. I had hoped my head's quick motion would fling the tear off, unnoticed into the deep-pile rug, but Alex, never missing a thing, pulled me close to him and hugged me in that comforting, reassuring way that only he could do. I felt safe again. Loved.

And, again, in that way that only he could do, he read my mind.

"Amanda, no matter what happens in my life, your picture will always be there. Just like you."

I felt an upwelling of anger in me. Anger at myself. Anger at Alex. Anger at the world. Then I thought of what Jimmy Carter once said, that life is unfair, and I had to laugh. I laughed at the thought of a peanut farmer-turned president uttering one of the most profound thoughts in the history of the world. He was right, life wasn't fucking fair.

Alex didn't say a thing. He took my hand and eased me along, out of the bedroom, along the artfully silent corridor and down another hall to his kitchen. He sat me down across the large countertop on a minimally Italian high stool, refreshed my martini and his, then shuttled a procession of bowls out of his glass-faced refrigerator, fired up the flames, and began the process of turning the ordinary into the extraordinary.

As I watched him sauté, fling, and toss meat and vegetables into bowls and then skyward, it struck me that the one thing that was so devastating about our divorce was the realization that I was giving up living with such an extraordinary individual. He cooked, he climbed sheer rock walls, he cycled, he photographed, he sculpted, he read, he wrote, he made love in an extraordinary way—everything like a man with a year to live, squeezing out every minute of every second of every day. It was like living and being married to Michelangelo and then having to give him up. Knowing that you couldn't live with a genius anymore, but you could have one right next door or across town didn't help much. And, yes, the irony that the only genius I could think of at this moment was also a homosexual didn't escape me.

We talked about real estate a little—we couldn't help it. Mostly the crazy stuff we ran into, or houses with incredible mid-century architecture. We talked about me getting sued. We talked about going to see some of the exhibitions in Los Angeles. The LACMA. The Getty. MOCA. It was like old times . . . almost. I just couldn't have him again. Not 100 percent. I guess I had to settle with ninety percent of the total . . . not a bad deal, considering. It is better to have loved and lost than never to have loved at all. Tennyson was right.

My cell phone rang.

"Amanda Thorne."

". . . Cathy Paige here . . . you got me thinking . . . lunch the other day . . ." came the broken conversation on the other end of the line.

"Cathy, I'm not getting everything you're saying. You're going in and out."

". . . lied . . . don't have my electronic key . . . missing . . . maybe lost it . . ."

"Cathy?" I pleaded. "Cathy?"

". . . at Pappy and Harriet's . . . Pioneertown . . . figure out . . . Doc."

"Cathy, you're dropping out. What about Pioneertown?"

". . . Monica Birdsong . . . other . . . clear my name, too . . ."

"Cathy, could you call me later when you get home? I just can't hear you now."

And the call dropped.

Alex looked at me. "Trouble in Pioneertown? Wagon train broke down on the way to the Donner Pass and she's running short of food?"

"Cathy Paige called me. I think she's up at Pappy and Harriet's."

"Let me guess, she's in a band called the Rockin' Realtors and she's testing out her new act?"

"No, it sounds like she's doing a little investigative work herself."

Alex was marshalling meat and vegetables in and out of frying pans like a general in an all-out battle. God, that man could cook!

Alex could see that my mind had shifted noticeably after the phone call.

"What's wrong?"

"I don't know, just a feeling."

"Cramps?"

"Close. Woman's intuition."

"And that feeling is . . . ?"

"I don't know . . . something strange . . . something's off."

"It's not the asparagus, is it? I paid a lot to get white asparagus this time of year."

"No, the asparagus is fine. Everything you do is always fine . . . God, I miss you," I said as I had yet another rosemary-vegan martini. Oops, that last part just slipped out. I meant it to sound like I missed Alex like an old friend, but it came out sounding like "marry me."

"I miss you, too, Amanda. You know that."

"I do."

"It's just so frustrating . . . you know . . . you and I . . . life."

" 'Tis better to have loved and lost than never to have loved at all."

"That's too spooky. I was just thinking that a minute ago."

"You know, we could always tell what each other was thinking."

"Let's put it to the test, Alex," I said, smiling. "What am I thinking about right now?"

Alex leaned over the counter and looked deeply into my eyes.

"Coelacanths."

"Correct," I answered, not knowing what a coelacanth was.

"You don't know what a coelacanth is, do you?"

"I didn't say a word."

"No, but I could see it in your eyes and on your face. And I can read your mind just like you can mine."

Indeed, he could.

"See, I'm good."

"Yes, you are," I said with a wink.

Alex stopped his cooking for a minute . . . the only sound came from the slowly bubbling sauces and fry pans.

"Amada, you know you will always be first in my life. No one will ever replace you. And you know, you will always have me."

I hesitated. "Well, not *have* you. More like, have you near me . . . have you to talk to whenever I need some support. Or have you when I need a gorgeous man on my arm for parties."

"And that's different from being married how?"

"Good point. Touché, Alex."

Dinner was superb, dessert sublime, and the after-dinner sauterne was heavenly. We talked about the problems of dating, of eating alone, and all the new adjustments one has to face when finding oneself suddenly single again. Despite our intentions that I should sleep over that night, I decided it was best to go home to my own bed.

I went home that night feeling just a little more at peace with my situation and a little more feeling not so alone. I slept well that night, dreaming that I had climbed a huge mountain naked. What would Freud say?

Tomorrow was just another day. I wished.

The next morning, the doorbell rang at 6 A.M. I threw on a robe and suspiciously approached my front door, peeking through the peekhole. A nervous Detective Becker stood on my doorstep, looking around as if for suspects lurking in the bushes behind him.

"Detective? You're working this early in the morning? Or did you join Jehovah's Witnesses?"

"When was the last time you talked with Cathy Paige?"

"Last night. She called from Pappy and Harriet's in Pioneer-town."

"Do you know what time that was?"

"Let me get my cell phone . . . I'll tell you from the call log. C'mon in."

He followed me over to my kitchen counter where I had carelessly flung my handbag from the night before. I punched some buttons on my phone.

"Eight forty-five P.M. Is Cathy in some sort of trouble?"

"Do you recall what she said to you? Exactly."

"Exactly? That would be difficult."

"How's that, Amanda?"

"Good, you're calling me Amanda."

"That's your name, as I recall. Plus, calling you Miss Thorne makes me sound like a detective with a big moustache from a British mystery series."

"Then continue to call me Amanda and I will continue to call you Ken."

"I've been working hard on this case. Could we get back to Cathy Paige?"

"It was difficult to get everything she said because her cell phone kept going in and out. Let's see, she said she was up at Pappy and Harriet's . . . something about Doc she was looking into . . . oh, she needed to clear her name . . . and oh shit, this is important . . . she doesn't have her electronic key . . . she said it's missing . . . or that she lost it. I think that was it."

"Hmm," Detective Becker mumbled as he wrote in his little notebook. Yes, just like a TV detective, he wrote in a little notebook that flipped over at the top. So cute.

"Okay, Ken. Now I'm getting a sense Cathy Paige has become a real suspect in this case after something she did last night."

"She's not a suspect anymore, Amanda."

"And why is that?"

"She was found dead this morning. Poisoned."

"Poisoned!" I exclaimed. I just couldn't believe it. Two in a row . . . It began to actually dawn on me that what Detective Becker said to me before was absolutely correct: The culprit in this case wasn't fooling around. Up until now, I had treated this whole matter like it was some kind of game. Yes, someone got killed, but it must have been some kind of fluke. Doc got croaked by mistake. Maybe the poison wasn't intended for him. Maybe he drank it by mistake. Maybe this was all a bad dream. People didn't get murdered in Palm Springs. Yes, they killed themselves driving their cars into palm trees, or drove off cliffs and plunged into deep canyons, or drank a vat of martinis and fell into pools and drowned, but people didn't get intentionally killed here. It couldn't happen in a city this small.

A thought sprang to my mind.

"Ken, did you talk with Mary Dodge yet? Can she account for her whereabouts last night?"

"I did. She was drunk and passed out."

"You're joking!"

"Nope. I shouldn't be telling you all this."

"I won't tell a soul."

As I said this, I knew it was a lie. Alex would soon know. But it occurred to me that I could use my feminine wiles to get information from Becker. Plus, it couldn't hurt. I was really beginning to like him. He was sexy. Carried a gun. Had a nice, firm ass under those tailored trousers of his. And oh, those ice-blue eyes of his. The Siberian husky thing. They actually sparkled, and when he looked at you with those great blue eyes, it was like he was peering inside of you, like he knew secrets you would never tell anyone. Yet he would keep quiet . . . much more than I could guarantee.

"She was drunk?"

"Four martinis."

"Four? From what I heard that would be an aperitif for her."

"So she's a boozer?"

"All Realtors are."

Becker looked surprised.

"You're not a very good detective if you didn't know that, Ken," I said, using his first name, I noticed more and more—dropping the Detective part. "It's the pressure. Buying a home is, for most people, the biggest purchase they will ever make. So people are on pins and needles all the time. Sellers, buyers. They get into fights all the time and you have to referee them. Plus, it's the hours. You work all week long, weekends, you get calls all hours of the night from clients up in arms about something. You have no life."

"Does that mean I don't get a date?"

"*That*, I'll make time for," I said with a sly wink. Hey, I wanted information and I wanted to have our first date. Two birds with one stone.

"So you don't remember anything else that Cathy said when she called last night?"

"No, I think that's about it. If I remember anything else, I'll call you."

"Okay, I have to get going now. Lots of people to talk to. Bye," he called as he turned and walked down my front sidewalk, dodging the construction debris Edwin had left lying all over it. "Oh, and about that date tonight? We're still on for seven-thirty."

"I'll be ready," I replied. And, indeed, I would be. "Dressed to kill." Oops, unfortunate phrase.

CHAPTER 14

Is That a Glock in Your Pocket or Are You Just Happy to See Me?

It took me the better part of the day to figure out what to wear to dinner with Ken. If I dressed too suggestive, he'd think I was a slut. On the other hand, too conservative and he'll think I'm playing hard to get. Or worse, that I'm frigid. Or a prude.

Ken was a very good dresser. Period. And the fact that he was a homicide detective *and* a good dresser made him rarer than a sincere compliment at an Academy Awards party. I had to be sexy, but smart and sophisticated at the same time. And nothing to catch on my skirt, dress, blouse . . . or shoes. No buckles on the shoes. I eventually settled on a white drapey lycra Norma Kamali diaper dress with spaghetti straps and wafer-thin white sandals. Big, dangly gold hoop earrings. Sophisticated with just a whisper of slut. Perfect. Then I waited.

I heard his car pull up in my driveway. His choice of a car was good: a classic, 1965 black Lincoln Continental with the suicide doors. Like Alex's cars, it was polished to perfection. I was going to like this guy. After peeking through the blinds, I raced back down the hall from the guest bedroom to the living room so he wouldn't know I was spying on him as he drove up.

Through the side windows on each side of the front door, I could see him pushing the doorbell and waiting. Of course, like everything in my house, the doorbell didn't work. I saw him repeat his efforts. Then came the knock. His just-hairy-enough knuckles knocking on my door.

"Oh, Ken, I didn't hear you drive up," I said coyly.

"Maybe you didn't hear because you were too busy peeking through the blinds in your guest bedroom."

I turned redder than a snapper filet. "Boy, you don't miss a thing, do you?"

"I wouldn't be any good at my job if I did. Are you ready?"

"Sure," I answered, grabbing my purse and standing at the door, waiting for Ken to open it for me. And like a gentleman, he did.

He took me to my favorite restaurant: Pesca's. After we ordered, he sat next to me at a table for four. Not across from me. Next to me. Romantic. Alex used to do the same thing. He looked deeply into my face, making me blush. I, as usual, broke the silence.

"So tell me about the case. Are you going to pounce on Mary Dodge any minute? Kick her office door down and spray her with a storm of lead from your AK-47?

"I can't talk about the case."

"Oh, c'mon. I've told you everything I've found out."

"You should, Amanda. That's your role. You're a citizen. I'm a detective. My role is to listen to what citizens have to say and keep my own mouth shut."

"Oh, pllllleeeaaassse? Will it help if I whine a lot?"

"Nope."

"How about if I promise to share my scallops with you?"

"Nope, not a word until the grand jury reveals its verdict. How do you know you're getting the scallops? You haven't even opened your menu."

"I looked at the menu online this afternoon. It saves time."

"Are you in a hurry?" he asked playfully, catching me off guard.

"Not tonight. I have all the time in the world."

"So do I," he responded, flashing me a slightly suggestive smile.

Suggestive not in an overt, sexual way. Suggestive in the way that he liked me more than a little. This guy was a gentleman, a quality I liked, unless I was horny and had three glasses of wine in me, which was my plan for the evening.

Uncomfortable, I shifted the conversation back to the case. (Why did I do such things when I was shy?)

"So how can you have dinner with me when I'm involved in your case?"

"You're not a party of interest."

I let out a big sigh or relief. "That's nice to know."

"But I am interested in you."

"Is that why you have that bulge in your pocket?" (Shit, why did I get so familiar—and vulgar—so soon? I guess the cocktail was really starting to work. I'm really not that kind of girl, but when I feel people getting close to me, instead of slyly seducing them, why do I pull the rug out from under them?)

"That's a gun."

"Nooo. Are you carrying a gun right now?"

"I was just kidding. I'm not carrying right now. There's one in my car right now, though. In a gun safe."

"Are you expecting trouble tonight?" *Good, Amanda, be coy.*

"Nope. Unless you want to make it."

"Just a little. Oleander."

"Oleander?"

"Yes, oleander. Doc was poisoned by it."

"And how did you know that?"

"I have my sources."

"Good sources too. Regina Bell?"

"How did you know, Ken?"

"I searched your neighbors on one of our databases. I know she knows everything and everyone."

"You searched me on the Internet?"

"Part of my job. Remember, you were a suspect until recently."

"Until recently? Am I off the list?"

"Pretty much."

"So you believe me that I had nothing to do with Cathy's death last night?"

"Not just *believe*. I have proof. I know where your cell phone was last night . . . over at Alex's."

"And how do you know that?"

"I had the cell phone company triangulate your phone last night."

"Triangulate?"

"Taking the reading from several cell-phone tower locations."

I leaned forward into the candlelight. "You're impressing the hell out of me. Go on. Is this while I was talking to Cathy last night . . . during her call?"

"No, your cell phone sends a *ping* every 15 minutes . . . that's how a call to your phone knows where to go. The tower receives a ping that says Amanda is nearest this cell phone tower . . . send any calls to here. That's how rescue personnel can sometimes find people . . . if the accident victim leaves his or her cell phone on and it has a good signal. They triangulate the signals from three towers, and find the intersection of three signal strengths."

"So you knew I was at my ex-husband's last night?"

"Yes."

"Okay, Mr. Smarty Detective. What if I went over to Alex's house, left my cell phone there, and drove to wherever Cathy was and poisoned her?"

Ken took a sip of the wine that had been brought to the table by the waiter and gave it a thumbs-up. "It's possible, but you're a Realtor."

"What's that got to do with it?"

"Well, it's not just that you're a Realtor, but you're a good one. You always have your cell phone with you. You would have taken it with you if you left your ex-husband's house. It's a strong habit all good agents have."

I took a drink as well. "Ken, nothing happened at my husband's—ex-husband's—last night."

"I know that," Ken said.

"What did you do, plant a bug in my tampon?"

"Tracking device. Accurate to twenty feet."

"So it doesn't bother you that I was at Alex's?"

"No, why should it?"

"Because we were once married."

"And you're still both in love with each other."

"You're probably right."

"I know I'm right."

"And that doesn't bother you, Ken?"

"Not at all."

"Why's that?"

"Two reasons. Reason number one: He's gay."

"And the second?"

"I know I can give you enough reasons to stay interested in me."

"Let's toast to that," I said, lifting my wineglass to clink.

And that's the way the rest of the evening went. Me trying to get information, him steadfastly refusing, and the both of us flirting shamelessly.

It was a perfect evening. I hadn't knocked the table over; I hadn't fallen. The restaurant hadn't gone up in flames. Everything was going fine. Almost.

Ken reached for his glass of red wine and knocked it over, the wine running like a lahar toward my white dress. A quick thinker, he reached under the table and pulled up the overhanging tablecloth, sopping up the spill just in the nick of time.

"There. Disaster averted."

I looked at him with a strained smile on my face.

"That wasn't the tablecloth. That was my dress."

Ken took me home, apologizing profusely for destroying my Norma Kamali while I chalked it up to another manifestation of Eagle Feather's curse. I did my best to make him feel better. When we got back to my house, I invited him in for a drink, showed him where the liquor was, then made a quick change from my poor, sad dress and into a linen jumpsuit.

We drank a little, listened to music (supplied by none other than Alex: Buddha Bar), and then began making out. Before long we were in bed. But we didn't make love as I had hoped. But Ken made me soon forget that. He wrapped his arms around me, making me feel safe and secure, tucked inside the curve of his body. It was nice to feel that way again.

CHAPTER 15

Unearthing a Dirty Little Secret

After I ate a wonderful breakfast that Ken cooked before I was up, I showered with him, dressed, then we parted for the time being. I went into the office and found Alex viewing properties on his laptop.

"Anything interesting?" I asked, throwing down my purse and coming around to see what he was looking at.

"As a matter of fact, I did find something of great interest."

"That listing?" I said, grimacing at seeing 932 Camino Norte on his screen. "Way overpriced, plus it has a lot of termite damage."

"Not that," Alex answered, clicking on a folder on his desktop. *"This."*

"It's a hedge. So what?"

"Take a closer look," he instructed me.

I squinted at the hedge, trying to see something significant. "Other than the fact that it looks like it was trimmed by a gardener with cataracts, I don't see anything out of the ordinary."

"Exactly."

"I don't get it."

"You just put your finger on the what's wrong."

"That gardeners with cataracts shouldn't cut hedges? Uh, don't hire gardeners who work at night? Uh, gardeners with

Parkinson's shouldn't be given hedge trimmers or defuse bombs? Help me, I'm dying here."

"This hedge belongs to Mary Dodge."

"So?"

"It's oleander."

"No shit! When did you take this picture?"

"This morning. I was taking pictures at our new listing on Stevens Road, and I was driving by when I saw Mary's hedge. I stopped cold in my tracks."

"So Mary could have cut down part of the hedge to make the poison for Doc and she had the gardeners cover it up by trimming it to make it look like it was a natural dip in the hedge."

"Look at this," he said, pointing to the portion of the hedge that looked like a tooth missing from a perfect mouth. "The problem is, the rest of the hedge is the same height all the way around, but right here, a portion is missing."

"This is so exciting, Alex. I mean it, I am really charged up. It's like the way things used to be," I said, and almost as soon as I had said it, I knew it was wrong. *Stop living in the past, Amanda. Move on.*

"The excitement doesn't have to stop, Amanda. Let's have fun with this."

"You mean you're not scared?"

"Have you ever known me to be afraid of anything?"

"Christian fundamentalists."

"I wore my TOO MANY RIGHT-WING CHRISTIAN FUNDAMENTALISTS, TOO FEW LIONS T-shirt when we drove through the South."

"I mean a different kind of bravery."

"Yeah, but other than that I have no fear."

"Furbies," I said, naming one of Alex's other mortal fears. Alex never trusted people who dressed up as big, furry animals—especially for sexual reasons. Come to think of it, these people creeped me out. Even weirder was the fact that I actually knew that people had such fetishes. I chalked it up to living with a soon-to-be gay man—there was little gay men didn't know about. Reason number 543 for marrying Alex: Sex with him was wild.

"So you really want to pursue this thing?" I asked.

"Absolutely. I could use a little excitement in my life," Alex replied.

"How about really adding a touch of spice?" I asked, almost giggling with glee.

"What are you thinking?" Alex asked.

"How about we break into Mary Dodge's office and do a little snooping? It would be so easy and they'd never know."

"Count me in. There's just something I have to do first."

"And what's that?"

"Get my ninja outfit back from the cleaners."

CHAPTER 16

Cream Rises to the Top . . . But So Do Turds

We decided to visit the queen herself first. Our primary objective was to see if we could get a better bead on Mary Dodge, and secondly, we wanted to scope out the door locks and alarm system.

As far as Palm Springs real estate was concerned, Mary Dodge, founder and President of Dodge & Dodge Realty was a star. She got the best listings from the best neighborhoods. She drove the right cars. She wore the right clothes. She got face lifts from the right surgeons. She even lived in the right house: Cary Grant's Palm Springs getaway. She was tall and statuesque. And she had a full head of sexy brunette hair, which she wore long. And it bounced in all the right places.

But not all was right in Mary-land. She was not well liked. Perhaps it was because she was the most successful Realtor in the Coachella Valley. Or maybe it was because she had pulled some questionable deals in her career. But whatever the reason, the rumors abounded—many of which were mostly true. She could be ruthless. She could be cold. Others said she was born without tear ducts. Old-timers called her by another name: the Dodger, a reference to the many lawsuits she had been hit with over the years. While it's true that any Realtor, over time, will eventually face a lawsuit of some sort, Mary had endured more than her share. She liked to counter the rumors by saying that a person doing her volume of sales was just more likely to be sued—it was a pure consequence of the mathematical odds. So let's suffice to say that Mary was both feared and hated at the same time, a reaction that suited Mary just fine, because both had been instrumental in helping her get ahead.

Of course, a person dedicated to this pursuit of a career had to put up with minor inconveniences such as three divorces. And children so emotionally fucked up, people said Mary ran a tab at the various rehab clinics that made the Palm Springs area so famous—or infamous, shall we say. But, no matter. There's nothing that a little money wouldn't solve, or hide away, be they aging, sagging faces or petulant, ungrateful children. Mary was a star. More importantly, Mary was determined to remain one. Whatever the cost.

Mary, who was usually too busy to see anyone—most of all, clients who had listed their houses with her—agreed immediately to see us.

We were ushered into her office by a very red-and-teary-eyed Anne Clexton, who didn't say a word but held open the door to Mary's cavernous inner sanctum and motioned to two very comfortable client chairs that, while comfortable, were noticeably much less comfortable looking than Mary's. They were also much smaller than Mary's and lower to the ground. Hitler used to pull this trick (the irony not lost on Alex and me). Mary leaned back in her cathedral-sized office chair and pulled Concerned Look with Sadness #59 out of her desk drawer and put it on her face. She shook her head.

"When is all this going to end?" she said with all the emotion of a soap-opera starlet. She pursed her lips in concern, switching to Concerned Look with Sadness of the World #604.

But it was her smile that said it all. Every time she smiled, it looked like she was being forced to pass a large and uncooperative turd past a sphincter that was only familiar with dainty loads. You could literally see the pain on her face as the corners of her mouth folded back on themselves, exposing a row of pearly-white incisors that looked well-adapted to tearing the flesh from zebra carcasses or agents foolish enough to turn their backs on her. Her eyes were another story. She had the concentrated look as if she were depositing a clutch of eggs in the abdomen of one of her rivals, to hatch at a later time and feed upon their host.

"Mary, Alex and I are trying to get to the bottom of this, as I'm sure you would want too."

"Absolutely, Cathy was a good employee. Ten years," Mary said.

"Eighteen," I corrected.

"Whatever," Mary replied. "She was a good employee," Mary continued, saying all that she needed to say.

A good employee, I thought. *Not friend.* I began to think Mary had modeled her life on that of a robber baron of the late 1800s. What? My carriage ran over and killed your four-year-old son? Here. Have $5. No, take $10 and have him buried properly. Enjoy.

Alex jumped right in.

"We all would like to see this criminal brought to justice. Amanda here because Doc was poisoned in her listing. You, with all those land deals up in the Chino Cone."

Alex's remark had a profound effect on Mary. Well, as profound as an emotion could exhibit on Mary's demeanor. Her fingers tightened on the end of her armrests ever so slightly while you could actually see a wave of frost skitter up across her skin. I decided not to look at Alex after uttering this statement, instead choosing to watch the subtle reactions skating across the surface of Mary's cadaver-like, pale skin. Mary regained her ice-like composure. Despite global warming, glaciers all over the world began heaving a collective sigh of relief: Their leader was back on the throne.

"Alex, I do a lot of deals *all* over town . . . not just in the Chino Cone."

Alex joined in the game, throwing on Slightly Repentant Face #294.

"Mary, I wasn't trying to imply that you had any connection to Doc Winters's death. I was just saying that people—and the police—are likely to assume there might be a connection. So I think it would be in everyone's interest to band together to solve this mess . . . and catch this person. Then we can all go back to selling homes."

This comment seemed to calm Mary, since selling homes was all there was to life, wasn't it?

"Alex, I am not the only listing agent representing sellers up in the Cone. Ed Jensen has sold fifteen lots."

Good, Mary, turn on a colleague, like a cornered mafioso.

It was my time to speak up. "Mary, I know he's one of your clients, but do you have any reason to think that Marvin Sultan is connected with this?"

"Marvin?" She hesitated. Realizing that the jig was up, she continued, "No, not at all. Marvin is a shrewd businessman, but one thing he is not is a murderer."

She smiled at the two of us, then looked past us at something going on over his shoulder. I saw her shake her head ever so slightly. Turning around, I saw a man with an upright dolly, stacked high with identical boxes, all of them marked with a religious cross on them. I turned back toward Mary, who looked pained at what I saw, but then when didn't she? Another large turd passed, I guessed. Or had it?

"Listen, I will do whatever I can to help clear things up.

But I think that trying to involve me or Marvin will lead to a dead end."

An unfortunate choice of words. Or perhaps completely planned.

"Like I said," Mary spouted, "Marvin is a businessman. Why would he want to jeopardize everything he's built up to kill someone over the sale of some lots?"

Alex was clearly frustrated at Mary's inability to change her story. "Mary, a lot of money is at stake here. There are millions to be made. This is the most valuable piece of land left in Palm Springs . . . practically the only large plot left . . . and it's a prime piece of land. Fantastic views, right up against the mountain. Each lot would be priceless."

"Like I said before, Alex, murder is unnecessary. Now, if you'll excuse me, I have some clients I have to go and see. Please keep me in the loop if you discover anything that could be of help."

Mary's remark said it all: I am not going to lift a painted fingernail to help you two meddlers. It also seemed to imply that she wanted this unpleasant matter over with so she could get down to business full throttle. Catching Cathy's killer wasn't as important as making money.

Alex and I were seen out of the office, with Mary walking us to the door to the outside. She wanted us out, that much was evident. As soon as we had gotten into Alex's car, we shared our observations.

"So what did you see over my shoulder? What was going on there, Amanda?"

"You're not going to believe it, but ol' Mary almost took a dump when she saw me catching those boxes being wheeled into a closet."

"Boxes?"

"With crosses all over them. When the guy who was pushing the dolly saw that I saw him and his cargo, he hightailed it into the closet faster than a Log Cabin Republican and closed the door behind him. I'll bet Mary's got a kilo of coke in there. Or the chilled hearts of her victims, for snacking on while watching TV."

"Well, I think we need to make a visit back here to see what Mary has to hide."

"When?" I asked, rubbing my hands together in anticipation.

"About thirteen hours from now."

"Count me in."

CHAPTER 17

To Catch a Thief

I drove home to have lunch, but before I could even enter my house, Regina appeared at my back, smiling from ear to ear.

"C'mon," Regina said, her face brightening with anticipation. "We're going to see Helen Hatcher."

"Regina . . . why?"

"Because I know that Helen is up to her watermelon-sized tits in this mess. I wouldn't put it past her to kill Doc just so she could stick it to Mary Dodge. And I know that you and Alex were just at Mary Dodge's."

"How did you know that? We just got back."

Regina smiled coquettishly. "I have my sources."

"Now, Regina, do you think Helen would kill someone just to clear the way for her to move in on Mary Dodge's territory?'

"Absolutely. Amanda, darling, this might be a small town, er, city, but these fucking broads would do just about anything to get ahead. In a way, they're like businessmen. They think that making the deal and earning a lot of money is the most fun you can have with your pants on. Most of them are castrating bitches, so no man with half a set of balls will even stick it in them, so some of these women turn to business as a way to climax. They get an orgasm whenever they get another commission check."

"Well, that's an interesting theory, Regina," I offered, not wanting to sound like I was turning on my own kind.

"It's not a theory. These women are all over the place. You should have seen them in Hollywood. You think that Miss No-Wire-Hangers Joan Crawford wanted some guy's pole in her hole?"

"Well, I . . ."

"Only if it got her somewhere. She wasn't interested in sex. She wanted money and power. That's what you gotta understand, Amanda. For some of these broads, murder is just another business deal. It's just that someone upped the stakes."

"Gee," I added thoughtfully, "when you put it like that, I can't wait to see the Hatchet."

Helen Hatcher, like Mary Dodge, was another example of women who had gotten into the Palm Springs real-estate market in the eighties and nineties, when you almost couldn't give homes away. But like the odor of a bad fart in an elevator, they lingered for far longer than most people wished. Yet, their businesses grew and grew and grew despite the fact that once most clients signed up with them, they never saw the principals again. They basically did a good business by the sheer weight of the fact that their lawn signs were all over town and the fact that, in 2005, you could sell homes with only one wall standing . . . if they were in the right part of town.

Helen was one of these dinosaurs who wasn't aware of the approaching meteorite that would soon end their Jurassic period of fame.

I'd seen Helen around town before, but only from a distance. From up close, I got a much closer read, and what I saw wasn't pretty. Helen was plump, but at the same time big framed, like a woman whose ancestors pulled plows themselves. She also had frosted, swoopy, Dallas, Texas, sprayed-in-place hair that came to a sharp point over her right ear. You could open cans with it. As if the hair wasn't enough, Helen used a peachy, dry pancake makeup as her primary cover, topped off with blush that Helen apparently spread around her face with a trowel—no brush for this woman. There wasn't a single discernable feature on this chick's face besides her nostrils and lips. No lines, no wrinkles, not even a measly pore that hadn't been cemented in. Her face looked like an off-color, cheap plastic doll from a sweatshop in Shanghai. And to complete her over-the-top billboard presence was lots of gold jewelry so inert it wouldn't offend anybody, and those hideous silk dresses that hung like her face, formless and featureless.

Now, I'm the first woman to give in to cattiness. Let's face it, we women can sometimes be absolutely vicious to each other. But Helen was one of those women who tried *way* too hard at covering up flaws, only drawing attention to what she thought was a masterful cover-up, like an incompetent magician sawing a woman in half, blood pouring out from the mystery box. You couldn't help but look . . . and be horrified.

Now, to her background. Helen's fierce determination to get sales earned her the nickname of the Hatchet. And to this day, she proudly displayed a bloody hatchet that had been given her by Mary Dodge back in the lean years of 1992. Mary had it beautifully framed in a box with a glass front, mounted on a black velvet background, complete with fake blood dripping from it, coagulating in mid-drip. It was one of Helen's prized possessions. Not because it helped reinforce the idea that she could be ruthless when it came to getting listings, but because Mary Dodge had given it to her, one killer recognizing another.

Speaking of the killer instinct, I worried about what Regina might say as we were seated across from Helen's desk, piled high with folders.

"Nice hatchet," Regina commented, pulling the pin out of the grenade. "You used that thing lately?"

"No, not recently," Helen replied sweetly, crossing her plump fingers that ended in blood-red fingernails on top of the desk in front of us. The gold, ostentatious rings clicked as she threaded her fingers together.

"Well, it looks like it was planted in someone's skull a few hours ago," Regina added, continuing her assault.

Helen smiled sweetly again. Again, too sweetly. I'm glad she had her hands on top of the desk in plain sight, where I could see them. I'm sure they were more at home holding a snub-nosed .38.

"Amanda . . . Regina . . ." Helen began, her face as sweet and demure as a nun hiding brass-knuckled hands behind her back. "I know you've come to ask me questions about me being involved in the Chino Cone, but I'll tell you right now, well, that there's nothing to tell quite frankly."

"To be frank, I didn't know you were involved . . . until you just told me." Touché me.

"Amanda, let's cut the crap," Helen whispered. "Any Realtor with half a brain in this town is in a mad dash to snap up and assemble land up in the Cone. It's the largest land grab in this city since the 1940s. It's not illegal to buy and sell land, you know."

"It is when someone gets poisoned because of it."

"Amanda, dear, do you actually think I would poison someone just to get another sale?"

"Ah, let me think about that. . . ." I replied comically.

Helen let loose a tightly controlled, pursed smile as if to say ha-ha, very funny.

"Mary Dodge is snarfing up land like a beggar at a banquet. So is Ed Jensen. And Martha Bickerson. *Even* Evelyn de-half-Witt," Helen added, punctuating the fact that the stupidest

Realtor in town had jumped on the bandwagon. "Everyone is in on it."

"Helen, do you think Mary Dodge could be involved in the murder of Doc Winters?"

"I won't answer that question."

"Okay, I'll ask a different question. Do you know anyone who would want to murder Doc to try and frame Mary?"

"Everyone in this town."

"Could you narrow that down a little?" Regina jumped in.

Helen smiled demurely. "Okay, anyone who isn't in a coma." Helen chuckled.

"She's hated that much?" I asked.

"*That* much. But a lot of people hate me too," Helen threw in, with a mixture of boasting and pride mixed in equal portions. After all, people hated Mary for a variety of reasons, but she wasn't going to let Mary get all the attention. "Mostly, it's just jealousy. Lots of people in this city resent a successful woman," Helen said, playing the sexist card, when it clearly wasn't warranted.

I decided to play Helen a little, since she seemed to be in a confessatory mood.

"So who hates you, Helen?"

"Loser Realtors. You have to watch your back all the time, every minute. I don't even trust my own team sometimes."

"Infamy, infamy, they all got it in for me," Regina recited, probably a line from one of her acts.

Another very-funny, ha-ha from Helen.

Helen crossed her plump fingers on her desk in front of her, thumping the desktop and signaling that the interview was over.

"Now, as much as I would like to stay and chat, I have some new listings to attend to," she announced.

Regina and I looked at each other for some sign of agreement, but Helen had decided that the interview was over and we were to leave.

"Helen," I said as we were being escorted out of her office, "if you remember anything that might be useful, you can call me anytime," I offered, handing her a business card.

She took the card in her hand and waved us good-bye. The card, I assumed, would quickly end up in the trash. Putting it in a shredder would require too much effort.

As I drove Regina home, we both conferred that we had again learned almost nothing.

"So we now know that everyone hates Mary Dodge."

"Check," Regina replied.

"And that everyone wants a piece of the action in the Chino Cone."

"Check."

"And that Mary Dodge is in cahoots with Marvin Sultan."

"Check."

"And that's about it. We're not doing a very good job, are we?"

"Check."

"I guess I'm no good at this sort of thing. I was just expecting someone—anyone—to give us a clue that would break this whole case wide open."

"That only happens in the movies. I know . . . I was in them. Did I tell you about the time Billy Wilder stuck his hand down my pants?"

I was not in the mood to hear yet another of Regina's sordid and unprovable Hollywood stories, so I merely responded that I had, indeed, heard that one.

Regina was quiet for a moment.

"How about when Robert Mitchum asked me to wear a saddle for him?"

"You told me that two weeks ago."

Regina wasn't convinced. "Are you sure?"

"Yes, you said you got saddle sores, Regina."

"Oh, right. How about the time Dean Martin burned me with a cigarette?"

"During sex?"

"Unfortunately, no. I think he was drunk."

"You told me that one."

Regina was quiet again.

"How about stopping for a drink at my place?" I offered.

"I thought you'd never ask."

I plied Regina with cocktails for an hour or so until she said it was time for her afternoon nap. No matinee today for her. I loved Regina dearly, but if I kept this pace of endless cocktail hours, I would have to drive my liver over to the Betty Ford clinic.

I worked for a few hours from what I laughingly called my home office, returning calls and prepping some mailings to drum up new business. I had dinner, watched two back-to-back episodes of *The Golden Girls*, then got ready for our burglary.

Breaking into a real-estate office sounds like a daunting task, but actually, it's quite easy for two reasons: First, there are so many agents coming and going at all hours of the day and night, firms never leave their security systems on. Second, they're cheap, so the locks on the doors are never very good.

When we arrived at Mary Dodge's office, the parking lot was empty and the office was desolate, lit dimly by the dull glow of fluorescent lights. Alex, using nothing more than a stiff piece of thin plastic, had the back door open in less than ten seconds. The rest would be easy.

We stood in the hallway, watching the security system control for a good two minutes just to be sure it wasn't going to go off silently. After a few minutes had passed in silence, we both breathed a sigh of relief and headed down the hall to Mary's office. Her office door was locked, but Alex had that opened in even less time. Alex went right to her to desk, opened the top right-hand drawer, and fished around inside for a few seconds, triumphantly producing a set of keys. Each key was labeled as to its purpose—after all, Mary was a Realtor. You got in the habit of labeling every key for those agents who were so stupid, they could be confused by a door having more than one lock. Don't laugh. Over the years, I've handled hundreds of phone calls from agents who had no idea which way to turn a key in a lock to throw a bolt into the strike frame.

We decided to find out what was in the boxes that Mary was so concerned about us seeing. Like magic, the set of keys quickly opened the closet door and we went inside, turning on the light and closing the door after us.

"This is so exciting! I want to see what Mary is trying to hide," I said, as Alex deftly slid his open sesame piece of plastic under the taped lid that held the box closed.

I was breathing harder, hoping to find some dirty secret that would lay bare the secret to Mary's success. Bullets? Aztec mummy heads? Decorated ceremonial knives used to slit the throats of rival agents? Alex reached inside the box and lifted out a rectangular object rolled up in brown shipping paper. He slowly unrolled the object until it sat there in the palm of Alex's hand.

It was a statue of Saint Joseph—one of the oldest superstitions associated with selling homes. And Mary believed in them enough to have boxes of them in her office. And while we both made fun of them, wielding them like swords against each other, I secretly wondered if they were just partly the reason for Mary's phenomenal success. Or was poison a more effective business plan must-have?

"Okay, enough fun. Let's go look over some of Mary's contracts. What I want to know is how much Marvin is paying for those lots up in the Cone. I get the feeling he bought them on the cheap."

"Cheap? Why would someone sell a lot up there for cheap? They're irreplaceable."

"They are *now*. But when Marvin was scooping them up, people were probably dumping them at rock-bottom prices. I'm sure they were convinced that their land would never be worth anything more than a place for jackrabbits to take a shit."

"Good thinking, Alex. That's why Marvin and Mary are the only reasonable suspects."

"Mary was quick to mention Ed Jensen. We don't know his story . . . yet."

"I'll make a note of it. Investigate Ed."

"Good," Alex agreed, making his way for the door, which, oddly, didn't budge.

"What's wrong?"

"The door seems to be stuck."

"Stuck? We just opened it. . . . How could it be stuck?"

"Well, Miss-Know-It-All, it seems to be locked from the outside."

"And I take it we're on the inside?"

"Correct, Amanda."

"Okay, well, just use your magical piece of plastic and let's get out of here."

Alex pointed to the door lock, which was covered by a heavy metal pry-proof plate.

It didn't look good. "Now, who the fuck would put a tamper-proof strike plate on the inside of a closet?"

As we mulled this over, Alex looked around the room for an answer that would presumably be printed on the wall.

"I see why," he suggested. "Look . . . there . . . on that one wall," he said, pointing to a faint outline on the far wall. "This used to be an entrance hall of some sort, so this was an exterior door, or it was an entrance door from a hallway when this was a suite."

"Oh shit! So how are we going to get out?"

"Break the door down, I guess."

"Oh great, and have Mary come in tomorrow morning and see a broken door to a closet that we just happened to see the day before with all kinds of cloak-and-dagger drama."

"You have a better idea, Miss Thorne?"

"Uh," I struggled, trying to think of something while looking up at the ceiling. "I've got it! The drop ceiling!"

"You think you're going to climb over the top? I'll bet that the walls here go all the way up to the roof."

"Well, let's see if they do. Here, give me a lift up."

Alex joined his hands together. I put my right foot into his hands and he hoisted me up rather quickly. So quickly, in fact, that my hand went right through the ceiling tile and broke it in half, showering us with a flurry of what was probably asbestos flakes.

I peered above the drop acoustic ceiling and saw that we were extremely lucky. For some odd reason, the walls of the closet only went to the drop ceiling, so I crawled out toward the hallway beyond and to freedom. As I was lifting the ceiling tile in the hallway to make my escape, I could hear the metal ties that connected the metal gridwork to the ceiling popping around me like firecrackers. Seconds later, the whole of the drop ceiling structure collapsed, leaving me stranded, doubled over the closet door—half in, half out.

"Are you okay?" Alex shouted into my shoes.

"I'm fine. I think I have a permanent crease in my abs, though . . . I wonder if I can do this in two more places, then I won't have to do crunches ever again."

"Can you drop down without hurting yourself?"

"I think so. . . . Let me turn around and I'll drop down feet-first. I guess I should have gone that way to begin with." I managed to squeeze out of my constricted abdomen. Like turning a full-sized octopus around inside a paper cup, I managed to turn over on my ass and point my feet downward for the fall, which happened faster than I thought.

"OW, GODDAMNIT!" I shrieked as my feet hit a coffee mug that had been knocked off the desk when the ceiling crashed down below me. "FUCK! FUCK-FUCK-FUCK-FUCK-FUCKKKK!"

Above my wimpers, came Alex's calm voice from the other side of the door.

"I take it that didn't go well?"

"Shhhhhiiiiitttttttt! I think I broke my foot."

More calm voice. "Uh, Amanda . . . could you open the door so that I could help you?"

"Sure, I'll just . . . OW!" I turned the doorknob and Alex poked his head out like a turtle, testing the area for predators.

"Here, let me look at your foot. Which is the one that hurts?"

"THEY BOTH HURT."

"Okay, Miranda, we need to keep our voices down. We've just broken into the office of a murderess, we've destroyed the ceiling beyond repair tonight, and we've got nothing to show for it beyond knowing that Mary Dodge buries cheap, plastic statues of Saint Joseph made in China in front of million-dollar homes in order to sell them."

I had a moment of calm myself. "So what's your point?"

"I forgot . . . Oh yes, we need to keep our voices down. So both your feet hurt . . . which one hurts the most?"

"The right one."

He gingerly removed my tennis shoe and ran his hands slowly over my foot. God, that felt good!

"It's definitely swollen. Can you move it . . . twist it around?"

"Yes, now let me go. I'm ready to dance *Swan Lake*."

I don't know why, but I started laughing. Then Alex started laughing. Then I pointed at the shattered acoustic ceiling tiles that lay strewn around the office. It was clear that it was ludicrous that we would even try and clean up the mess. It was crazy. I mean, what were we thinking? It reminded me of the time Alex and I smoked some pot and stole the baby Jesus from a Nativity scene and replaced him with a Pee Wee Herman doll. Alex helped me limp slowly out of the office.

"Wait, what about the files?" I reminded Alex.

"What files?"

"The files. When you break into an office late at night, you have to steal some files—everyone does," I said with all seriousness on my face, then burst into laughter again, which caused Alex to start another laughing jag.

"We better get you home and get some ice on that foot of yours."

"Look, Alex, I was kidding about the files at first, but maybe we should take a look. If Mary's spearheading a big project to buy up land in the Chino Cone, she's got to have a project file on it."

"But what about your ankle?"

"It's okay for now. Help me look through her office."

I hopped, hobbled, and twisted down the hall to Mary Dodge's office.

"Wait a minute," Alex blurted out as I was about to open a drawer in Mary's imposing desk. "The file's probably out here in the files near Cathy Paige's desk; after all, Cathy was her right-hand woman."

"Good thinking," I added, as I hopped back toward Alex. We turned on a lamp and shined it toward the file cabinets, then began rifling though them.

"Oh my God, Mary has files on agents from other offices."

"Recruiting?"

"No, shit-list files."

"Noooo!" Alex said, slowly and incredulously.

"Yes . . . newspaper and magazine articles, police reports, DUIs, Department of Real Estate Disciplinary Actions . . . She's using these for blackmail! Ho-ho-ho, what do we have here? Amanda, slash Alex Thorne!"

"A file on us?"

"You bet."

"What's it say, what's it say?" Alex whined as I plowed through the file.

"Shit! Nothing juicy. Just printouts of our more spectacular listings. The Markham house, the Bette Davis house . . . wait a minute here . . . printouts of both your house and mine . . . the listings from the Multiple Listing Service . . . with pictures of our homes, inside and out, before our renovations . . . they're all paper-clipped together with the words *personal home* written on the topmost page. Oh, Alex, this is getting creepy. From these, she can piece together the layouts of the rooms in our homes. This chick is really nuts."

"Okay, okay, we can take care of ourselves, Amanda, can't we? Now, let's find the Chino Cone file, make some copies, and get out of here. How's the foot?"

"Still hurts. It's swelling."

"Then let's get out of here now," Alex said, concerned.

"No, no, I'm all right for now. Let's finish what we started."

"Hey, hey, hey, look what I found," Alex claimed cheerfully, waving an overstuffed folder in the air. "Chino Cone. I'll go make some copies of the documents; you stay here and keep looking for more juicy stuff."

I was fascinated that Mary was so obsessed with her competition that she bothered to collect all these files. Then it dawned on me: These might be personnel files, information gathered on prospective future employees, to find the good ones and weed out the bad. Nah, I thought. I was giving Mary too much credit. It was like Martha Stewart. You don't have that many people hating you unless at least some of the vicious stories you hear about that person are true. Although the story of Martha running over baby chickens in anger because the farm-fresh eggs she bought for her show were fertilized and accidentally hatched—that's probably made up. Probably.

Alex was running off a stack of copies from the sound of it. He returned a few minutes later with a folder absolutely bulging with paper.

"I got it all. Maps, letters, newspaper articles . . . all right here," he said, patting the folder affectionately. "Off we go."

Alex lent me a shoulder and we lurched like drunken sailors toward the door. We made it to the car, threw the folders inside, and were about to get inside when a brilliant beam of light flashed in our faces. From the look on the policeman's face, I could tell this was going to be a long night.

The next morning, when Detective Becker saw to our release from the police station, we strode out into the brilliant sunlight. Well, *strode* isn't quite the right word. Hobbled is more like it. My foot still throbbed, despite the fact that I had an ice pack on it for the remainder of the evening, supplied by Palm Springs' finest.

As Alex and I sat in the car, the motor off, replaying everything that happened in the last few hours, we started laughing again. God, it felt good—even better than his muscular, but soft hand when it caressed my foot after the accident. To laugh with someone who knows you almost as well as you do yourself. Sharing a laugh—it's not just a term.

"Boy, we're lucky that Becker has the hots for me. Otherwise, we might still be in there," I said, thumbing toward the police building.

My comment produced the most profound effect I could imagine: Alex looked like I had just slapped him across the face. Seeing my concern for his reaction, he brightened up immediately, chasing the clouds away from his expression.

"Amanda, I'm happy for you. I really am."

"Alex, we've had *one* date. One. It's not like we're getting married tomorrow. I like him, but it's waaaay too early to tell. How about you?"

"No one special. Just looking around," he said, smiling. Smiling with a tiny sadness showing in an almost imperceptible downturn in the corner of his smile.

I reached over and kissed his cheek. "You'll find someone." Alex rolled his eyes.

"Oh, c'mon, Alex. With your charm, wit, and dashing good looks, you could have any man you want."

"That's the problem. I don't want just *anyone*. I want someone like you: someone extraordinary. Someone who gets my all my jokes, cries at the same things—someone who . . ."

". . . can finish your sentences for you?" I jumped in.

Alex let out a sigh. "Yes."

"Let's get off this topic," I interjected, fearing that if we went down this path any further, we'd both end in tears. I switched gears. "I can't believe that Mary Dodge didn't press charges."

"Oh, *I* can. Now that she knows that we know what she knows, she wouldn't dare, you know?"

"Would you run that by me again? You lost me somewhere after the fifty-yard line."

"We have the goods on her; from knowing about her shit-list files to our grand-slam Chino Cone file, we now have our own shit list on her. And she knows it."

"Well put. So should we go over to my place and go over our documents with a fine-tooth comb?"

"Let's. But one request," Alex uttered.

"Yes?"

"Could we go to my place? The last time I was over at your place, I ended up with a half-inch nail in the sole of my shoe."

"You got it."

As we sat at the counter in Alex's kitchen, me poring over the documents and Alex making blueberry pancakes, it hit me what was going on up there in the Chino Cone—a lot more than anyone guessed.

Not only was Mary Dodge fucking over the city, but Ed Jensen was fucking her and Marvin Sultan over. Ed, it seems, was buying up lots that hopscotched across Marvin's assemblage, like rotten teeth in a supermodel's mouth. He was deliberately buying up, at highly inflated prices, lots in between the ones Mary was snapping up for Marvin, preventing him from having an uninterrupted development that he could bulldoze to his heart's content.

Alex looked up from his grill for a moment. "You mean someone else is as cutthroat as Mary? I'm surprised that he isn't dead because of it."

I thought for a moment. "You know, Alex, that was really brilliant what you just said about him not being dead."

"What's so brilliant about it?"

"Maybe it isn't Mary Dodge who's behind all this."

"You think Ed is our man?"

"He could be. Think about it for a moment. Suppose he has the same idea as Mary Dodge and Marvin. And a client like Marvin. So he murders Doc to pin the thing on the two of them. And if it works and they end up in jail, then he buys up what's left at fire-sale prices."

"Yeah, but your theory falls down when you consider that it wouldn't take long for the cops to figure out that he's in it up to his neck too."

"Good point, but you have to admit, it's possible that Ed is our culprit. If he pins Doc's murder on Mary and Marvin, he stands to clean up."

Alex held up his spatula like he was taking an oath. "I'll admit it, your theory could prove to be correct."

"Well, this seemed to be such a simple thing. The killer was Mary Dodge. Then it was Mary Dodge and Marvin Sultan. Now it could be Ed Jensen," I said, looking out to the tiny patch of lawn beyond Alex's pool. "I guess we're not doing such a great job as detectives. We were born to sell homes."

Alex gave me a look of puzzlement. "What do you mean we're not doing such a great job? We've uncovered information that Detective Becker is probably just drooling to get his hands on. And we're about to uncover more."

"A visit to Ed? How about noon tomorrow?

"You bet."

"You read my mind," I said.

"That's what makes us such a great team."

"I knew you were going to say that." I added.

Chapter 18

A Flaming Heterosexual

The three worst things in the world that you can hear are, in this order:

3. "The condom broke."
2. "For your information, I'm his *wife* . . . or didn't he tell you?"
1. The worst, however, is a sound. It is the sound of a smoke detector shrieking somewhere in your dark house at 2 A.M.

That is what I awoke to. At times like these, the first thing you think about is whether you forgot to turn off a stove burner before going to bed. Then, as you're racing to put slippers on your feet, the next thought that goes through your mind is the toaster, followed by an unextinguished candle, an electrical short, and finally, a carelessly tossed cigarette. But since I hadn't lit a candle in my house in ages and don't allow smoking in my house, my mind raced back to the stove. I ran through the house, madly flipping on lights to see what was setting off the detector that clung to the ceiling just outside my kitchen. *Oh*, I thought, as I saw the bright orange flickering coming through my front window, *my front door is on fire.*

Knucklehead started barking wildly just because there simply was something exciting going on. Doors, of course, rarely catch on fire by themselves, so as I flew over and fumbled at trying to free my fire extinguisher from its wall holster (Yes, I have a fully charged fire extinguisher in my house. Everyone should, so sue me for being prepared.), the ominous thought sprang into my head that someone deliberately did this. Or did they? Perhaps a flaming bag of dog poop gone wrong? No, no, it couldn't be. Well, my doorbell wasn't working, so if someone threw the bag on my front porch and rang the bell . . . No, that was silly, I thought as I kicked the front door open to get the flaming plane of wood away from the door frame and doused it with everything the fire extinguisher had to give. Four minutes later, satisfied that the door was out and the charred overhang wasn't going to combust, I called the fire department, then Detective Becker. Of course, I repeatedly told the dispatcher at both phone numbers that the fire was out and I was okay, but that didn't stop two industrial-sized fire trucks and Ken's unmarked police car from screaming down my block with sirens wailing for everyone within a six-mile radius to hear. You'd think they were trying to put out a flaming 747.

As a crew of firemen and Ken converged on my house, I stood there, unable to speak, pointing toward the charred hulk of what was left of my newly refurbished mid-century door with the central doorknob. (It's not easy to find replacements for a door like that.) All I could do was point. Then the tears welled up in my eyes and I just went to pieces.

Ken approached me and put his arms so tenderly around me, I didn't know they were there until he pressed me to his chest and squeezed just a little, just enough to make me feel safe. I continued crying for some time, partly because of the shock of having my house and my life violated so viciously, and partly because I just liked being held by him and I was so thrilled to know someone like him was interested in me. Sometimes turning on the waterworks is the perfect tool that every woman should have in her female arsenal.

"There, there," Ken cooed. "Everything's going to be all right. I'm here now."

And you know what? I believed him.

Ken spent the night with me. Not sitting in his car outside my home, but in my bed. We didn't have sex . . . again. He just held me, and I for one, was more than happy to curl up inside the wonderful cove of his just-hairy-enough arm, which spent the night shielding me from whoever was planning to do me harm. After Alex and I had divorced, I had a few one-night stands with some guys I picked up, and instead of finding them wild and exhilarating, I just found them tawdry and sad. I was willing to take my time and I liked that Ken was doing the same. Two minds, one thought. But considering my past propensity of sleeping with gay men, I did have to ask the question to Ken.

"Ken, you *are* straight, right?"

"Yes, I'm straight. But if you want me to be gay, I'll be gay . . . if that will help me win favors with you. I'll go get the fabric swatches out of the trunk of my car."

"I didn't really doubt you, it's just that, well, with us not making love . . . Don't get me wrong, I love falling asleep in your arms, I just felt that maybe I wasn't attractive—"

Ken held up a hand. "Stop right there, missy. I don't seem to remember being handcuffed to your bed last night. I've spent two nights with you of my own accord."

"Oh, Ken, I never do handcuffs on the first or second date. Next time."

"I'm holding you to that. Amanda . . . ?"

"Yes, Ken?"

"I'm a divorcé, just like you. I want to take my time getting to know you. I don't want to rush into anything. I want to think with my head as much as my heart. And I want you to do the same."

I gave him a salute. "Yes, sir."

"I want, more than anything, to be your best friend in the world first. Lover second."

"That's exactly what my husband said when we started dating."

"C'mere, you," he said, grabbing my hand and placing it on his crotch, which was welling up with excitement. "Does that feel like the reaction of a gay man?"

Alex had no trouble getting a stiffy with me, I thought. But I kept my thoughts to myself. "Nope, no, it doesn't."

I think one of the reasons so many women choose not to date is because there are so many jerks out there. I was never good at math, but the chances of encountering more than a few of them were high. My chances, however, were abnormally high. So high, in fact, that I wish I had the same odds in Las Vegas. I would end up owning the town.

Of course, a psychologist would probably suggest that believing that you had a high chance of meeting dickheads was just that—all in my head. The reality, I had to reluctantly concede, was that I allowed myself to be attracted to guys who weren't a good choice. Or, more correctly, that I attracted the wrong kind of guys, and worse, that I allowed them to get over my dickhead filters (barriers, to you in therapy).

Matt was one of them. No, he was *the* one. He came before Alex. Right before. Matt was an asshole who had mesmerized me. We met at a real-estate open house at an over-the-top, overpriced tract mansion in West Bloomfield Hills shoehorned into a tiny sliver lot so that the builder could say his house was on the lake. It was—all forty feet of waterfront. Matt, well, I thought he was energetic, charismatic, and gregarious. The reality, which few of us see, was that he was manic-depressive, schizoaffective, and shallow, in that order. But I was a fool in love. And we all know what happens when we suspend our own good sense of judgment: We end up as just another link in the chain, chain, chain of fools. And me, I was the weak link, no doubt about it. I was so smart in school but so dumb when it came to relationships. I spoke French, German, and a good amount of Italian by the time I graduated college, but the one thing I couldn't do is translate what Matt was really saying.

MATT: I'm gunna say something crazy. Now, don't have a stroke.

WHAT HE WAS REALLY SAYING: I'm crazy.

HOW I WOULD TRANSLATE IT: I am about to propose something that, because of your low self-esteem and years of psychological belittling from everyone from your twisted old-country grandmother to Mrs. Lacey, your third-grade teacher who made you stay after school for two hours once a week practicing your cursive *l*'s and *t*'s on the schoolroom chalkboard, you will initially realize is insane, but because of the aforementioned psychological dysfunction that cripples you to this very day, you will accept as brilliant and breakthrough because I said so. Because I am schizoaffective, and thankfully, most people like yourself don't realize this very real psychological disorder even exists and certainly can't see it when it's staring you in the face, I perceive everything I do as utterly wonderful and create such an air of assuredness concerning my actions, weaker people accept what I say and do as the result of a talented mind, which is what it is.

HOW OTHERS WOULD TRANSLATE MATT:
Amanda, this guy's nutz with a capital Z. He spends
money—mostly yours—like a drunken congressman,
he's created more drama than Shakespeare, and he gets
in and out of friendships whose duration can only be
measured by atomic clocks.

ME: You don't understand him. No one does. This is
just the kind of exciting relationship I need to help me
branch out and expand my horizons. I am trying to learn
to think bigger, to not be so overly careful. I need to take
risks in order to move onto higher things in life.

Never mind that I was, in fact, living with a man who fell
into instant friendships with people, showing how lovable he
was, only to drop them weeks later in a fury when they looked
at him sideways. Or that I, with Matt's help, was burning
through money that I had so carefully stored up like a chip-
munk expecting a brutal winter. I was becoming a woman
under the influence, ditching the one rule in life that one
should always follow: Follow your own instincts. Matt was
putting a shine on a turd and I was buying it.

There's an old saying: Live with a crazy person long enough
and you'll end up there yourself. Before our breakup,
Matthew had made me so crazy, I got drunk one night and
drove my car at 130 miles an hour on the freeway, hoping to
accomplish I-don't-know-what. Die like Lana Turner in *The
Bad and the Beautiful?* Get arrested like Bette Davis in *The
Star?* Luckily, I didn't get pulled over, I didn't get into an accident, and I made it home safely, until I pulled into my driveway. I got out of the car, vomited several times on my lawn on
the way to my front door, and promptly fell asleep on a living
room couch. Little did I know I had left my car in neutral with

216

the key in the ignition, which, minutes later, pushed by the physics of Murphy's Law, rolled down the driveway, plowed through a line of mailboxes, and ended up in Cranbrook Lake. Enough was enough.

Being nonconfrontational by nature, I decided to have the Mother of All Fights in order to push Matt out of my life, but fate intervened. Matt was having an affair with a bimbo behind my back. When crazy people have made a shambles of a life, they do what crazy people have done since the dawn of time: They move on to destroy a new life. So now you know how relieved I was when Alex stepped into my life and pushed Matthew out. Or came to the rescue, really.

In college, Alex, instead of taking all the dreary, skull-numbing classes that would eventually land him in a cubicle in an accounting firm or marketing behemoth, took classes that interested him. Especially those that gave him insight into human nature, he said. So he took a lot of psychology. A lot. Eventually, that's what his major was, but he never pursued that line of work. As he told me over and over, abnormal psychology gave you insights into how the world really worked. With those tools, you had a leg up on the world that few others had. It was seeing what was really going on in people's minds that held the key. As it turns out, his entire family took the same route. At last, I figured out what made his family so self-assured, so confident, so successful. It was as if they had the golden key to life that evaded the rest of us.

Anyway, to get back to the story, it was Alex who started showing me what was really happening in my life because I had given up my free will and followed Matt like Whitney Houston tagging after nutcase Bobby Brown.

And little by little, Matt began to recede in my life, the final push occurring when Alex packed up the last of Matt's things and had them delivered to Matt's bimbo girlfriend's apartment. So, as a result, I have never looked back. More important, I have never forgotten.

So it was with this trepidation that I kissed Ken, got him to trust me and let me go about my day, unprotected, but he demanded that he return at the end of the day. Twist my arm.

He got in his car and headed back to the department. I got myself ready and hopped into my car. I had a lot of catching up to do. In fact, I had several offers on 2666 Boulder Drive, despite the fact that there had a been a murder there. I disclosed the fact, but people wanted to buy. It was 2005, after all . . . everything was selling.

I turned on the radio and adjusted the air conditioning, blasting it to cool down the car. I had never felt the air blow on my legs quite like that. Or maybe it was my panty hose. Still, it tickled.

Then I saw something that made my blood run cold. Dozens of small, black peas were crawling on my ankles. Black widow spiders. Females.

A tiny eternity passed. Should I beep the horn? No, black widows don't like vibrations. Smash them? No, I'll risk getting bitten if I miss and rile them up. So I just sat for a minute. Okay, think. Unless I try and grab them or provoke them, they won't bite. They don't know my leg from a log. Well, a little bit. My leg is warm, but a log is not, unless it's been sitting in the sun, but nonetheless, no black widow spider would bite a log, so I was safe for the time being. Why was I thinking these thoughts? Plus, if one did bite me, I wouldn't die, but probably get very sick. But then again, what if a lot of them bit me all at once? What if they gave off some kind of pheromone, some chemical or scent that made the other spiders go into a biting frenzy? My mind was running away with me. Okay, stop wondering and start thinking. Think clearly. Okay, black widows don't like vibrations—that's why they hide in piles of things that don't move. Okay, my car is vibrating right now . . . not a good thing. First thing, Amanda: Turn off the air. I reached over slowly and turned the air conditioning off. Next thing: Turn off the engine. I reached over to the steering column and turned off the motor. Done. Good. Black widows don't like light, so I must open the car doors if I can, because the lights will come on in the car and so will the ones in the door panel; plus, the sun will drive them back into the dark, under my seat. I got the driver's side door open easily enough. I reached around slowly to the door behind me, pulled the door handle, and pushed the door open. I pushed it a little too hard, and the door opened to the end of the hinge, bounced, and slammed shut with a mild bang.

Fuck!

I looked down and the bang of the door must have vibrated the one spider hanging upside down on my calf, because it seemed to have lost its footing and dangled by one leg from a thread in my panty hose, then dropped to the car floor mat. I turned around again, pulled the door handle, then pushed the door behind me again, and this time gave it just enough of a push to keep it fully open, but not enough to make it bounce back closed. Next, I leaned across the center console and opened the front passenger door and pushed that open. This door bounced at the end of the hinge, but I was ready for it. My hand dove into my purse and pulled out my long comb, which I used like a sword to stop the door from banging shut. Success. The last door, the back-seat passenger on the other side of the car was too far away to risk opening. I had three doors open. Then I waited. Nothing happened for the first few minutes. I think the spiders were still confused about being in a car in the first place and not under a pile of wood or junk, or hiding in a crack in a rock wall. But the light started to work its magic. One by one, the spiders dropped from my legs and crawled with an agonizing slowness under my seat or up-hill, past the brake pedal, and up into the bottom of the dash-board where they disappeared.

I waited another 15 minutes, fearing to move just yet. As I looked around, I finally realized that Becker had driven off some time ago, not even knowing that I was in danger. Then, as gingerly as a bomb diffuser, I swung my legs slowly out of my door and held them as rigid as two long poles, inspecting the undersides of my legs to make sure all the spiders were gone. I then got out of the car and slowly walked into my house, through it, and into the backyard, where I slowly and carefully removed my clothes, then jumped in the pool just to be sure. I stayed at the bottom for as long as my breath could be held, all the while rubbing my legs and ass and crotch vig-orously—don't want any spiders to take up shop in those crevices. My oxygen spent, I popped to the surface, nude, but free of the creepy things.

From nowhere, Edwin appeared at the edge of the pool, oblivious to the fact that I had no clothes on.

"Miss Thorne, I'm having trouble finding fittings for that fancy European toilet you want me to install."

Ken came screaming back to my house five minutes after I phoned him to tell him what happened. He almost kicked the door to his car open and bounded up the driveway toward me, throwing his arms around me and knocking the can of bug spray out of my hand.

"Thank God you're safe," he gushed. I was in the Ken Safe Zone again. I loved it. He held me for some time, then sure that the danger had passed, released me but kept his hands on my arms, as if to assess if there was any damage.

"I'm okay," I answered a little too breathlessly. So sue me.

Ken had that effect on me. Plus, he was really squeezing me. I needed to get some air back in my lungs. I bent over and retrieved the can of bug spray. "I try so hard to be green, but I'm afraid I opened fire on the assailants," I said, holding up the can like it was a Beretta 9mm semiautomatic. "It was self-defense."

"Shit, you are brave, Amanda. Any other woman would have panicked and been bitten. You did the right thing."

"Now my car is going to smell like Raid. I really bombed the bitches."

"No, your thinking was brilliant . . . using the light to drive the spiders back into hiding."

"Aww shucks. Twern't nuthin," I said, kicking a bit of dirt from my driveway with my Prada loafer.

"I'm going to have a patrol car posted outside your house for a while."

"Why, because you think someone tried to kill me?"

Ken shook his head. "No."

"That's funny. I was thinking the same thing. You don't kill someone by setting their front door on fire. Or by putting spiders in someone's car. It seems like an amateur. So what do you think it means?"

"I don't know yet," he replied, scrunching up his eyebrows in that adorable way of his.

"A warning?"

"A warning against what?"

"Against me . . . us snooping. I mean, Alex and I pretty much brought the house down at Mary Dodge's office."

"The ceiling?" he said, giving a little chuckle. "That was pretty funny." He reminisced a while, then changed gears. "Listen, Amanda, I have to get going on another homicide. Are you going to be okay?"

"Sure. What's the homicide?"

"Elderly woman hit her husband with a frying pan. Said she couldn't stand living with him another minute more. Bam!" he said, mimicking an elderly woman hitting an imaginary head with an imaginary frying pan. "You just never know when someone's going to snap, do you?"

"No, you don't. And that's what makes this world so damn interesting," I added.

"Dangerous, too," Ken added.

"There's another angle we haven't considered," Alex said, brightening with a new theory.

"And what's that?"

"Monica Birdsong killed Doc to get her hands on a lucrative piece of business."

I balked at Alex's idea.

"I balk at your idea, Alex."

"Because you think she doesn't have the smarts to carry off a murder?"

"That woman doesn't have the brains to brush her teeth. I think she nails her toothbrush to the wall and puts her mouth on it while she moves her head back and forth."

"Yeah, but look at Anna Nicole. Thick as a post, but she managed to nail that oil billionaire. You just have to have the right incentive."

I chuckled. "Yeah, bleach-blond hair, cantaloupe tits, and the ability to dance on your back with an octogenarian."

"So I say we pay Miss Birdbrain a visit."

"Yes, let's. This should be quite entertaining."

CHAPTER 19

Why Do Birds Suddenly Appear?

The next morning, our car pulled onto Snow Creek Village Road, a tiny private community plunked right at the northern base of Mt. San Jacinto. I mean, right at the base. Doc's house looked like it was built by a hobbit—a hobbit with a fondness for Jack Daniels. There wasn't a straight line in the building. The roofline wobbled back and forth, dove down here, and zoomed up there. Porthole windows dotted the walls, their placement about as haphazard as the roofline.

A pack of dogs greeted us with unorganized barking, wagging tails, and some kicking of dust. They made a lot of commotion, but seemed friendly. Monica emerged from the house wearing Daisy Dukes, even though the day was actually on the cool side, especially with the strong winds that constantly raked this area northwest of Palm Springs. Monica extended her hand, which, I noticed, sported a particularly large diamond. Guessing offhand, I'd say about two-and-a-half carats. Even more interesting was a shiny red Maserati sitting in the driveway.

Alex kissed her hand in the Continental style. Monica giggled like a little schoolgirl.

"So fancy, Mr. Thorne!" she tittered.

One of the dogs came over to sniff my leg, then proceeded to hump it.

"Oh, Sparky really likes you!" Monica exclaimed as she made no effort to stop Sparky's amorous motions. I just started walking until Sparky fell off.

"Come in, you two. I have some tea just brewed and some sweets," she said, leading the way with her birdlike frame.

As I followed Monica across the threshold, something flew at my face, circled my head, then flew across the room and settled on a high shelf, where it watched us intently.

"Oh, don't mind him . . . that's Poe . . . he's a little black-throated sparrow. Doc and I took him in because he had a broken wing. Cost us eleven hundred dollars to fix his wing, but it was worth it. The little guy is just about mended and ready to fly off, aren't you, Poe?" she asked the terrified bird while blowing him a kiss. Monica motioned for us to sit down . . . on rocks cemented into the floor. What was it about rock chairs here in the desert? I think it all started with Albert Frey, our late, local famous architect.

The inside of the house was decorated in early Witch's Lair. Alex and I sat down, with me first looking to check if the sparrow had left a present on the seat. All clear. Monica took her place on a wooden bench that looked like it was still in the process of growing. I looked for roots at the end of the bench legs. Nothing. On another rock sat a tray with a homemade set of stoneware so ugly it looked like it still had some stones lodged in it. The tray was inscribed with Monica's florid signature, so it was safe to assume that Monica made it. While blind. And missing thumbs.

"Would you like a cup of tea?" she offered.

"Yes, certainly," we both said at the same time. Finally, something normal about this place.

"It's mandrake fruit tea. It's poisonous if eaten in larger quantities, but one cup of tea won't hurt, will it?"

Alex and I threw each other sideways glances, then put our cups down and smiled.

"Help yourself to some glazed buns. I just made them this morning," Monica offered with a sweep of her hand.

I figured she couldn't have put wolfsbane or some other ingredient in them, so I picked one up, but not before hoping that the white splat on the top of the bun was frosting and not something plopped there by Poe. Luckily, it was. Frosting, that is.

"So, Monica," I started, "Alex and I are here because we want to get to the bottom of who killed Doc."

"Mr. Thorne, nothing would please me more."

Alex leaned forward. "Monica, who do you think killed Doc?"

Without a moment's hesitation: "Marty Sultan."

"You seem very sure about that," Alex replied.

"Absolutely. Doc and that blood-sucking jackal have been at it since Marty decided to come out here because he hadn't destroyed enough in Los Angeles. This was open territory, and the locals here aren't prepared for his viciousness. Well, I for one, am going to stand up to him. . . . I'm going to carry on without Doc, and I'm not going to rest until I see that snake in prison."

I jumped in. "Monica, I urge you to be careful. Whoever did this is willing to stop at nothing to get their way. I've had several attacks on me already."

"You don't seem to be scared, Amanda."

"I'm not a direct target, Monica. But you are."

"So why would someone attack you if you're not a target?"

"Monica, that's the $64,000 question. I wish I knew the answer. To keep me scared and warn me not to poke my nose where it doesn't belong."

Monica replied, "Obviously that doesn't seem to be working. After all, here you sit."

"Good point. No, it hasn't."

Alex spoke up. "Monica, it seems that you're quite clear on who killed Doc. But is there anyone else you can think of who might have resorted to murder to get even with Doc?"

"A Realtor with a lot at stake in buying up land in the Chino Cone."

"Anyone in particular come to mind?"

"Mary Dodge, Helen Hatcher."

"Interesting," Alex muttered. "Why?"

"Because they're involved with buying up land and assembling it into one big parcel to put up some ridiculous hotel and golf course for rich people. I went with Doc once to talk to Mary Dodge in her office. She was very polite, telling us that Palm Springs needed a five-star resort to bring more taxes into the city coffers. To bring more jobs."

"And how did Doc respond to all this?" I inquired.

"He said that, in doing so, we'd destroy one of the big reasons people come here . . . for the unspoiled mountain views, the wildness at our doorsteps. 'Who wants to look up at another goddamn golf course and mega mansions?' was what Doc said. And he's right. Look at what happened to Sedona. It's just a suburban neighborhood of ugly houses building right up to those beautiful rocks. It's destroyed forever."

"It sounds like Doc was getting a little hot under the collar with Mary."

"Doc had a temper . . . sometimes. He could get so angry with people who had no sensitivity for the environment."

"So what was the outcome of the meeting?"

"He threw a handful of M&Ms in her face," Monica said, stunning—and amusing—both Alex and me.

I couldn't let this one go. "He threw M&Ms in her face?"

"Yeah, it was kinda funny. Mary just kept repeating the same thing about needing a five-star resort and condos and private homes to raise Palm Springs to a world-class resort destination. She didn't raise her voice, but Doc got so frustrated because she kept repeating the same line over and over, he reached into a bowl of M&Ms that was sitting on Mary's desk for clients, grabbed a fistful, and hurled them into her face."

Alex looked at me for a reaction, then turned back to Monica. "And how did Mary Dodge react?"

"Like I said, it was kinda funny. She was shocked at first. I think it was the first time anyone had ever stood up to that bitch. You could tell she wasn't used to it because she didn't know how to react.

After what seemed like minutes, she told Doc and I to leave her office."

Alex pursued a little more. "Did anyone else in the office see this?"

"What, the M&Ms? Oh yeah! The windows in Mary's office are all glass . . . you can see right into her office from just about everywhere. Every member of her team saw it. The funny thing, one of them was smiling. I guess there are people on her own team who want to see her get her comeuppance."

"That seems to be the general consensus. The top producers are always watching their behinds," I added.

"Well, if I were Helen Hatcher, her behind wouldn't be hard to hit."

I was impressed. Monica managed to make a funny.

"Can I ask you one more question, Monica?" Alex ventured.

"Shoot."

"Do you think that anyone in Doc's organization had a grudge against him?"

"If by what you mean *organization*, you mean Save Our Hills, no. Everyone is nonviolent. We love animals, trees, nature."

"Don't get me wrong, Monica, Amanda and I are long-standing members of the Sierra Club and the Nature Conservancy, but some of the most violent acts have been committed by people supposedly dedicated to the environment. Hummers have burned; animal testing facilities blown up."

"Mr. Thorne, you're not a Republican, are you?"

"Oh God, no. But I don't think violence ever solved anything, even if it means making a point."

"Sometimes, it *is* necessary . . . to protect the environment, since it can't protect itself. We have to pick up the sword for it from time to time."

"Well," Alex said, turning to me, "unless you have any questions, Amanda, I think I've learned a lot. How 'bout you?"

"I have one, Monica, and I hope you won't take this personally, but it seems like a lot of people are donating a lot of money to Save Our Hills," I said.

"Yes?" Monica answered, clearly not aware of where this question was going.

"Well, where is all the money going?"

"Whatever do you mean?" she asked sweetly.

"What I'm trying to get at is that with so much money in Doc's hands, someone might try and kill Doc and get their hands on it."

"Oh, that's silly," Monica replied, covering the massive rock on her wedding finger with her other hand. "It's all in an account Doc set up to fund his work. It would be impossible for someone to take it. They'd need Doc's signature and mine."

Mine. The word resounded in my head over and over. Now the bank would need only one signature. Hmm.

"So Save Our Hills is a charitable foundation?" Alex asked, jumping in.

Monica was becoming noticeably uncomfortable, squirming in her chair. Either that, or her thong underwear (which I'm convinced was all she owned) was creeping up her ass crack.

"Doc had some lawyers looking into what was needed to set it up. Doc had been struggling for so long on almost nothing, then when Marvin Sultan proposed Marvin Gardens, the money just came pouring in. I mean, just pouring. So he opened an account and put everything in it."

Alex, who knew a lot about everything, lobbed the next grenade.

"Monica?" he started. "Unless Doc had a non-profit organization or a charitable foundation set up, he couldn't open an account under them."

"So, you're saying . . . ?" Monica ventured.

"That all the money was probably in a checking account in Doc's name."

"Well, yes. The contributors made the checks out to Doc," Monica replied uneasily.

"So all the money that was contributed is being . . . was being held by Doc in a personal banking account?" Alex finished.

"Sure. Listen, the contributors all knew that their money was going to fund Doc's work. . . . That's why they made the checks to Doc personally. There wasn't any organization to make the donations to."

I had heard enough. Anything after this point would just be excuses and avoidances. "Monica, thank you so much for taking time out of your day and at such a terrible time for you."

"It's not terrible," she objected with a smile.

"Not terrible?" I asked.

"Doc's not dead," she stated as a matter of fact, like one would report it was sunny outside. "Doc's energy has gone onto a higher state."

"I see. Well, thank you for everything, Monica," Alex said.

We got up to leave, but as I rose and walked toward the door, Mr. Black-throated Sparrow got agitated and made a wild circuit around the room, depositing a nice splotch of bird doo on my right shoulder.

Monica was quick to turn tragedy into triumph. "That's supposed to be good luck."

"Or a sign that Eagle Feather's curse strikes again."

"What?" Monica giggled.

"Nothing," I replied. "I hope your bird gets better," I said, while secretly wishing that once he was set free, he'd fly into one of the rotating blades of an electric fan. Don't get me wrong. I love animals . . . just not this one.

The rest of the day was pretty much routine. Calls to clients, writing up an offer on a house, ordering new lawn signs. By the time I reached my house at the end of the day, I was exhausted. I slipped into bed early and fell into a deep sleep. Around 2:30 in the morning, I was awakened by Knucklehead's barking and growling. After what had been going on in my life, I had to carefully check it out. I moved from darkened room to darkened room, peeking out between the slats of my tasteful microblinds. Nothing in the front yard. Nothing on the south or north sides. The backyard . . . it seemed clear. I waited for a while in silence, listening to Knucklehead's agitated breathing, wanting to bark, but I kept my hand resting on top of his nose. I waited a few minutes. Nothing. I thought about venturing out, but since nothing seemed amiss, I felt it was safer to be inside than expose myself to a lunatic waiting in the shadows. I told myself that it was probably just an animal or that owl I've seen sitting atop our telephone poles from time to time.

I got into bed and read for a while, then turned out the light and went back to sleep. No more barking.

At 6:00, I arose to find—surprise—another cloudless, sunny day. Opening the blinds, I saw nothing out of the ordinary. My car seemed untouched. Nothing flaming in the front yards. The backyard was fine. Just a bunch of clothes floating in the pool. Topped up by bleach-blond hair.

I went into the kitchen, ground some coffee, and started my F.A. Porsche-designed coffeemaker for a nice cup of java to start the day. When I heard the machine belch its last volcanic puff of boiling water, I pulled out the carafe and poured a cup of wonderful, delicious coffee, the substance that would bring me from slumber into the world of the living and the awake. In went some half and half. Wonderful. I sat at what would soon be my Caesarstone kitchen counter. I looked out the window into my disheveled backyard and pool that would soon be completely torn apart, reshaped, replastered, with a spa set into the corner, splashing water in a neverending fountain of tasteful splashing and zen-like background noise. I would have to do something about that body floating in the pool.

. . . body in pool.

. . . body . . .

Oh Christ!

Twenty minutes later, Becker was standing next to me in my kitchen while the crime scene investigators were milling around the backyard, photographing details, putting clues into plastic bags and carefully labeling them.

"Let me guess, Amanda," Ken whispered, "you were reenacting scenes from *Sunset Boulevard* and things got out of hand?"

Ken was being funny at a time when I really needed it. Just then, a car raced up in front of my house and out popped Alex. Ah, the two men in my life that I really needed right then.

Alex threw his arms around me, letting me know everything was going to be all right.

"*Sunset Boulevard?*" Alex ventured, raising his eyebrows.

"I did that one already," Ken said. "Hi, Ken Becker, Homicide."

"Alex Thorne, adventurer."

I extended my hand for Alex and Becker to shake. "Amanda Thorne, perennial victim."

Ken shook my hand first, followed by Alex.

"Glad to know you, Amanda," they both said, each in their turn.

Alex craned his neck to see the coroner supervise two cops pulling a body from the water. "Monica Birdsong?"

I put my left index finger on the tip of my nose and pointed the right index at Alex.

"I was afraid that was going to happen," Alex added.

"Me too," I added. "From the minute we left her house, I felt Monica was in over her peroxided head. I just wish I had checked my yard better last night when Knucklehead went berserk."

"It wouldn't have made any difference, Amanda. She was already dead before she was dumped in the pool."

"You mean someone dragged her dead body, somehow, into my backyard and tossed her in the drink?"

"It looks like that. There are dragging marks on the concrete from the street curb to your pool. Since you don't have a side gate . . ."

"I did have a side gate . . . that is, until Edwin took it down to have it re-welded."

"Exactly," Becker admitted. "It was easy to drag Monica into your backyard. Plus, she was a very petite woman."

I had an idea. "So whoever dragged Monica would have left footprints?"

"None. The assailant stayed on your concrete and pool decking the entire way."

"So what do I do now?" I asked.

"I'd begin by adding a little more chlorine to your pool," Alex replied.

"You go about your normal day. And at night, I'll be staying here," Ken stated. "If that's okay with you, Alex?"

"She's yours now," Alex said, planting a kiss on my cheek. "Just remember, she hates it when you pee in the shower."

Ken couldn't stop laughing.

"It doesn't bother you, my ex kissing me in front of you?"

"No."

"It doesn't make you jealous?"

"No, from what I remember, your ex-husband is gay."

"But it doesn't bother you that I was once in love with him?"

"Not *once*. You still are."

"So you've noticed that, too, huh?" I said.

"Yes."

"And you're not afraid of that?"

"No."

"Why?"

"Like I said before, I'll give you plenty of reasons to want to be with me."

CHAPTER 20

Real Whores Drive Nice Cars

Ken spent the night, making me feel safe, happy, and horny . . . no sex again, but I have to admit, I enjoyed every minute with him.

The next morning, we showered together, ate breakfast together, and Ken bade me good-bye with a passionate kiss that made me remember him for several hours. While I was throwing a load of laundry into the clothes washer that still gave me electrical shocks, the phone rang. Alex wanted to take another step in our investigation. I agreed.

At 11:30, Alex picked me up because my car still smelled like Raid. We headed over to Ed Jensen's office at Desert, Inc. Ed greeted us promptly and we followed him down the hall to a corner office, where from his spacious corner office, he could stare out at his car, a baby blue Bentley, sporting vanity license plates that read, CALL ED.

Ed motioned for us to take seats. Ed followed suit, but when he sat down, his unbuttoned shirt spread wider, revealing a gold chain decked out with none other than a gold pig head . . . with devil horns. It wasn't that I thought Ed was involved in some kind of devil worship, it's just that the look he gave me at Cocka2's was like that from a soul completely empty of humanity. Like emptiness staring you in the face.

There was very little in life that scared me, but the look I got that afternoon still makes my blood run cold.

Of course, I wanted to be sure about Ed being the psycho drag queen. As Alex and he made small talk, I sized up Ed's height, eyes, distance apart, his ears. No doubt about it—the two were one in the same.

I rejoined the conversation when Alex decided to drop the bomb.

"Ed, as you know, Amanda wants to clear her name, so we couldn't help but notice that you've bought up a lot of land for a limited liability company in between the parcels Marvin Sultan has purchased.

"There's no law against that," Ed said as casually as if he had proclaimed that the sky was blue.

"We're getting that from everyone we talk to," Alex replied.

"Well, it's true."

I jumped in. "Ed, I knew you were at 2666 Boulder Drive the day of the murder."

"I've already been over all that with the police."

"But we'd appreciate it if you'd tell us what happened."

Ed let out a sigh of exasperation. "The day before Doc died, your listing popped up on my phone, I have a client who wants to buy in Caliente Sands, so I was in my car, I drove over, went inside your house, looked around, and left. The end."

"The listing popped up on your phone?"

"I have an e-mail notification when a property that matches my search criteria comes on the market."

"So you didn't see anything out of the ordinary when you went in the home?"

"No."

"And you locked all the doors and windows when you left?"

"Of course. I double-checked."

Seeing that we weren't going to get anything more out of Ed concerning 2666 Boulder Drive, Alex took a different tack.

"Ed, you don't happen to hold a grudge against Mary Dodge, do you?"

"No more than anyone else in this town."

"So the fact that you're buying up land in-between the parcels Mary's buying for Marvin Sultan—for much higher prices—has nothing to do with sticking it to Mary?"

"It's just good business practice."

"And very profitable for you," Alex said.

"I don't do what I do for charity."

"You also bought some of the parcels for yourself . . . isn't that right, Ed?"

Ed gestured toward his Bentley with a wave of his perfectly manicured hand. "That car isn't going to pay for itself."

"So if it turns out that Mary Dodge and Marvin are convicted on charges of murder, your land will skyrocket in value."

"I didn't consider that when I bought the parcels for myself—neither did my client. But now that the possibility has raised its head, I'm just thrilled," Ed said with a malevolent smile, a smile as twisted as his total-dismemberment frown I received at Cocka2's.

Alex tried one more angle. "Not that I don't already know the answer to this question, but who do you think killed Doc?"

Ed smiled again, an awful smile. "Isn't it obvious? Mary Dodge. She has the motive—money—and she has Marvin behind her to do her dirty work. She doesn't even have to get her lily-white hands dirty."

"Ed, let's suppose Mary and Marvin croaked Doc. Aren't you afraid that by the way you're buying property up in the Cone, you could be next?"

"I'm not afraid of anything, Mr. Thorne. If I were, I wouldn't have gotten as far as I have in this business. Now, if you'll excuse, me, I have some clients to call."

And that was that. Alex and I went to a late lunch and discussed our brief meeting with Ed.

"Alex, remember the really spooky drag queen at Cocka2's? The one that looked at me like Satan himself."

"Amanda, there is no such thing as Satan. The only evil is what we as humans do to each other."

"Okay, the drag queen that looked at me like a cold-blooded killer?"

"Yes, yes, I remember. You said he really shook you up."

"Yes, well, that drag queen is Ed."

"Nooo."

"Yes."

"How do you know?"

"He's wearing the same gold pig head around his neck."

"Maybe it's just coincidence."

"Honey, I've seen all kinds of charms in my life, but I've never seen one like that. A pig head with devil horns. It's pure evil."

"Amanda, I hate to wreck your theory, but it probably means he's a pig. He likes sloppy, dirty sex."

Ever since Alex plucked me out of the coma I lived in before I met him, I've been exposed to a lot of things I never knew existed. But I felt that I was nowhere as naïve as Alex believed me to still be.

"Alex, I don't know about that. A pig? With horns?"

"It took you two years to realize that eyehooks in the ceiling over a bed weren't there for hanging plants."

"I knew that they were there for leather slings. And give me some credit, Alex. A lot of people in America still don't know that."

"Or that men can put their fists up places where the sun don't shine."

"That one took a few pictures to make me believe it. I was sure they were using Photoshop."

"The pig is most likely a signal to other guys that Mr. Ed likes sweaty, dirty, hot sex. And lots of it."

"But he drives a Bentley!"

"Amanda, sluts drive expensive cars. In fact, that's how most sluts end up owning them: because they put out. And besides, I seem to remember fucking you in a Rolls in the English countryside years ago."

"Oh, right. Moving on. Alex, none of this matters. We're getting sidetracked from the main point here."

"Don't blame me, you brought up the fisting part."

"Let's get back to the point. Ed is a drag queen. The landscapers said they saw a woman in a red dress entering Boulder Drive."

Alex looked at me as if I was crazy, brilliant, or both.

"That's crazy."

"Not so crazy. Who in their right mind is going to suspect that the woman seen going into Boulder Drive was, in fact, a man?"

"Crazy."

"No, think of it, Alex. The landscapers were mostly Hispanic. They don't have the cultural exposure to drag like some Americans do. They probably wouldn't even consider it. Plus, they were far enough away, no one could probably tell."

"Amanda, I have to hand it to you. It's a wild theory, but it's possible. In fact, if it's true, it's brilliant. Ed implicates Mary Dodge with her red dress and he gets off scot-free—and rich in the process."

"Alex, do you still have that recording of when you talked to the landscapers?"

"Yes, it's still on my smartphone."

"I think we need to get it translated. Roberto can translate . . . and I think I could use a little touch-up."

Two hours later, we were at Roberto's hair salon. Roberto, who had never met Alex before, was smitten with Alex from the moment we walked in. It was difficult trying to keep Roberto's mind on the recording and off Alex's crotch. Alex, sensing this, played only one sentence at a time. I wrote down the translation.

"Dees part, he say '. . . it was a woman, red dress, she walk very sexy, she have red hat, big red hat. She carry box into house when she go in. She carry box out about an hour later.' "

We could then hear Alex asking what kind of car she drove up in. You could hear several men's voices wavering in their answers, racking their brains. Then came the answer we were all waiting for: ". . . she drive up in square car . . . no, truck . . . like truck . . ." Then another voice correcting the man speaking, "SUV. Square and boxy . . . silver," Roberto translated. "Like toaster. I think he ees saying a Mercedes."

"Bingo," Alex said triumphantly. "A G-class. Exactly the kind that Mary Dodge drives."

"Maybe it was just the other SUV," I suggested. "The more rounded one."

"I believe it was the G-class. Like Mary's."

"I've got an idea, Alex. Let me make a quick call," I said, while Roberto hyperventilated near Alex. I dialed, then waited for an answer.

"Good afternoon, Desert, Inc."

"This is Amanda Thorne, I was just there visiting Ed Jensen and I think I scratched a car there. It might have been Ed's . . . you know the Mercedes SUV. In silver."

"Ed only drives a Bentley. And no one here has a silver Mercedes SUV," came the receptionist's reply.

"Are you sure?"

"Yes, I'm sure."

"You know what I'm talking about, don't you? One of those G-class Mercedes. The boxy ones."

"I know what you're talking about," came the slightly acerbic reply. "They cost over $100,000. Believe me, I can see every car that comes in this lot, and I haven't seen one of them in a long time. You might try Mary Dodge over at Dodge & Dodge . . . she drives one . . . in silver."

I thanked the receptionist and hung up.

"Well," I said, "Ed doesn't have a G-class. So I guess he's out."

"Why would you say that?" Alex replied. He obviously had another angle I hadn't considered. "He could've rented one. We need to check that out. Amanda, can you get on the phone and call all the rental car places in town?"

So instead of working like a good Realtor, I finished getting my hair spruced up and headed into the office, where I spent an hour or two calling every car rental place in the Coachella Valley. I found plenty, but the companies sensibly refused to give me the confidential information I needed. I gave Alex a call, who was out landing another listing for the two of us.

"There are dozens of companies that rent Mercedes G-class SUVs."

"And they wouldn't tell you if Ed Jensen rented one lately?"

"Right you are. So that was a dead end."

"Not necessarily, Amanda. At least we know the killer probably drove a G-class. In silver. I wouldn't call that a waste of time. And Mary does drive one . . . in silver."

"It looks like all the signs are still pointing toward Mary Dodge."

"And what's wrong with that?"

"It seems so obvious."

"I imagine most crimes are just that: obvious. It's probably just a matter of gathering enough evidence to convict. You can't nail someone with innuendo."

"And in-you-endo, as we all know, is Italian for sodomy."

"Who told you that one? Your mother?"

"The Pope, I think. He was drunk at the time. Threw up all over the Sistine Chapel."

Alex's face lit up. "I've got it. Ed Jensen did drive the murder car. But he didn't rent one."

"I suppose he broke into Mary Dodge's home, found her purse, got her keys, opened her garage door and her ten-foot gate, drove off with her car, killed Doc, and returned the car before Mary sobered up."

"Nope, but he *did*, indeed, drive a silver Mercedes G-class."

"But you said he didn't rent one."

"I did, because renting one would leave a trail of a credit card, a driver's license."

"Alex, maybe Ed had a boyfriend who did the renting."

"Nope, Ed has no boyfriend because no one can stand him."

"Good point," I replied. "But you did say he drove a silver G-class."

"I did."

"But how? C'mon, Alex, spill it."

"He drove a client's car."

"Brilliant, Alex."

"Yeah, it came to me when I was thinking about banging my knee in our listing over on Mirada Drive. You know, the Simons' house."

"Oh, I get it. They're gone all summer and into the fall, and they leave their expensive cars in the garage the whole time. Ed's clients wouldn't know if he took their car out for a spin . . . unless they wrote down their odometer reading, which I doubt."

"Exactly."

"So, Alex, I guess Ed is still a suspect."

"Correct."

"Well, good . . . I think. I wouldn't want this to be too easy."

CHAPTER 21

Amanda and Regina Take a Field Trip

The next day, after getting back from an early-morning ride of thirty miles on my bicycle, Regina invited me over for cocktails. It was 10:30. Okay, so it was a little early.

"Regina, I don't know what to do," I said with not just a little exasperation. "We've searched high and low, but we don't seem to be getting anywhere."

"Maybe that's the problem. We've been searching low."

"Low, I didn't think my life would get any lower until now."

Regina looked at me with more than a little pity. "What I mean is, we need to search high . . . as in the high desert. Yucca Valley, Joshua Tree, Pioneertown."

"You think?"

Regina smiled the smile of the Cheshire cat. "I think we'll find out a lot more about Doc than we're finding here in Palm Springs. Let's go. If we start now, we can maybe catch an act at Pappy and Harriet's Palace."

And so we went.

Regina and I made a quick clothes change into something less citified, then took Highway 62 up to the high desert. Winding our way up the long hill past Al Capone's old hideout in Morongo Valley and leveling out in Yucca Valley, Regina and I shared our plan of attack.

"I think our first stop should be the Institute of Mentalphysics in Joshua Tree," Regina explained. "Doc was into all this stuff. Plus, you can get a look at a few of the buildings. Much of the center was built by Lloyd Wright, the son of Frank Lloyd Wright. From what I know, Frank was supposed to design and build it, but he quarreled so much with the founder of the institute, Edwin Dingle, Frank wouldn't put his name on it. But no matter how much of the design is due to Frank or his son, Frank's signature is all over the place. You've never been there?"

"No, but it sounds fascinating."

"Now, remember, these people take this stuff very seriously, so we can't go making fun of these people."

"I think the plate just got called Ming by the vase."

"Amanda, are you inferring that I can't hold my tongue?"

"You can hold it, but you can also kill a person with one blow of it."

We crested the hill from the Morongo basin and slipped down the hill into Yucca Valley. People from the lower desert sometimes called it Yukky Valley since it didn't have the cosmopolitan air of Palm Springs, but it had its own kind of charm. If you could peer beyond the Walmart and Applebee's restaurant, you could see that Yucca Valley had the soul of a little western town. This soul is what attracted many New Age practitioners to the high desert. Low prices, wide-open spaces, cooler days and nights than in Palm Springs all contributed to a sizable population of people seeking spiritual fulfillment in any shape or form. We passed through Yucca Valley into Joshua Tree, the landscape changing little with the exception of the complete disappearance of commercial buildings lining the sides of the road.

"See those buildings up there on the left? Pull in there," Regina pointed.

We wound our way through a sizable parking lot that was mainly empty and pulled up to the office and gift shop. (What could you sell at a spiritual meditation center? Earplugs? Lotus blossoms?) We went inside and met the manager, a woman who introduced herself as Ohm-Ra. Regina explained our situation.

"I'm afraid there's not much I can tell you. Doc came here from time to time."

"Did he ever come here with anyone else? Like a woman?" I inquired.

"No, never. Doc was very much a loner."

"So he came here to meditate by himself?"

"Sometimes, but mostly he used the vortices."

My bullshit sensors went into alarm mode whenever I heard the word *vortex*. People raved about the vortices in Sedona, Arizona, but all I ever felt was perspiration. It's hot there in the summer.

"And what are the vortices?" I asked.

"There," she said, pointing out to the desert at nothing in particular. "We have over fifteen vortices on our holy grounds. The Labyrinth is running over 1.5 million cycles per second."

Even Regina was confused. "Excuse me?"

"Energy from the earth. Natural energy. Most people use them for divine guidance, healing, or inspiration."

Regina was clearly doubtful and the look clearly showed on her face. Fortunately, she was standing off to the side of the manager, so Mrs. Ohm-Ra didn't see this, nor did she see Regina smack her head with her hand, as if trying to jog her head back into reality.

"I have one more question."

"Yes?"

"Who do you think could have killed Doc?"

"You mean, who helped him pass from this life?"

"If you want to put it that way. I'd prefer to say someone poisoned him."

"I can't answer that," Ohm-Ra replied. "We try to avoid all forms of negation here. Now, if you'll excuse me, I have a busload of guests arriving in an hour from Ojai, California, . . . I must get ready to greet them."

Interview over. I looked at Regina, who was still incredulous.

"What the fuck just happened here?"

I shrugged my shoulders. "I guess we should go look at the vortices."

"If we have to," was Regina's reply.

Regina and I made our way onto the holy ground until we eventually came upon a circle of stones in the ground about 100 feet in diameter. I expected to see some fiery plasma suspended in space, sucking rocks and dirt into its gaping maw, like something from *The Matrix* or a Star Trek movie. But no, it was just a circle of stones. Even stranger, there were ten people walking inside the circles, some silent, some quietly chanting, some waving their arms around slowly, some wafting their arms up and down, as if blown by an invisible ether wind.

"This is fucked up," Regina commented none too quietly.

"Do you feel anything?" I asked.

"Yeah, hungry. Let's go get something to eat."

We had lunch at the Purple Lizard sandwich shop in downtown Joshua Tree. When I say downtown, I mean the collection of about twenty stores, restaurants, and unicycle and rock-climbing gear shops that make up Joshua Tree. As I munched my way through my Blue Job burger (bleu cheese on a hamburger . . . in case you had other ideas), I looked around at the collection of backpackers and eco-hippies that populated the place. It seemed so strange, thinking that in the midst of so much white trash lives this island of progressive culture. The draw, of course, is Joshua Tree National Park. Some come for the rocks to climb, some to meditate, some to bike. It's kind of wild, really. Like the billboard across the street, depicting a fire-ravaged drag queen lying dejected on the embers of a scorched landscape. The tagline read: FIRES ARE A DRAG. BE CAREFUL WITH FIRE IN THE PARK. I kid you not. This was on a huge billboard.

Regina and I finished our sandwiches, then headed off for a few New Age stores. We turned up nothing at Get Your Rocks Off, a psychic store specializing in crystals. Zippo at Kabala Valhalla. But our luck started to turn at New Age Concepts. The store owner, Bonnie, highly recommended a visit to Pappy and Harriet's. Turning north onto Pioneertown Road, we drove up through a brutal landscape dotted with yuccas and Joshua trees, passed a coyote out for an early-evening stroll, and up to Pioneertown for a drink at Pappy and Harriet's Palace, a saloon and self-described best honkey-tonk west of the Mississippi, for a drink before heading down to Palm Springs again.

We chatted up the bartender, Lisa, and hit pay dirt.

"Yeah, he used to come in here quite a bit," Lisa laughed. "I was so sorry to hear that Doc was killed. I'll bet that really shook up his girlfriend."

"She was murdered too. Just a few days ago."

Lisa looked at me wide-eyed. "Murdered? Oh my God! I don't believe it. Wow . . ." She let out a long sigh. "I guess you just never know, do you?"

"So he came in here with his girlfriend?" Regina inquired.

"Yeah, for a while it was almost once a week. He'd go out back with the woman he was dating."

"Where in the back?" Regina asked, pointing toward a corner of the bar.

"Not in the bar . . . outside . . . in the back . . . our backyard, if that's what you want to call it. Like he didn't want anyone to see them together."

It was my turn to jump in. "Why would you say that, Lisa?"

"Because when he came in by himself, he'd always sit right here in this room and watch whoever was playing pool."

Regina and I looked at each other as if we'd both discovered something important. But what?

I took a chance. "That's odd. I would've thought he'd sit out front and center with Monica. I mean, she is . . . was . . . kind of a bimbo, but she was attractive in her own way. A man who looked like Doc would want to show off someone like Monica."

Lisa looked puzzled. "A bimbo. I wouldn't call Doc's girlfriend a bimbo. She seemed very plain to me. Painfully plain, if you asked me."

Now I was puzzled. "Are we talking about the same person here?"

"Yeah, Doc's girlfriend . . . Monica, that's what you said her name was."

"He never introduced her?"

"No, never. That's another reason I felt like he was hiding Monica."

I turned to Regina, who was looking rather muddled. "Maybe Doc was embarrassed that Monica was such a bimbo."

Lisa, who was busy washing the jelly jars Pappy and Harriet's used for beer mugs, paused her dunk-and-dry routine.

"Maybe I've got a different definition of bimbo, but this girlfriend was no bimbo. Maybe you're thinking of another girlfriend."

"He never had one before Monica," Regina added.

"Oh."

"Well, I don't care what you say about Monica, she was no bimbo. This woman was in her fifties, just a little heavyset . . ."

"Stop right there, Lisa," I said. "Heavyset? I don't think Monica even tipped the scales at over one hundred five, maybe one hundred ten."

"Oh no. This woman had to weigh about, say, one hundred fifty, one hundred sixty."

"Holy shit," Regina whistled.

"Lisa, what color was her hair?"

"Dark. Brown I'd say."

"Not blond?"

"She could have colored it. But, no, this woman's hair was brown."

"Bingo," I said, grabbing Regina's arm. "Wait a minute, Lisa. I've got a picture of someone I want you to look at. It's on a business card, so it's kinda small, but I want you to look at it."

I pulled out Mary Dodge's business card and handed it to Lisa, who studied it for a few seconds before handing it back to me.

"Definitely not her . . . that woman looks like an Orange County bitch, if you ask me."

I put the card back into my purse dejectedly. "I know it was a long shot. I couldn't see Mary Dodge with Doc. But I had to ask."

"Who's the chick with the bouncy hair on the business card?" Lisa asked.

"Mary Dodge. She's a very successful real-estate agent in Palm Springs."

"Well," Lisa started, "she looks like she could kill. That smile doesn't fool me one bit."

Regina was starting to put the pieces together. So was I.

"So it looks like Doc had a girlfriend before Monica," Regina surmised.

"Regina, why would he be so concerned with hiding her? He wasn't ashamed of Monica from what I've heard."

"Maybe he had two girlfriends at the same time, so he had to keep a low profile when he was out in public with Madame X."

I turned to Lisa again. "Lisa, do you remember when was the last time Doc was here with his girlfriend?"

"About nine months ago. Maybe eight."

"Regina, wasn't that about the time people said Doc hooked up with Monica?"

"Amanda, I think you uncovered something there. Wait a minute. Holy shit! We might have a disgruntled girlfriend here. Doc is seeing this woman that he's ashamed of; then he dumps her for a bimbo! Madame X then decides to get revenge and she kills first Doc, then Monica. Maybe this whole mess has nothing to do with saving the hills or Martin Sultan!"

"I think we're on to something here, Regina. But what I don't understand is why Doc went to such lengths to hide her."

Regina's face lit up like the Christmas tree at Rockefeller Center. "I've got it. He was protecting his career!" Regina exclaimed, using her fingers to put air quotation marks as she said the word *career.*

"His career? His only source of income was his eco protests."

"And what would be the worst kind of person to date when you were making your living at trying to save the Chino Cone?"

I said the words slowly, "A Realtor."

"Right. He was dating someone in Palm Springs who sold properties. He had to keep that a secret. If word got out, it would ruin him."

"Okay, Regina, let's assume this is all true. Then who could it be? Lisa here said it was definitely not Mary Dodge. It could be anyone. I've got it! Maybe it *was* Mary Dodge and she disguised herself when she came up here. That seems kinda farfetched. But Mary is the type to stop at nothing to sell land up in the Chino Cone."

"Oh, right. You've got a point there. What do you say we head down to the valley? I think we've found out all we can find here."

"Sounds like a good idea. And I think a call to Alex is in order. Then Ken."

We both got into my car and started the long ride down to Palm Springs.

Just then, my cell phone rang.

"Hello, Amanda Thorne."

"Amanda? It's Anne . . . Anne Clexton. I called your office, but they said you were up in the high desert today. I didn't know you had listings up there."

"Oh, Regina and I went up to do some investigating. What can I do for you?"

"I just thought about something concerning Mary Dodge . . . it seems like such a small thing . . ." Anne said, then cut out. She came back on for a second. "It's not really important, but I'd like to talk to you about it tomorrow . . . no rush . . . but it might be important . . ." she said, cutting out a final time. We were coming down out the hills and reception was spotty.

I hit the Redial button, but no answer. Damn those hills. When we got to the bottom of the hills and came out onto the plains of Desert Hot Springs, my cell phone rang again.

"Anne?"

"No . . . it's Alex. What have you and Regina been up to? How did your trip up to Joshua Tree go?"

"Alex, Regina and I solved it!"

"Solved it? The murder . . . murders?"

"Yes . . . well, not exactly, but we're close. Doc had a girl-friend nobody knew about. We think Doc dumped her for Monica Birdsong, setting the jealous girlfriend into action."

"Wonderful! Who is it?"

"Well, we don't know that yet. But at least we know it's a woman. Well, maybe. It *is* Palm Springs, after all—gender-bender central."

"Wonderful," came the reply. "We've narrowed our search down to fifty percent of the population."

"Oh, come on, Alex, be reasonable. At least we're getting somewhere. Oh, and Anne Clexton called me just before you and said she remembered something about Mary Dodge. I think our suspicions were right from the beginning." There was a bunch of static on the line. "Alex, could you call Ken and tell him that there was another girlfriend. I'm still having shitty reception even though we've just come out of the hills."

"Amanda, I think that . . ." and the phone went dead. The cell phone display told me what I already knew: Call dropped. My phone dropped another bomb: low battery. Damn.

We arrived back at The Curse and I pulled into the drive-way.

"Regina," I said, hoping that she didn't want to invite me over for cocktails. "Thank you so much for helping me today. I think we're really close to solving this thing. I can't thank you enough," I said, kissing her on her forehead. "I am ex-hausted . . . it must be that high-altitude, clean air," I stated, even though Joshua Tree was only about 3,000 feet higher than Palm Springs.

Regina made no fuss. She looked tired as well. She stood on her tiptoes and gave me a kiss on the cheek.

"Good night, honey. And for fuck's sake, lock your doors from now on."

I winked at her. "You bet. I'm going for a swim, then a shower, then straight to bed. No more Avon ladies with flame throwers. This case is about over . . . thanks to you."

I made my way home. Edwin was out of town again, trying to get his brother out of jail again. I fed Knucklehead, who went ape shit when I got home (but then again, when didn't he?), got out of my clothes and into a long, white, terrycloth bathrobe, and went out to the pool. I swam around for a while, taunting Knucklehead to get in the pool, but as usual, he hemmed and hawed about getting into the water. Feeling sorry for him, I got out and sat in one of the outrageously expensive outdoor chairs I had gathered around a table, then lit up a cigar. I developed a taste for them, like most things in life, from Alex. It wasn't just the sex scenes involving cigars that made me take them up. I think it was the rebellion. Even in 2005, most women didn't smoke cigars, or if they did, they smoked the little feminine ones "for ladies." Fuck that. I lit up an Ashton Half Corona and sat puffing great clouds of smoke into the starry skies. Not bad, I thought. I'm divorced, but still here. Alex is working with me again. Good. Houses are selling like hotcakes. Ken seems crazy about me. Life is good.

CHAPTER 22

Play a Little Tune for Me, Bernard Herrmann

I drifted and dreamed for some time until my cigar was down to the bitter end. I stubbed out my stogie and went inside to take a hot shower and to wash off the chlorine. Oh shit! I forgot to plug in my cell phone; the battery was probably dead. I found the charger and plugged the phone in. Life was good.

I was about the enter the bathroom in the master suite, when I heard Knucklehead barking and whining at the dining-room door. He got so excited that I was home, he forgot to go out and pee, so I ended up leaving the door open so he could go out into the backyard, sniff around, and let loose a stream of pee that rivaled the Colorado after a heavy spring thaw. No wonder nothing wanted to grow in my backyard.

I went into the master bath, dropped my robe on the toilet seat, and stepped into the shower, pulling the curtain closed—my Keith Haring shower curtain, signed by the artist months before he died. I opened a new package of Kiehl's cleansing bar (soap to you) and turned on the water. The water cascaded down on me like a million little rainstorms, washing away the worries, the cares, the feeling that I was some kind of gigantic loser.

From above the roar of the shower, I could hear Knuckle-head barking. Probably a bat or a sun spider he had seen. He barked at anything. Just then, I felt a breeze flow through the shower, which was strange. I closed the door before I got in the tub. I turned to see a figure advancing toward the shower curtain, chef's knife in hand, raised high, ready to strike. The figure threw back the shower curtain and I was confronted by none other than . . . than . . .

"Anne Clexton!"

Anne didn't waste time. She smiled at me with a psychopathic grin, then started to slash at me with the knife, but years of training in Isshinryu karate taught me what to do. With my left hand, I tore the shower curtain down from its hooks and wound it around my hand, making a defensive weapon to absorb the blows. Then, with my right hand, I grabbed her at the wrist and twisted to the right as I flipped my entire body around, the leverage twisting the fuck out of her wrist. Anne held on to the knife for dear life and tried slashing at me again and again. I pointed my fingers in the classic karate spear position and hit her in the windpipe hard. She stood for what seemed like an eternity, then wobbled backward slowly. It was time to deliver the pièce de résistance. I turned to see Alex's gift to me while honeymooning in Paris: a 10-inch ceramic figurine of a man with an enormous cock that dispensed—what else—cream rinse through his penis when you pumped his head. It was vulgar in the extreme, but I kept it as a memento of his sense of humor, which, like mine, was severely twisted. I grabbed the figurine by the cock and swung it fast, bringing it down on Anne's skull with a sickening crack. She stared at me with eyes lolling around like a shook-up doll, then tottered backward and collapsed.

A second later, another figure burst though the door. Not Mary Dodge, but Alex, followed a minute later by Ken. Even though I had been naked in front of these men before, I covered myself up with the shower curtain, which, to my chagrin, was slashed in several places.

"Goddamn bitch. She's going to pay for this. This was signed by Keith himself."

Alex looked down at the shattered figurine, its cock clearly detached from his body.

"To make a joke here would be superfluous."

He was right.

CHAPTER 23

A Million Little Pieces

Ken went down to the station with Anne while more police department investigators took a thousand pictures, drew a hundred diagrams, and dropped a dozen pieces of evidence into dozens of labeled plastic bags. I could see the trial now.

"If it please the court, I would like to enter into evidence this ceramic cock, used to subdue the defendant, Anne Clexton."

"A ceramic cock, counselor?" the judge would ask.

"Yes, sir, it was used to dispense hair conditioner for the witness, Amanda Thorne."

"Very well, counselor. The court clerk will label the cock Item A."

Maybe I could ask for the Witness Protection Program to spare me the embarrassment.

Alex and I stayed up all night. Me, I was too wound up to sleep, and Alex just wanted to be there since Ken couldn't.

We opened a bottle of champagne and spent the night talking, reliving old times. We each fired up a big, fat Arturo Fuente Hemingway Masterpiece and puffed away, laughing and reliving the places we'd celebrated life together: Chile, New Zealand, Kenya, Iceland, Russia. Oh God, it was all just too wonderful. The Egyptians have a saying that to speak of

the dead is to make them live again. Perhaps they were thinking about memories too.

"Oh shit!" Alex said. "We really had some good times, didn't
we?"

"The best . . . the absolute best," I replied. "I don't think I
will ever enjoy myself like that again," I added, turning to
look at Alex, who was seated right beside me. For fifteen thousand millennia we looked into each other's eyes, feeling that
closeness that only comes from one soul touching another,
completely, reverentially, carefully, tenderly.

We heard a car drive up in the driveway, and the moment
was gone. Like two guilty lovers almost caught in the act, we
moved to different sofas while Ken knocked on the door and
then entered.

"Well," he said, beaming with pride, "we have a full confession."

"That's wonderful, Ken!" I exclaimed, wanting to kiss him,
but feeling that it would be cruel toward Alex in light of what
almost happened between Mr. Thorne and me. I stayed seated,
letting the congratulations do its work without making Alex
feel left out. I did motion to a chair beside me for Ken to sit
down. What would Freud have said? That I was still in love
with Alex, but falling for Ken, too, and I was positioning myself right smack in the middle of them? That I wanted to hear
all about Anne's confession and was seating Ken in the middle
so that all could share? Maybe. I decided to be in denial.
Sometimes a chair is just a chair, I told myself.

Ken started breathlessly rubbing his hands almost with
glee. "Where do I begin?"

"To tell the story of how great a love can be?" I started.

"The sweet love story that is older than the sea?" Alex continued.

Ken, still riding high from bringing in Palm Springs's most

notorious killer in years, seemed confused. Then his eyes brightened. "Shirley Bassey would be proud," he added. "Or Andy Williams."

A knowing look passed between Alex and I. He got it. Goddamnit, he got it.

"Your theory about Doc having another girlfriend was correct. I have to admit, I wouldn't have seen it myself. He was dating Anne Clexton for two years; but because she was a Realtor and worked for Mary Dodge, he couldn't chance anyone finding out, since that would destroy his credibility in the eco-community. Plus, now that money was starting to really roll in with their contacts in well-heeled places, there was even more at stake. So, at some point, Doc meets Monica and falls head over heels."

"Or maybe Monica makes sure Doc falls head over heels, since perhaps she's discovered a new wellspring of financial wealth," Alex suggested.

"That's certainly possible," Ken conceded.

"Oh, it's more than possible," Alex replied. "We saw the rock on Monica's hand the day we visited her . . . and the red Maserati. I think she knew she had hit the jackpot."

Ken continued, "So Doc dumped Anne for a woman much younger, sexier, and skinnier than her. Anne is furious and decides to get revenge. At the same time, she really hates Mary Dodge for a whole host of reasons. Anne told me Mary cheats her, belittles her, and takes all the glory, delegating Anne to one notch above a secretary. So Anne decides to get revenge on Doc, Monica, and Mary. One stone, three birds."

"It's brilliant in its simplicity. Simple if you see the reasoning behind it, but completely clouded by the red herring of the Chino Cone, which had nothing to do with it," I said.

"Exactly," replied Ken. "So Anne starts setting up Cathy Paige to become the fall girl, so to speak. She started stealing

Cathy's things, putting them in different places—trying to make Cathy nervous and jumpy as a cat. Oh, get this . . . Anne was putting Vivarin tablets in Cathy's coffee to make her even jumpier."

"Now it makes sense, Ken," Alex said. "When we went to see Cathy, she said the coffee must have been a cheaper brand . . . that it was bitter. But she offered mugs to us, and they tasted fine. She must have only put the tablets in Cathy's coffee."

"Correct again. So Anne sets her plan in motion. Anne picks a house that is somewhat isolated, yours being at the end of a cul-de-sac, with heavy foliage in front. It's also vacant, with no owners inside; plus, Caliente Sands is so new, almost no one lives there yet, so there aren't a lot of witnesses to see what Anne has planned. Over the course of several months before D-day, Anne goes with Cathy to check up on Mary's listings, looking over Cathy's shoulder to get the Personal Identification Number for her electronic keybox. When Mary Dodge is called by your client, Amanda, to list 2666 Boulder Drive, Anne intercepts the call, sets up an appointment, and doesn't tell Mary about the listing appointment and lets Mary miss it, guaranteeing that Mary doesn't get the listing."

"Oh, I see," I commented. "If Mary got the listing, it would be a little too close to home for murder. After all, Mary wouldn't murder someone in her own listing. . . . And this would be just another way to stick it to her hated employer."

"More or less," Ken agreed. "A day or two before the murder, Anne calls Doc and threatens to tell everyone about their relationship, which would ruin Doc. She tells Doc to be at 2666 Boulder Drive to talk it over. She cuts several branches from Mary's oleander hedge to implicate Mary and boils up a poisonous tea for Doc. That night, Anne makes a quick trip to your place, gets into your car—*because you don't lock your car*—

and pops the hood and cuts your battery cables. The day of the murder, she steals Cathy's electronic key from her desk, puts on a red dress, which will implicate Mary, drives over to a client listing that Mary has in South Palm Springs, borrows a silver Mercedes G-class SUV being stored for the summer in a client's garage, and drives over to Caliente Sands. She parks down the street just in case someone remembers a license plate number, but she struts down the street, throwing just enough sex into her walk so that the landscapers notice her. She is carrying a box filled with Danish and poison Earl Grey tea. When Doc arrives, she gives him a glass of the tea, knowing that it's his favorite, and even better, that the bergamot in Earl Grey tea will mask the taste of the oleander. Anne also knows that Doc—and this is something I didn't know until yesterday—has a history of irregular heartbeat. She gets as much tea into him as possible while she stalls him with talk about him dropping her. About twenty minutes, the tea starts to work on Doc, and he falls to the floor, probably suffering seizures and uncontrollable muscle shaking, destroying much of the furniture. When Doc has finally died, Anne gets an idea to introduce a red herring into this scene: She grabs a handful of rocks from the planting bed in the backyard and stuffs them into his mouth to make people think a message of some sort is being conveyed. Kind of like a warning, like leaving a horse head in someone's bed."

"Then," I continued, "she leaves the house, carrying out two fab-fifties glasses belonging to my stager because she doesn't want to leave traces of the poison behind. It seems like a sloppy cover-up, Ken, considering the lab will only take a day to figure out what killed Doc."

"You're not thinking, Amanda. There's another reason for taking the glasses and not breaking them."

I thought for second, but like standing at the chalkboard in eighth grade in front of my lesbian algebra teacher, Miss Franklin, wishing for an answer to a quadratic equation to come to me, I saw only a blank.

Alex rescued me. "Fingerprints. Even if the glass is broken, the prints are still there. And that could be a fatal mistake for Anne."

"Correct," Ken said. "So Doc is dead, Mary is under suspicion, and everything is going according to plan. Then Cathy Paige throws a monkey wrench into the works by confessing to Anne that she remembered that Doc had another girlfriend: Anne herself. I'm guessing that Anne had Cathy sworn to secrecy, but when she knew that Cathy was too dangerous to let live, she pulled out the poison again."

"Which helped Anne in a perverse way, since it helped to divert suspicion of Doc's murder followed by Monica's directly. Another red herring in the way. It was Anne who set your door on fire and put the black widows in your car. More red herrings. But those two attacks made me suspicious. They seemed so amateurish. And they didn't make any sense since you weren't involved in the Chino Cone protest movement. That's when I started to doubt that theory. I'm not sure why Anne did those attacks. . . . I guess you can't always expect an psychopathic killer to be logical. Perhaps by being illogical, she helped to confuse the motives for the killings."

"So let me guess the last part. Anne goes to visit Monica on some pretext of confessing something about Mary Dodge that would solve Doc's murder. She visits Monica and poisons her."

"With castor beans . . . nasty poison. It makes oleander look like child's play. She ground it up and probably put it into Monica's tea. Or maybe told her it was an herbal tea, and Monica, not being the brightest bulb in the chandelier, trusted her. Since Monica had no heart problems, it took longer for the symptoms to show. Anne said she waited three hours in Monica's house for her to die."

"Jesus, creepy," I said. I mean, what else could you say?

"Then she dragged Monica to her car, drove her over here, and dragged her into your backyard and tossed her in the pool. Again, why you? I think you became a convenient dumping ground for victims . . . and I think in her mind, Anne thought that if enough attacks happened to you, the police would begin to think there was some kind of pattern. Again, a red herring . . . confusion on top of confusion . . . in her own crazy way, brilliant."

"And the rest we know," I ventured. "By sheer coincidence, she found out Regina and I went up to Pappy and Harriet's and would possibly uncover her past with Doc . . . and the whole thing would come unraveled."

"And that, as they say, is that." Ken then looked at Alex, then at me, then back at Alex, as if waiting for one of us to make a move, or to say something. What was next? He knew the case had been resolved, but the conflicting emotions between Alex and I hadn't.

As usual, Alex was always the gentleman with impeccable radar.

"Well, it's been quite a day," he said, putting on a yawn and an arm stretching that wouldn't have fooled anyone. But it was the right thing to do at the right time. And that, in a nutshell, was Alex. "I'd better be going."

He got up to give me a kiss on my forehead, but not before knocking over a tall vase with flowers, which, in turn, knocked over a bottle of champagne, which knocked over another bottle, smashing all three fluted glasses, and upending an ashtray and its contents.

Alex was aghast. "I'm so sorry, Amanda."

"I'm actually quite happy," I admitted.

"Happy?"

"Happy it was you and not me . . . it means the curse on me is over."

Alex smiled, gave me a kiss on the forehead, shook Ken's hand, and congratulated him on a job well done. And he left, driving home alone while I might have the man of my dreams right here in my arms.

That night, Ken finally made love to me and it was terrific. Absolutely terrific. Like Alex would have. I have to admit, during the sex, I did think of Alex briefly. And that was the wonderful thing about having been in love with someone once. They never really leave you. They will always be a part of you. But at some point, you have to move on. And that night, I did. Sort of.